SURVIVE TO FIGHT

Also by Billy Billingham and Conor Woodman

Call to Kill

BILLY BILLINGHAM

AND CONOR WOODMAN

SURVIVE TO FIGHT

HODDER &
STOUGHTON

First published in Great Britain in 2022 by Hodder & Stoughton
An Hachette UK company

3

Copyright © Steel Eagle International Ltd and Conor Woodman 2022

Maps by Rosie Collins

A CIP catalogue record for this title is available from the British Library

Hardback ISBN 978 1 529 36460 6
Trade Paperback ISBN 978 1 529 36461 3
eBook ISBN 978 1 529 36462 0

Typeset in Bembo Std by Manipal Technologies Limited

Printed and bound in Great Britain by Clays Ltd, Elcograf S.p.A.

Hodder & Stoughton policy is to use papers that are natural, renewable
and recyclable products and made from wood grown in sustainable forests.
The logging and manufacturing processes are expected to conform to
the environmental regulations of the country of origin.

Hodder & Stoughton Ltd
Carmelite House
50 Victoria Embankment
London EC4Y 0DZ

www.hodder.co.uk

PART ONE

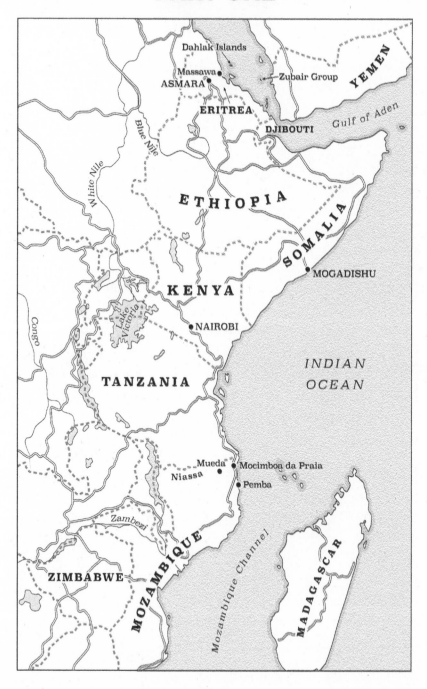

PART ONE

ONE

Niassa Game Reserve, Mozambique

Matt Mason waded through the dark grey mud, carrying a length of coiled rope over his head. One false step could be his last.

The watering hole was thirty feet in diameter and five feet deep, and sharing it with him was a five-tonne bull elephant, who, despite being almost beyond the point of total exhaustion, was still more than capable of crushing Mason to death. The beast had got itself trapped in the mud and was now slumped to one side, two of its legs waving pointlessly up into the air. When he was only a couple of feet away, Mason cast the rope high into the air, biting his lip as he watched it loop and land squarely over the front foot of the elephant. Before it could move, Mason pulled his end of the rope, and immediately, all around him, the crowd roared their approval.

During the time that Mason had been in Mozambique, he had changed more than at any point in his life since he'd joined the forces. Five years in the Parachute Regiment followed by twelve in the SAS had turned him into a lethal force with skills beyond those of any ordinary soldier and yet, three short months in the African bush had opened his mind to a whole new world.

His life now couldn't have been more different to how it was after his discharge from the army. He'd returned to Hereford from operations in Yemen and moved the last of his possessions from the family home to a one-bedroom flat near the centre of town. Although he and his wife Kerry had parted amicably, it had been hard to say goodbye to his son and to the house where they had all lived together since he'd joined the SAS at twenty-two. Almost as hard as it had been to say goodbye to his daughter Joanna when she left for naval college in Devon.

Mason had thrown himself into his newfound bachelorhood with some enthusiasm, spending his evenings catching up with old squadron buddies in the Barrels, before hitting Rubik's nightclub and, more than once, rounding the night off with a punch-up outside the Commercial Road kebab shop. It was after one such scuffle, which resulted in a local farmer going to hospital, that Mace had come to his senses; at thirty-five he simply couldn't return to the life he'd had as a seventeen-year-old before he'd signed up. That would only end badly. He had to move on before he landed himself in serious trouble.

Many lads struggled with civilian life after leaving the special forces. It was hard to settle into a new routine, expected to fend for yourself. Mason might have been able to take out a man at over a thousand yards with a sniper rifle, but the everyday things in life, from making an appointment to see the dentist to paying his phone bill, were completely new. In the army, things like that were done for you, someone was always on hand to help before you even knew you needed it. On the outside, you were on your own. Money in particular had become a concern. Not that the army had paid very well, but at least when you were in, you were getting paid, rain or shine. On the outside, you had to find your own work, which wasn't as easy as it had been back when Iraq and Afghanistan offered lucrative security jobs to guys with Mason's particular skills.

Mace had turned to his old pal, Gordie, who'd served with him in Afghanistan before getting out to start his own security business. Gordie had thrown Mace a lifeline with a gig in Mozambique, drilling a new batch of rangers on the Niassa Game Reserve just across the Tanzanian border. Initially, the contract had been for six weeks, but when Florence Dubois, the posh old girl who ran the place, asked him to stay, he'd gladly extended his trip.

To say that Matt Mason was undergoing a bit of a renaissance in Africa wouldn't be an overstatement. Six months under the hot African sun had bronzed his skin, while his hair and beard had grown longer than ever before. A diet of red meat three times a day combined with heavy physical exercise had added twenty pounds to his muscular frame so that he no longer looked like the skinny kid from Walsall. Meanwhile, his mental outlook had changed even more than his physical appearance.

For most of his adult life, Mason had experienced the world as a place to do battle. The planet's flora and fauna had often been collateral damage in his never-ending scraps with the bad guys. He'd seen stretches of rainforest reduced to a hole in the ground by aerial bombardment, jungle village streets littered with dead cows and goats caught in the crossfire, shores of white-sand beaches piled high with the carcasses of dead fish blown out of the water. War's ability to destroy everything in its path knew no bounds. Now though, he was connecting with the natural world in a way that he'd never imagined possible.

Every day, Mason's routines took him on a new adventure. He missed many aspects of life in the Regiment, but he had found comfort in bringing its professionalism to his new work. Whether it was checking the new security measures he'd put in place around the reserve, or training the men in the deepest parts of the bush, the job brought him face to face with zebras, giraffes, and buffalo not to mention a myriad of mesmerising flowers and birds. Mason had begun to see a beauty that he'd not had time for when he'd been a soldier. He had discovered in himself a source of pleasure that he didn't know existed. Every new encounter with the natural world around him brought him closer to a sense of peace that he had never known. And there was one animal in particular that had truly captured Mason's heart – the elephants.

Florence had called Gordie for help when the elephant situation on the reserve had reached crisis point. By the time Mace arrived in-country, the near two thousand elephants that had roamed the park five years ago had dwindled to fewer than five hundred. It was the same sad story across the whole East African region.

The culprits, of course, were poachers engaged to take down elephants for their tusks. The demand for ivory from the Far East was insatiable and despite various international bans and embargoes, the price of elephant tusk was at an all-time high. The job of protecting elephants in the real world had fallen to the reserves themselves and as the bigger, wealthier game reserves in Kenya and Tanzania had spent big, militarising their rangers, taking on the poachers with ever-increasing force, the smaller reserves had become easier targets. The poachers had refocused their efforts to where they met with less resistance, which currently meant Mozambique. The country was riddled with poverty and corruption from the old days of the civil war, and the financial resources of its game reserves lagged far behind those further north. The result was that its elephants were vulnerable to the men who came at night with guns. It was Matt Mason's job to change all that.

The huge elephant let out another bellicose roar, lifting its trunk in the air before slapping it down again on the mud, spraying dirty water in a high arc, all over the crowd. People screamed and scurried for cover. Mason could see that the life was draining from the beast, in less than thirty minutes it would run out of energy altogether. If he was to save it from drowning in the mud, he had to coordinate his men fast. He whistled to Joseph, his newly appointed head ranger and the most competent man he had.

'Leavers, Joseph!' he shouted.

Joseph, a slender but strong, bright-eyed young man, with a roguish smile that seemed permanently etched on his face, waved to a group of uniformed rangers who were standing along the bank. Each man bore a ten-foot length of thick bamboo and on Joseph's signal, they inched forward in a line and plunged their poles deep into the mud. Still waist-deep in the muddy water below, Mason guided them forward, edging their poles gingerly into the space behind the thick spine of the elephant.

Satisfied with the set-up, Mason held up a hand to instruct everyone to hold their positions. The men braced themselves, while Joseph ran along the bank, shouting at the onlookers to move back, pushing them away with a dismissive wave of his hand. It seemed as though the whole village had come to the watering hole to watch the action. Over a hundred people were gathered, jostling, craning, climbing to get a view of the crazy white man in the water with the bull. Among them, the headman, Mwamba Kiba – Joseph's father, tall, heavily built, greying a little above the ears – watched it all with a wry smile. He had to hand it to the Englishman; he was determined.

Mason had become popular with the locals. The first thing he'd encouraged Florence to see was that they stood no chance against the poachers without the help of the community. The Regiment had taught him that. Winning hearts and minds mattered above all else, especially when you were in a combat situation on someone else's turf. Shortly after arriving, he'd increased the park's manpower, employing Joseph as his deputy and using old military contacts to source new uniforms, boots, and Bergens. He'd convinced Florence to spend money on a dozen AK-47s as well as five reconditioned G3s with night scopes. He'd built an assault course for physical training, a classroom, and several new sentry points and covert hides in the bush.

But the main thing that Mason had built was camaraderie. The poachers were much better funded than the reserve, so if he had any chance of defeating them, he needed the community to take a stake. He had to make them see that the elephants were their own, and today was a prime opportunity. Mason had no doubt that getting the bull elephant out of the watering hole would help to get everyone behind the cause.

He scrambled out of the hole, drenched head to toe in mud, beard dripping lumps of brown goo onto the ground as he ran around to the front of the elephant. He reached down and grabbed the rope that he had thrown over the enormous front leg, shouting to the crowd to move back. Joseph reversed the digger down the hill and Mason hooked the ends of the rope around its mechanical bucket, securing it with two strong knots.

Everything was set. Mason crouched onto his haunches and looked the elephant in the eye. The poor wretch looked forlornly back at him and he could hear its laboured breath above the noise of the crowd. He knew it was terrified, confused about what was happening to it.

'I need you to help us,' Mason said to the elephant, his voice calm and reassuring. 'You can do this.'

The elephant let out another low, sorry sigh as Mason lifted his hand so that Joseph and the rangers could see him. When he dropped his hand again, it was the signal to act.

At once, the men heaved, throwing their whole weight behind the poles, levering the back of the elephant up above the surface of the mud, tilting it back towards the vertical. Mason waved to the villagers to help and the crowd responded, crushing in behind the rangers, adding their collective weight to the big push. Meanwhile, Joseph worked the digger, lifting its mechanical arm, straining the ropes tight against the mass of the beast, using its full power to drag the elephant, legs first, towards the bank.

The crowd roared, drowning out the sound of the digger's diesel engine and the elephant bellowing its disapproval at the discomfort of being dragged through thick mud. Mason took hold of the ropes and added his own weight. Every kilogram counted.

'Come on!' he roared at the beast. They were at full capacity, everyone giving it everything, doing all they could do to help, but Mason knew ultimately the animal's survival depended on it helping itself.

Again, the elephant trumpeted at the top of its lungs. Several children in the crowd screamed, others began to cry. Mothers pulled the small ones close to them, while their husbands pushed in tight behind the rangers, adding more weight to the collective effort to push the elephant back to its feet.

By now the bull was reaching out one of its front feet for the solid edge of the bank. It strained hard against the ropes, pulling the digger backwards. Mason realised that it was in danger of taking it down into the mud with it. He ran around the edge and snatched a pole from the nearest ranger, manoeuvring it a few feet to the left, changing the angle a little.

'On me!' he screamed, calling the men around him to help.

The change of direction did the trick, giving the elephant just enough forward thrust to lift its other front leg out of the mud and scramble up onto the hard ground. With two feet in and two feet out, it balanced precariously, gasping for another breath before, with one enormous heave, it hoisted itself out and stood on the bank dazed, like a boxer who'd taken an upper-cut and lost all sense of where he was.

The sight of an adult bull elephant standing on its feet was enough to send most of the villagers running for cover. Only Mason ran the other way, realising that he had limited time before the elephant regained its composure. Drawing his machete, he sprinted towards the digger, slicing through the ropes. Moments later, the five-tonne brute raised its trunk again and, with an ear-splitting cry, lolloped off into the bush, away from the humans, to return to its own family.

Mason slumped down against the digger, using the last of his energy to raise a hand in triumph as the crowd began to dissipate. The show was over, but Mason hoped they would appreciate the significance of what they'd achieved today. He looked up to see the village headman walking towards him.

'Impressive work, Mason,' Mwamba Kiba said, offering him an outstretched hand.

Mason shook it as Joseph appeared from around the other side of the digger. 'Couldn't have done it without this man,' Mason said, patting the young ranger on the back. 'He's a credit to you, Mwamba.'

'He's a good boy,' Mwamba smiled. 'You have a son?'

'Yes, Sam. Back in England with his mum,' Mason nodded. 'And a daughter, Joanna who's away at sea. Joseph reminds me of her. Strong. Determined.'

Mwamba smiled although no part of him enjoyed hearing his eldest son compared to a woman. 'You're a proud father,' he said, diplomatically.

'Very,' Mason replied. 'My kids mean everything to me. Even more than the elephants.'

'Good!' Mwamba laughed. 'Now, come. Tonight you will eat with my family.'

Mason picked himself up and followed the two men back along the track from the watering hole. A wave of exhaustion crashed over him, but the sound of people up ahead, laughing and singing, raised his spirits. When they reached the village, he took a seat near to the fire and Joseph passed him a cold beer. His thoughts drifted homewards again. He missed Sam and Joanna. He couldn't wait to see them again and tell them all about this place, about Joseph and the elephants. But most of all he couldn't wait to tell them both how proud he was of them.

TWO

Dahlak Islands, Red Sea

The *Golden Falcon* was close reaching under its staysail while the mainsail, with one reef in it, was almost full to bursting. Captain Ben Warmington, a tall, curly-haired Irishman who'd learned his craft sailing off the rocky Antrim coast, manned the bridge, working the colossal one-hundred-and-three-metre-long superyacht to windward as the seas beat hard into the bow. He was relieved at how easily they were achieving eighteen knots without heeling over much at all. The owner, resting in his private cabin on the upper deck, should at least be happy that they were remaining level at speed. He and his guests could enjoy their champagne without worrying about their glasses sliding off surfaces or even tumbling overboard themselves when they'd had one too many.

Although Ben was the skipper of the *Falcon*, the boat belonged to Wei Lun Chow, a Hong Kong-Chinese businessman, who'd engaged him and his crew to pilot the boat from Cairo to the Dahlak Islands off the coast of Eritrea. Chow and his entourage, two Russian security guys and four Chinese 'models' were set on enjoying a spot of scuba diving in one of the most remote and inaccessible spots in the Red Sea. The problem was that, as is often a billionaire's wont, the destination had changed at the last minute.

Ben sighed as he replayed the rather frank exchange he'd had with Chow minutes earlier. The problem was that when you were making a year's salary in a fortnight and getting to sail the third-largest sailboat in the world, there wasn't a lot of leverage to say 'no'. Chow had suddenly wanted to dive the reefs around the Zubair Group, a collection of volcanic islands two hundred miles further south, less accessible and, in Ben's opinion, considerably less safe than the Dahlak Islands. But despite the skipper's protestations, the billionaire had been very insistent and Ben had reluctantly swallowed his tongue. Now, as he tried to recover his calm, he resolved to focus on the positives – he was sailing the *Golden Falcon* in near perfect conditions.

The *Falcon* was pure genius. Its steel hull supported a lightweight aluminium superstructure, designed by the world's best marine architects, Nuvolari Lenard. It combined outstanding sailing performance and state-of-the-art technology with exceptional space, comfort, and luxury. With a beam of more than five metres, it could accommodate sixteen VIP guests in eight luxury cabins. Along with the master suite on the upper deck, there were two queen-sized berths on the lower deck and four guest staterooms below, with separate dressing rooms, his and hers bathrooms, and a private gymnasium. Finally, tucked into the bow, were the six bunk rooms that housed the *Falcon*'s eighteen crew.

As well as the Filipino chef and a dozen of her catering staff, Ben's crew entailed his first officer, Paul Woods, a potty-mouthed Ozzie with an unnatural ability to read the wind, and two deckhands: Jim, a massive Kiwi, who looked like he'd been weaned on steak; and Ben's treasured protege, Joanna Mason, or Jason as she was known on board. She was a brilliant young sailor from Hereford, who'd crewed for Ben many times before, including last year at Cowes where they'd won the Triple Crown. She'd proved herself to be a gifted tactician and it was Ben who had convinced her to come on this trip, even though it meant moonlighting during her shore leave from the navy. She probably shouldn't be there, but he was glad she was.

'Jason,' he called her from behind the huge chrome wheel. 'Trim that fucking line, will you.'

'Skip,' replied the young woman on deck, ducking in and out of the lines, her blonde ponytail peeking out from the back of a black baseball cap. She knew the skipper was in a bad mood and that the best thing to do in those circumstances was keep your head down while you waited for him to calm down. She skipped lightly between the yards, pulling the lines tight, forcing the boat even closer to the wind. She tilted her head upwards to the sky, taking delight in how the gust instantly filled the sail, lifting the near-one-hundred-tonne vessel effortlessly over the crashing waves.

Joanna breathed in the warm sea air and felt good about her life. She'd passed out from Britannia Royal Naval College three days before and been offered a commission to become a junior naval officer. She'd breezed through training. Over the last few months, she'd worked her body hard and she felt fitter and stronger than ever before. She'd learned to shoot the SA80 rifle, aced navigation (not surprising given her experience sailing since the age of nine), walked the leadership reaction course, and scored the highest in her year on the physical exam on the wilds of Dartmoor. Joanna Mason embodied exactly what the navy wanted. She never made a song and dance about things, she got her head down and completed tasks with zero bullshit, smiling and exuding a positive mental attitude, always taking time to offer encouragement to her classmates, which also made her likeable within the group. By the time she graduated, she'd been singled out as the outstanding cadet in her year, winning the coveted Queen's Sword Award.

When she got back to England she had to decide whether or not to accept the commission. Ordinarily, the navy would never agree to a delay; but when Joanna had asked for time to consider, given her enormous potential, they had made a rare exception. She now had a week to make up her mind. If she signed up, then it would herald the start of a minimum of three years in the navy. But she didn't want to think about that yet. For now, she only wanted to be there on the deck of the *Golden Falcon* under sail in the Red Sea.

She looked out across the horizon and thought about her father. He'd recently moved to Mozambique and she wondered what he might be doing now, a couple of thousand miles away. Thinking of him made her feel guilty all of a sudden because her decision to stay away this Easter had been born out of not wanting to deal with her mother's sadness as much as wanting to sail again. Although her parents had broken up 'amicably', her father seemed to be dealing with it better than her mum. Every time she called home, her mother and Aunty Sheila seemed to be sinking another bottle of Chardonnay and moaning about the state of the men on offer in Hereford. Her mother was still a good-looking woman, and she'd find someone else. Joanna just didn't want to be around her much until she did.

Fortunately, the days on board the *Falcon* kept her mind on other things. Work began at 6 am, cleaning everything from deck to hull, removing bird shit and salt spray, wiping down dirty fingerprints from surfaces, removing evidence of anything that made the boat look less than brand new. Eight o'clock was the daily crew meeting when Ben would brief them on the route and activities for the day. As the most experienced of the deckhands, Jo was usually required to then help Ben and the first officer sail the boat; but when they were anchored, she could just as easily be asked to prepare the jet skis or help the guests with their diving equipment. She was there to do whatever the client required and she worked hard without complaint, happy to be at sea and even happier to pocket the two grand she'd earn from the fortnight's work.

She walked back to the bridge and stood alongside the skipper, glancing sideways, trying to judge if he was out of his funk yet, noticing how his eyes darted back and forth along the horizon. She could sense that he was still a bit edgy, probably nervous about their bearing, unhappy that the client had overruled his advice. Everyone on board had heard how angry Mr Wei had been when Ben tried to push back, and nobody liked to hear the skipper being shut down. Unfortunately, that was often the way when you were sailing someone else's boat.

'Thanks for asking me out here, Skip,' she said.

'Wanted you to see what you'd be missing,' he said, not taking his eyes off the horizon.

'The navy said I can still take time out for racing.'

'Hmm,' Ben replied.

'You think I'm doing the wrong thing.'

'I think you have talent.'

Jo's cheeks reddened a little. She wasn't used to receiving praise, not least from Ben Warmington. 'Thanks, Ski—'

'Ssh,' he interrupted her. 'Here, take this.'

He moved aside, handing her control of the wheel while he grabbed his binoculars and scanned the horizon. Jo squinted to make out what he was looking for, but there was nothing that she could see with the naked eye.

'Great,' he said, lowering the glasses again. 'Just, fucking great.'

THREE

Pemba Port, Mozambique

Wang Li Lan pulled her headscarf tight as she crossed the
road opposite the Mosque and hurried past the Italian restaurant towards the port. Pemba felt like a town on the
edge and she could sense fear everywhere. In the last week
alone it seemed like the population had doubled as more
and more refugees piled in from the countryside, seeking
shelter and safe passage across the sea.

She was, by some way, the slightest woman in Pemba,
which combined with her fine black hair and pale alabas-
ter skin, marked her out immediately from the rest of the
locals. As she reached the harbour's security gate, the guard
moved to let her pass but she paused, as she always did to
address Filipe, the old blind beggar, sitting in his usual spot,
white stick between his legs, thick curly grey hair wildly
protruding from under his Taqiyah.

'Good morning, Filipe,' she said, dropping a couple of
centavos in his begging bowl. 'What's the news?' More
than once, Filipe had proven to have his ear to the ground
better than the local news agencies. Foreign journalists
were now banned from northern Mozambique and even

the local guys daren't venture much north of Pemba anymore.

The old man smiled at the sound of Li Lan's voice. The men in the port had told him a hundred times that the young woman was Chinese, but he found that hard to reconcile with the voice he heard, which was pure Kiunjuga, the Arabic Swahili that the traders from Zanzibar used. Filipe often wondered if those who had told him that weren't having a bit of fun at his expense, pulling the old blind man's leg.

'Al-Shabaab massacred a whole village near Mucojo last night, Miss,' he said, his face crumpled in a look of deep anguish. He shook his head solemnly. 'Not long now before they reach Pemba.'

Li Lan sighed. Mucojo was less than a couple of hours away. If the Islamists were already there, then she had even less time than she'd hoped. She thanked Filipe and continued through the gates, taking the path along the dockside to her office.

She might not have looked like your average Tanzanian, but Li Lan was born and raised there, on the island of Zanzibar. Her mother had given birth to her only daughter soon after she and Li's father moved from Shuidong in Guangdong province, Southern China in the early 1990s. Li's father, the son of a poor fisherman, had followed his dad into the seafood industry, and when the opportunity came to move to Africa, he took it. Since then, he had grown his business into one of the largest sea cucumber exporters in the Indian Ocean region. Chinese people's appetite for eating the slug-like animal's flesh had exploded in the past thirty years. When Li's two elder brothers left Zanzibar to focus on growing the customer base in Hong Kong, it had fallen on her to take over the supply side of the enterprise. Three years ago, Li Lan officially became Operations Director of Wang Trading Company and her old man had finally been able to put his feet up and enjoy his old age.

She wasted no time in making her mark on the business, investing in sea cucumber fisheries not only in Zanzibar but also in Mozambique and Madagascar. She set up an office in Mozambique because it was undoubtedly the new growth market. The white teatfish, a variety of sea cucumber particular to Mozambique waters, could reach fifty dollars per kilo wholesale in Hong Kong, while housewives in the seafood market would pay five or ten times that depending on size.

But everything was about to change because Pemba, the town that had long been a stronghold of the Makonde people, was facing a very uncertain future. Mozambique was almost the last African country to become independent in June 1975 after a long and bloody ten-year struggle that culminated in civil war. The victorious Marxist party had taken power of a country with few resources. That was until they discovered twenty billion barrels of gas off the coast of Cabo Delgado. A large French multinational oil company secured drilling rights and, soon after, billions of dollars went missing while development in the region stalled. Deep resentment grew as the jobs that were promised never materialised and the people in the north realised that politicians and western corporations planned on getting rich while they saw none of the cash.

The Islamists, calling themselves Al-Shabaab, jumped on the opportunity, highlighting the gross injustice of the deal, recruiting the region's poor young men, who had no hope of a better life. They were offered real jobs – fighting for Al-Shabaab – and thousands took up arms to fight against the corporate overlords who they were told were robbing them of their birthright – the huge gas and mineral reserves under their feet, being plundered by international companies and corrupt politicians. Within months, an army had been raised and now the gas project was in danger of being overrun.

As the jihadists expanded their area of control, they butchered all resistance in their path. If Felipe was correct, then the port could fall to them any day, and if that happened, Li Lan's business in Pemba was finished. She would have to flee along with everyone else.

She unlocked the door to her office, a prefabricated single-story unit bolted onto the front of an old brick warehouse that opened directly to the loading area where Pemba's visiting ships docked on the jetty beyond. Li Lan checked her watch. It was 7.15 am, which meant it was the middle of the afternoon in Hong Kong.

When she got to her desk, she dialled an international number that she knew by heart. After a couple of rings, she heard a voice on the other end that she knew well enough not to feel the need to say hello.

'We have to move,' she said.

'It's not time yet,' the voice replied.

'No more delay. We could lose everything, Oo.'

'The buyer don't want a part consignment, sister.'

She held the phone away from her ear. Her big brother, Oo, had never been good at listening to her. Five years in Hong Kong hadn't helped with that.

'There's a ship leaving for Mombasa on Tuesday,' she said.

There was a pause on the end of the line. She knew her brother well enough to know that he was working out all the angles. She'd worked them out already, but she waited for him to catch up.

'Okay,' he said finally. 'We can try. I'll call him. Be ready.'

She hung up the phone with a heavy sigh and removed her headscarf, shaking out her jet-black hair. She reached into her bag and opened the flask of tea that she had brought from home. A cup of green tea marked the real start to the day and after she had taken a sip, she felt a little better about the situation. Her brother would come through for her. He always did. Three days should be enough to complete the order and get the goods to Pemba in time to make the Tuesday shipment. As long as his people were ready, then it was possible.

When she'd finished her tea, she went back to the office door and locked it from the inside. She lowered the blinds and then let herself through the back door into the warehouse. To anyone else the smell of drying sea cucumber would have been unbearable, racks upon racks laid out in the gloomy hangar, releasing their pungent sour and salty aroma. But the stench no longer even registered with Li Lan and she passed by oblivious to it, concentrating instead on finding the right key from the several that she kept on her keyring. When she reached the far end of the warehouse, she unlocked a heavy metal door and pushed it open.

Li Lan knew exactly where to find the light switch in the blackness. The small storeroom had no windows and the door she'd opened was the only way in and out. When she hit the lights, a single strip-light overhead blinked on and off a few times before settling down. She focused on the contents – two rows of large grey-white elephant tusks lay side by side on the floor. Li Lan's eyes ran along them, counting in her head as she did so – a little over two hundred tusks in each row, less than one hundred short of a full consignment. As long as her brother's people had been busy, she could be safely out of Pemba by the middle of next week.

FOUR

Dahlak Islands

'Ooooooooooooooooh,' Wei Lun Chow screamed out, half in agony, half delicious ecstasy, as the tip of a single feather flittered down his naked back and over his buttocks. He shivered from the sensation, pulling a little against the silk ties that tethered him face-down to the bed. Chow loved and loathed being tickled in equal measure. At that precise moment, he gave himself over to it and relished the contradiction. In doing so, he felt all the tension of the last few days ebb away.

The main suite on the *Falcon* was opulent to the point of gaudy, having been personally designed by Lulu Lytle, the London socialite and designer. African rosewood panelling had been imported from Gabon, and the furniture individually sourced from Europe, nothing more recent than the sixteenth century. The bed, solid oak, had previously been that of Louis XII, while the chandeliers, customised originals from an estate in Scotland, were repurposed specifically for the *Falcon*'s low ceilings. The soft furnishings, produced exclusively by Soane of London for the *Falcon*, included thirty momme mulberry silk bed sheets embossed with the Cantonese characters 周伟伦 – Wei Lun Chow.

Sitting astride Chow in the middle of the French king's old bed, was one of his guests, Mae Yin, a nineteen-year-old woman from the southern region of Guangzhou. Mae Yin moved to Shenzhen three years previously to pursue a career in modelling, but had found greater economic success working as an exclusive escort for Chow. She and her three colleagues lived together in an apartment in Hong Kong, at his expense, where they were free to spend their time (and Chow's money) as long as they remained on standby 24/7 to accompany him when and where he chose – any time, anywhere, any way.

'A-Rest-O-Mo-Men-Tum,' Chow cried out, his voice slightly muffled by the pillow in his face. Mae Yin knew very well what this command meant, having heard it many times before, and she dutifully tickled Chow with the feather again, only slower this time, giggling with faux delight over his renewed cries for mercy. He was paying her handsomely to indulge this fantasy and she was more than happy to oblige. It made a pleasant change from the things her previous client had expected from her.

Chow had explained at some length why that particular feather was very precious to him. It was the actual peacock feather used by Professor Gilderoy Lockhart, played by Sir Kenneth Branagh in the movie *Harry Potter and the Chamber of Secrets*. A movie she hadn't seen. Chow had recounted how he'd acquired the prop (anonymously) for a considerable sum, through a specialist auction house in Los Angeles, along with various other Potter memorabilia.

He had purchased these things because he had very specific sexual needs, which he liked to call for in the form of Harry Potter spells, all of which he knew by heart. He'd watched every single one of the movies several times because magic excited his obsessional tendencies.

The Chinese billionaire had very specific obsessions. Harry Potter came a close second to boats. He'd been fascinated with everything maritime since he was a child when his father had been a ferryman on the Star Ferry, carrying passengers across the Victoria Bay, from Hong Kong Island to Kowloon. That was before Chow got rich and bought his parents a luxury penthouse on the waterfront in Tsim Sha Tsui, from where his dad could watch his old ferry crossing the water back and forth to Wan Chai Pier.

Money had changed everything for the Chow family. Chow had left Kowloon for the mainland with precious little of it at sixteen. He found work at Freight Tech, one of China's largest shipping companies, working in the warehouse. At night, he'd studied, teaching himself how to code, eventually well enough to land an intern job with Huawei in Shenzhen. Ten years of hard graft at China's foremost tech company had eventually led to a promotion into the Huawei AI development team. A couple of years after that, he'd spotted an opportunity that he knew was too good to share with his employer.

Chow's lightbulb moment came when he realised how AI could save the shipping industry a lot of time and money. He quit Huawei, secured seed funding from a Taiwanese investor, now his business partner, and worked day and night to develop a neural network-based screening tool that allowed major shipping lines to detect suspicious cargo. He called the product SinoCheck, AI software that could scan keywords in booking documentation and cross-reference them against international regulations to identify dangerous shipments of everything from arms to drugs. Today, Sino-Check monitors more than half of the world's shipping cargo every day. In the process, it made Wei Lun Chow a very, very rich man.

Mae Yin moved back as Chow pushed his buttocks back and up into the air and cast another spell, 'A-Kwa-Ee-Ruck-To.' She knew this drill well. This was her cue and she reached around to give him his final relief. Chow slumped forward onto his belly with a satisfied moan. The diminutive tycoon lay flat on the silk sheets while the other three women appeared with tubs of warm soapy water and together set about meticulously cleaning his whole body. When they were done, he would take a nap while the *Falcon* completed the journey to the Zubair Group for some scuba diving later in the afternoon.

Chow's most recent obsession was a fascination with exploring life below the sea. Over the past couple of years, he'd dived most of the world's greatest dive sites including Sipadan and the Palau Islands, the *Yongala* and *Thistlegorm* wrecks and the Blue Hole of Belize. Now he wanted to take things further, to visit sites that nobody had dived before. Top of his list was Zubair. As the epicentre of two decades of war, it was thought that reefs around Zubair could be the most unspoilt in the whole world. In a couple of hours,

Chow would become the first person since the 1990s to see if that was true.

He told the women to leave him alone. As he closed his eyes, he heard a firm knock on the door. Irritated with the interruption to his routine, he told Mae Yin to tell whoever it was to go away and, with a deferential bow, she left to convey his message.

Chow closed his eyes again, but he could still hear voices in the corridor. He couldn't sleep while he could hear people talking. He gritted his teeth in frustration. It sounded as though one of the crew was arguing with Mae Yin. And he could also hear the voice of his security guy, Vlad. After a minute, frustrated that this interruption was going to ruin his whole afternoon, he stood up and marched to the door, flinging it open.

'Can you shut the fuck up,' he said in his unusually high register.

Everyone did exactly that. Chow's angry gaze moved from Vlad to Mae Yin to the girl from the sailing crew. They were now all standing, dumb, looking back at him until finally, Joanna spoke up.

'The captain wants these two on deck, Mr Wei,' she said to Chow, motioning to the muscular Vlad and his tall, gangly colleague, Sergei.

'We don't work for the captain,' said Vlad.

Chow looked even more irritated than before. His nap had been ruined by this bullshit. And again the captain was putting his own agenda before the man who was paying him. 'Go, see what he wants,' he said, with a dismissive wave of his hand. He'd already decided that he would never use

Ben Warmington again, either on the *Falcon* or any of his other boats. He would be giving a much smaller tip than usual too.

Vlad nodded to Sergei and the two Russians followed Joanna back upstairs. Mae Yin lowered her eyes, offering Chow an apologetic bow, but he wasn't in the mood for forgiveness, he was already slamming the door.

FIVE

Niassa Game Reserve, Mozambique

The Toyota Hilux made light work of the potholes that peppered the dark red muddy track running east of Patrol Tower Six. The sun was low in the sky, so Matt Mason, sitting in the front passenger seat, pulled down the visor to help him see. He lifted the radio to his ear, listening to the chatter on the airwaves. His men had reported hearing gunshots minutes before and now they were triangulating, relaying the information back to Mason so that he could establish the source. He looked down at the map, quickly calculating that the shots must have come from the area around one of the smaller watering holes on the river running parallel to the northern border.

He radioed the control room and told the duty ranger, George, to look for elephants in the immediate area. Nearly all of the herds were tracked closely using GPS-satellite tracking devices, attached to one of the oldest in each family. Once the GPS collar was fitted, the animal's whereabouts could be followed using a satellite phone, but the codes were strictly protected and changed every day. Only Flossie, Mason, and the ranger on duty that day ever had access.

The radio crackled as George called out the coordinates for the only herd he could see in their immediate vicinity. Mason pointed to his left and Joseph, his right-hand man and by some distance the most talented of his rangers, span the wheel sharply, launching the 4x4 down another track that headed north. He accelerated hard, forcing the four men standing on the back of the truck to hang on for dear life. They were under orders to be prepared for imminent engagement. Even though poachers worked fast, there was every chance they would intercept them before they had time to escape. But as the vehicle turned the corner, Mason saw they were already too late.

In front of the vehicle was a scene of abject horror. Lined up along the southern riverbank lay the carcasses of six dead adult elephants, their bodies still and lifeless. A lone baby elephant stood among them, crying a sorrowful peal, laying its body down on the heft of what must have been its mother, caressing her with its trunk. Another four juveniles watched from the water, jittery, fidgeting, also mourning the loss of their elders. The cadavers were already covered in flies, feasting off the exposed flesh, now rotting in the heat. In the coming days, they would feed an army of predators. Hyaenas and vultures would come and strip the bodies back to bone. But for now, the family was alone with the dead.

Joseph pulled the Toyota to a stop and Mason climbed down onto the silty mud. He walked over to the largest beast and saw how the blood was still pouring freely from where its face had once been. The animals' trunks lay in a discarded pile to one side. The poachers had butchered them all, sawing off their faces so as not to waste any of the valuable tusks.

In the ten weeks since he'd been on the reserve, this was the first time Mason had lost an animal and he wasn't prepared for the way it made him feel. He felt shocked, sick, sad. These magnificent beasts had done nothing to anyone and yet here they lay, slaughtered in cold blood, cut down in their prime. *For what?* So that someone on the other side of the world could have a fancy pair of chopsticks? In his seventeen years in the army, Mason had seen more than his fair share of death. He'd seen friends blown to pieces, men die in the dirt in front of his eyes, but the sight of the elephant torn apart for no good reason saddened his heart deeply.

He crouched down and dipped his finger in the fresh blood that was oozing from the elephants' remains. He could still feel its warmth. The animal was not long dead. He was suddenly aware of his own breath and his racing heart. His blood was boiling. A feeling that he thought he'd left behind in the army was stirring in him again. It was anger. This injustice couldn't be allowed to stand. He couldn't let such a gross act of destruction go unpunished. He would find the people who had done this and he would stop them from ever doing it again.

'We are too late,' Joseph said, standing next to him, looking down at the wretched animal and shaking his head forlornly.

Mason wiped the blood from his fingers and looked around, surveying the site like it was a crime scene. Two sets of tyre tracks ran right up to the dead elephants. They were deeper than the ones made by the Hilux meaning that the poachers were carrying more weight. Judging from how one of the tracks ran askew, he also guessed that the vehicle's suspension was probably off.

He examined the ruts in the mud, noting where they had turned around before taking the road east through the tree line. Something troubled him about it all. How could the vehicles have been so close? There were six watering holes along this stretch of river and no guarantee that you'd see elephants at any of them. Plenty of paying guests came back disappointed after a day out looking for them. A group of poachers would ordinarily have to stalk a herd on foot for days and hope to get lucky, so to drive straight to a watering hole and find a group of adults? It was too lucky.

'Back in the car,' he said, to Joseph's surprise.

'But Mason—'

Mason was no longer listening, he was addressing the men on the back of the Hilux, barking orders at them. 'Weapons made ready, fingers off triggers, stay alert!' he said before he turned back to Joseph, still standing over the dead bull. 'Let's go!'

Moments later, they were on the road heading east, speeding along in pursuit of the elephant killers. Mason's nose was back in the map. The Hilux was fast and the suspension was good, so with one hundred kilometres of mud track to cover before they reached the highway, even with a ten-minute head start, they had a good chance of catching up with the poachers. He removed an old Vector pistol from its holster. The Vector was a South African knock-off of the better-known Beretta, but it did the job just the same. He put a round in the chamber and clicked off the safety before he set about readying his rifle. He opened the window and leant out, lining up the AK-47 in the direction they were heading. He began to run through the potential courses of action, but before he got far, the Hilux hit trouble.

As they turned the bend, Mason didn't see the tripwire laid across the road, nor did he see the homemade IED that it triggered. The device wasn't large but it was powerful enough to blow the driver's front wheel clean off its axle, sending the Hilux skidding nose-first into the dirt. Joseph wrestled with the wheel but he couldn't stop them careering off the track, and the vehicle came to an abrupt stop against the trunk of a mahogany tree. The men in the back were thrown heavily into the back of the cab while Mason and Joseph's airbags exploded.

Mason was dazed, but he pulled himself together fast. He reached for his knife and stabbed the airbag to create some space. As the air came rushing out, he heard gunshots. Two men appeared from the tree line on the other side of the road, striding confidently towards them, unleashing a volley of bullets in the direction of the Hilux. Their strategy seemed to be one of quantity rather than quality as the rounds hit pretty much every part of the vehicle, sending glass showering all over the inside of the cab.

Mason opened his door and slid down onto the ground on the far side of the vehicle, flipping onto his back and using his heels to push himself under the chassis. He eased the Vector from its holster and slid his hands up over his head. On his back, looking up, he could see the two shooters working their way towards Joseph's door, spent AK cases cascading onto the red mud. Mason dug in with his heels and pushed himself along until he was almost on the other side of the Toyota.

He paused for a moment, waiting until the firing stopped. He heard one of the men shouting orders in Portuguese and then the familiar sound of reloading weapons. Mason knew it was his chance to move and with a final push, he emerged from under the 4x4 directly beneath them. Just as they realised that Mason was there, he was looking up at them, pistol trained on the taller of the two men.

'Too late,' Mason said.

He double-tapped the trigger, placing a pair of bullets under the first poacher's chin. The second poacher turned to run, but Mason was too fast, firing twice again only this time into the base of the man's spine, causing him to fall heavily, rifle flying from his grasp. Mason leapt to his feet, shaking off the fragments of glass that had gathered in his hair. He strode over to the man lying on the ground. The bastard was going to die just like his mate, but he had two or three minutes of bleeding out to do first. During which time, Matt Mason had a few questions to ask him.

SIX

Zubair Group of Islands, The Red Sea

It's a common misconception that yachts are blown along by the wind, when in fact it's quite the opposite. The sail creates a barrier between low pressure in front and high pressure behind, which means the boat is sucked forwards. Knowing where the wind is blowing from, and at what angle, is critical to maximising pressure differences and, therefore, top speeds. There were few captains in the world better at it than Ben Warmington, but in the middle of the Red Sea, twenty miles shy of the Zubair Group, no amount of pressure would allow him to outpace two wooden-hulled skiffs with one-hundred-horsepower engines mounted on the back. Ben estimated that the pirates would catch them within a few minutes.

He handed control of the wheel to his first mate, Woodsie, and dialled Channel 16 on VHF radio, issuing a mayday distress call to anyone that might be listening. There was a clear protocol to follow in such situations and Ben knew it well – slow the boat, drop the sails, present arms. Moments later, Jo returned to the bridge with Vlad and Sergei, the two burly Russian ex-special ops guys who were aboard as Chow's security detail. Both looked like they'd been carved from granite. They had trained with the 22nd Spetsnaz Brigade, seeing active duty in Chechnya, Syria, and Crimea, before they moved into the bodyguarding business.

'Gentlemen, if you wouldn't mind,' Ben said, unlocking the secure weapons cache bolted to the floor of the control room. He removed four Steyr AUG bullpup rifles, light and accurate, perfect for the job he had in mind, and handed one to each of the Russians with a fully loaded clip. He took another for himself and then looked around the bridge for a willing volunteer to take the last one. Joanna Mason was the first to step forward.

'I know how to use it, Skip,' she said taking the rifle and loading the magazine before either of the other crewmen could say a word.

Chow came shuffling up onto the deck, his face red with fury, his short silk dressing gown barely covering his private regions. 'What the fuck is happening?' he asked, looking around, noting that the boat had changed course once again. 'I made my instructions very clearly, Captain.'

'I'm afraid we are making a bit of a diversion, Mr Wei,' Ben explained.

'Again? This is my fucking boat,' Chow said.

'Maybe not for much longer,' Ben replied half under his breath as he handed Chow the binoculars and pointed him in the direction of the two skiffs approaching off the stern. Without waiting for Chow to catch up with what was happening, Ben gestured to the others.

'Okay, you lot follow me,' he said.

The captain led the security detail and Joanna along the starboard side until they were lined up near the bow. He lifted the rifle to his cheek and looked through the sight, estimating that the go-fast boats were now less than eight hundred metres away and doing nearly forty knots.

'Drop sail. Bring her to starboard, Woodsie!' Ben called out.

As Paul Woods followed his instructions, Jim winched down the sails and the *Falcon* turned square to the wind so that Ben and the others were facing directly at the oncoming skiffs.

'Now, everyone, hold the rifles up,' he said, lifting his rifle in the air and encouraging the others to copy him. He held the Steyr high above his head, where he was confident the pirates could see it clearly. Non-lethal escalation. Be visible. Show arms. That was the protocol. If they followed it to the letter, then hopefully the skiffs would think better and turn around.

'We can take these guys,' said the shorter of the Russians, Vlad. A vein on his forehead was already pumped full of blood like it was piping adrenaline straight to his brain.

'And if they return fire?' Ben asked. 'This boat's aluminium. Believe me, it won't take a volley of AK rounds very well.'

The Russians exchanged sideways glances. Neither looked very comfortable with the idea of holding a rifle in the air when you could use it to shoot instead. But when Ben motioned again for them to lift their guns, they did it, albeit without looking entirely convinced.

'If they see we're serious, they'll give it up,' Ben said, confidently.

He'd heard stories of pirates attacking tankers in these waters, but on a tanker you had the advantage of height and cover, which gave you an option to return fire. Out on a yacht like the *Falcon*, where everything happened at water-height level, you had no ballistic protection and zero fretboard. The *Falcon* was designed for fun, not battle.

He held the gun up as high as he could just as a round ricocheted off the jib behind his head, another three rounds whizzed into the water, metres in front of him. Both Russians lowered their rifles and started returning fire, sending a volley of bullets back across the sea in the direction of the approaching skiffs.

'Cease fire, cease fire,' Ben screamed, but no one was listening. The Russians kept shooting at the skiffs, but they were still too far away to engage with any accuracy.

In the distance, Ben saw a muzzle flash from one of the pirate's guns as they returned fire. Again, bullets pinged off the *Falcon's* mast and tore through its hull. Ben dropped his rifle and bent double, holding his hands over his head as though they might protect him, while the Russians stood boldly still, continuing to fire until their magazines were empty.

Just next to them, Joanna Mason quietly dropped to one knee and aimed her rifle just as she had been trained to do. She made a small adjustment, changing the point of aim. She estimated the target to be a little over four hundred metres away so she increased the magnification to x6 and lined up the reticle pattern of her LPVO sight, allowing approximately four inches for the shot to drop over the distance to the target. She waited another moment for the boat to rise to the peak of the swell and then eased her finger over the trigger, releasing her breath as she squeezed it gently. Once. Twice.

Meanwhile, the Russians had begun to recheck their own settings despite Ben's pleas for them to stand down, but they were interrupted by the sound of the two shots. Ben looked down to see Joanna kneeling in position, eyes still looking straight down the barrel of her rifle. He turned and followed the line of her sight towards the oncoming skiffs and saw that the pilot of the first boat had slumped over so that his body was now leaning against the tiller. The skiff veered off course violently, throwing two passengers overboard. While another of the pirates wrestled to retake control, the second skiff diverted course to rescue the men floundering in the water.

Ben looked back to Jo again. She was completely still, maintaining her aim in case another shot was required, composed, focused, eye on the target, ready to strike.

'Good shot,' said Sergei, the taller, blond-haired Russian, in a gruff monotone.

'Jo?' Ben sounded dazed. He'd known Jo since she was fifteen, seen her develop into a truly promising young sailor, but he couldn't reconcile that with the woman he was looking at now, who had just calmly taken out a pirate with a rifle from four hundred metres.

'I think they're turning back,' she said. She continued to observe the target through her weapon sight. 'Yup. Definitely fucking off.'

She got back to her feet as the boats sped off, back from where they'd come. Satisfied they were no longer a threat, she disarmed her rifle, removed the round from the chamber, and applied the safety.

'Are you okay?' asked Ben.

'Yeah,' she replied, sounding unnervingly casual. 'Are you?'

Ben considered the question. He wasn't sure. His hands were trembling and he suddenly felt ice-cold despite the temperature being in the thirties.

'Skip, we've had a response to your mayday call,' Paul Woods had appeared by Ben's side without him even noticing. 'Looks military.'

They turned to see the *Falcon* was being approached from the west by an Eritrean-flagged gunboat. The grey steel vessel was moving at a fair clip, maybe fifty knots. Ben felt a wave of relief. He took Joanna's rifle and gestured for the two Russians to follow.

'We'd better stand down before they get here. I don't want to get into a fight about rules of engagement with the Eritrean Navy,' he said.

They packed the rifles back into the strongbox and Ben padlocked it shut again as the Eritreans pulled along their port side. The Super Dvora Mk II was a sixty-tonne Israeli-designed high-speed patrol boat equipped with a 20mm cannon. A tall, dark-skinned officer in a faded blue uniform appeared on the bridge carrying a loud hailer. He was flanked by four armed men on either side.

'Who is the captain?' he called out. The boats were less than five metres apart, so to Ben the hailer seemed a touch excessive.

'I am,' he said, stepping forward, holding up a hand.

'I am Captain Kidane of the Eritrean Navy. We heard your mayday call,' the officer replied.

'We were under attack,' Ben pointed across the water where the would-be pirates had made their escape. 'Two skiffs, they withdrew less than three minutes ago.'

The captain didn't turn around. He remained focused on Ben, weighing him up as he lowered the loud hailer. He exchanged a few words with the man standing next to him in a language nobody aboard the *Falcon* could understand. Finally, he lifted the hailer to his mouth again.

'We come aboard,' Kidane said, already directing his pilot to pull the gunboat alongside the *Falcon*.

'No,' the bigger of the Russians, Sergei, said. 'This is a bad idea.'

'The security of the ship is my responsibility,' Ben replied firmly under his breath, before he addressed the Eritrean officer again. 'Please, come aboard. We have nothing to hide.'

SEVEN

Niassa Game Reserve, Mozambique

The wounded poacher lay on his front, his head turned to one side, saliva dripping onto the dirt as he struggled for breath. A puddle of blood was slowly growing around him, thick red liquid oozing from two bullet holes in his back. His eyes were filled with fear, darting around as if looking for clues as to what might be happening, when the explanation was clear. He was dying.

Matt Mason crouched alongside him. 'Who do you work for?' he asked.

The man's eyes widened and he shook his head to indicate he wasn't going to answer. Mason looked disappointed, things were so much easier when people cooperated. He placed a finger directly into one of the bullet wounds and pushed hard. The poacher screamed out in pain as Mason repeated himself.

'Who's paying you?'

'Sim Ingles. Sim Ingles,' the man simpered, panting hard, trying to deal with the agony.

Mason wiped his finger on the man's shirt. He considered himself to be a pretty good linguist. As well as a few bits of French, Spanish, and Mandarin he'd learned in the Regiment, he spoke fluent Baghdadi Arabic and conversed happily in both the Dari and Pashtun he'd picked up in Afghanistan. But Portuguese? *Nehnuma.*

He searched the dying man's pockets and found a cheap Chinese phone, a wallet, and a key to a Toyota 4x4. When he tried to open the phone, it prompted him for a facial ID. Mason held the device close to the man's face and unlocked it, scrolled to the option he guessed meant, 'change passcode' and used the man's face again to permanently disable the phone's security. Happy that he could now explore its contents at his leisure, he returned his attention to the man himself.

'El jefe?' Mason asked, guessing that the Spanish word for 'boss' might be similar in Portuguese.

'O chefe?' he whispered, now barely able to catch his breath.

Mason shrugged. Sure, that was close enough. 'Si,' he nodded.

The dying man smiled. Maybe he smiled because he knew that what he was about to say would be the last thing he'd ever say. Maybe he smiled because in that moment he found a little peace. Either way, he took his last breath and answered, 'El chefe é Allah.'

A second later, he died.

Mason left him where he lay and returned to the Hilux. His men were taking stock of their injuries. They had some bumps and bruises but they were otherwise fine. Mason handed one of them the poacher's car keys.

'Find their vehicle. Quickly,' he instructed.

Joseph was in a much worse state. Mason dragged him from the cab, seeing how the IED had torn through the floor, filling Joseph's leg with puncture wounds from the shrapnel. The leg was now full of hot metal. Mason irrigated the wound with water from his bottle. Joseph let out a low moan as Mason flipped him over to take a closer look at the more urgent wound in his shoulder. Mason tore away Joseph's shirt and saw a clear exit wound. He considered that a bonus. The absence of a bullet at least bought them some time.

Seconds later, the men screamed up in the poachers' vehicle, an old Nissan Nivara pickup, which they'd found hidden in the trees. As Mason had suspected, the back of the cab contained a dozen tusks, freshly cut from the dead elephants on the reserve. They were still caked in blood and pieces of flesh. He pushed them to one side and lifted Joseph onto the back next to them, laying him on his front so that he could maintain pressure on the shoulder wound.

'Hospital!' Mason shouted to the driver.

They sped off in the direction of the highway. Once they hit the main road, they would turn south towards Montepuez, the only field hospital within three hundred miles. They were at least five hours away so Joseph's chances of making it were 50:50 at best. Mason held his water bottle to Joseph's mouth. The guy looked bad. Blood was still oozing freely from the shoulder no matter how hard Mason pushed down onto it.

Mason had another thought. The Golden Beach Hotel was less than an hour away. Since Mozambique had discovered the largest gas deposits in Africa just off its coast, the gold rush that followed had drawn in ex-pat contractors from around the globe. The hundreds of engineers and construction guys that flocked in to build the project's infrastructure needed somewhere to kick back when they got leave. As a result, the Golden Beach had a decent medical centre. Mason banged on the roof of the cab and shouted to the driver to make the detour. If Joseph had any chance, then the hotel was it.

Twenty minutes later, the Nissan pulled off the dusty track and picked up speed on the tarmacked road, heading south. They raced by villages and small towns, no more than collections of single-storey mud huts topped with corrugated iron roofs. Joseph passed in and out of consciousness, moaning weakly from the pain, mumbling incoherently while Mason eyed the tusks of the elephants.

He still had the poacher's phone in his pocket. He flicked it open and looked through the list of recent calls, an anonymous list of +258 Mozambique numbers. At least the guy had had enough brains not to save any names in it. Mason instinctively hit redial on the last number. *Why not? Let's see who picks up.*

As soon as he hit the green button, he heard the sound of two phones ringing, the one in his hand and another right next to him. It was coming from Joseph's pocket. He went through his jacket until he found a phone and read the name on the screen – João. Joseph had been passing the dead poacher information.

Mason felt sick. He'd trusted Joseph. Soon after he'd started work on the reserve, he'd gone to the village to speak with the headman, Mwamba Kiba. He had sat with Mwamba for hours, convincing him that the elephants should be a priority for the community. He'd tried to explain how preserving what they had would bring more wealth in the long run than the poachers could pay them in the short term. The headman had suggested to Mason that his son would make a good ranger and so they had struck a deal. Now he wondered if they'd played him for a fool.

To Mason, the elephants represented everything beautiful and noble about Africa. Like most Westerners, he felt they were deserving of all the effort and money needed to protect them. But obviously, that wasn't true for everyone. For at least one person, the young man bleeding out next to him, the elephant represented something different. Men like Joseph worked with poachers because, with so little else in life, elephants were simply not a priority. They were just another way to make money.

He scrolled down to the next number on the call list and dialled. It went immediately to a voicemail that sounded Cantonese. Mason couldn't understand any of what the woman was saying beyond the name of the business – Wang Trading Company, Pemba.

They reached the outskirts of Mueda and the driver honked his horn, swerving in and out of lanes, avoiding crowds of people in the street. Mason was shocked by the vast numbers of people he saw on the move. The last time he'd seen anything like it was in Syria where he'd helped Kurdish fighters to hold off an ISIS advance while whole towns were evacuated.

Everywhere Mason looked, families were walking, carrying what possessions they could, driving their animals in front of them. They had exactly the same hunted look in their eyes that those Kurdish civilians running from ISIS had had. They were fleeing something so terrifying that they had packed up everything they owned and ran. The Nissan stopped at an intersection next to an old man holding the hand of a young girl.

'Where is everyone going?' Mason asked

The old man looked blankly back at him. He spoke no English, but Mason's face told him all he needed to know.

'Al-Shabaab,' the old man said, pointing back the way he had come. 'Al-Shabaab está chegando.'

They swung a left onto a bumpier track that led to the coast and Mason saw a handwritten wooden sign that read 'Golden Beach 10.' Twenty minutes later, they came to a stop outside the perimeter fence of northern Mozambique's only deluxe resort. The Golden Beach was a high-end all-inclusive hotel with fashionably appointed, hardwood, single-storey cabins arranged around a circular restaurant building with a sprawling terraced bar that overlooked an infinity pool stretching all the way down to a private white-sand beach.

But Mason had never seen the place look like it did now. The gates were pulled shut and a crowd of local people, ordinary farmers from the surrounding villages, were clamouring to get inside. There was a sense of panic and chaos in the air. Some of the men were scuffling with each other, someone else was trying to climb the fence, another was banging his fists on the gate. Mason jumped down from the truck and approached cautiously.

'What the fuck is going on?' he asked one of the men in the crowd.

'Mister, Al-Shabaab is coming.' The man replied, his eyes wide with fear. 'If we cannot go inside, it will be big trouble for us.'

Mason didn't have time to discuss what exactly that trouble might be. 'Move aside,' he screamed to the crowd. 'I have a wounded man. Move!'

The tone of the Englishman's voice caused the people to stir. Behind him, the rangers were lifting Joseph down from the back of the truck and carrying him to the gates. Mason shouted to the driver to start honking the horn. Immediately, from behind the gate, a security guard, a big guy carrying an AR-15 over his shoulder, appeared at the hatch and addressed him directly.

'The hotel is closed, boss,' he said.

'Open the fucking gate,' Mason said as though he hadn't heard him. 'I've got a dying man here. Tell Maurice, Matt Mason's outside and needs urgent medical help.'

The name Maurice got the security guard's attention. Maurice, a flamboyant but ruthlessly pragmatic Frenchman had once been a doctor in the Médecins Sans Frontières. He'd retired years ago to set up the Golden Beach, and he and Mace had spent nights propping up the hotel's bar before now. The security guard closed the hatch again before the gates opened and several other security guards piled out, pushing the crowd back, creating enough space for Mason and his team to carry Joseph inside.

A young woman appeared from the main building and ran directly for Joseph, crouching down beside him to investigate his condition. She wore a white cloth apron over a blue nurse's uniform which looked to Mason like she'd stepped out of an old movie. A second later, she ran back inside, calling for help and the hotel concierge appeared, closely followed by a tall, handsome, big-nosed Frenchman.

'Matt Mason? *Incroyable*. It's good to see you, Mace,' Maurice said, shaking Mason by the hand. 'Maybe you arrive just in time to keep us alive.'

'I've got a man down, Maurice,' Mason said. 'Can you help?'

Maurice bent down to examine Joseph. He placed his head next to Joseph's mouth before placing his fingers against his throat to feel for a pulse that wasn't there. The ex-doctor sighed and shook his head.

'Non, I'm sorry, Mace,' he said. 'It is too late for this one.'

Mason deflated again as he watched Maurice close Joseph's eyelids. He'd seen many men die at war before, but it was one thing for a man to give his life for a cause, quite another to lose it for the sake of a few dollars. Whoever had put Joseph up to this was responsible, as far as Mason was concerned. The ivory trade was a cancer, and it was killing not only innocent animals but now a young man whose life could have been much more.

'I'd better tell his family,' Mason said. He was already dialling Flossie's number. It had been an eventful day and he had a lot of explaining to do to his boss, and a lot of bad news to tell her.

EIGHT

Zubair Group of Islands, The Red Sea

Joanna Mason took a hard shove in the back that almost sent her tumbling down the stairs. She managed to right herself only by laying a hand on the woman in front of her. The atmosphere on the *Falcon* had changed the second Captain Kidane and the Eritrean sailors came aboard. Kidane had demanded that everyone return to their cabins to collect their passports. After a close inspection, orders were issued, whereupon Ben, Woodsie, Jim, Wei Lun Chow, and the two Russian guards were taken to the bridge. Meanwhile, the Filipino catering staff, Jo and the four Chinese models were led below deck.

Before she'd been taken away, Joanna had begged to remain with the others but Kidane had refused. Joanna noticed how neither of the Russian security guys had looked very comfortable with it or indeed with anything that was going on. Since Ben had asked them to stand down, they had been giving each other the side-eye, like they were signalling secretly to each other. She had a bad feeling that things were going to turn nasty very soon.

One of the Eritrean sailors started shouting at the Filipino woman who was leading the line. He was a short, skinny boy, not much older than Joanna and his uniform was filthy, streaked with salt spray. She could smell his body odour even though there were at least eight other women standing between them.

He used the muzzle of his rifle to nudge each woman as she passed him, counting them off as they packed into the guest suite. The *Falcon*'s cabins were generously proportioned but it was still a squeeze for sixteen people. The Chinese women started chattering to each other in Mandarin. Jo thought they sounded like they were complaining but she didn't speak the language, so she couldn't be sure. Two of the Filipinos had been crying the whole time. The sound of two languages that she couldn't understand on top of whatever the Eritreans were speaking to each other was adding to Jo's sense of unease.

'What do you want with us?' she asked the smelly sailor.

'Be quiet,' he replied, placing a long thin finger to his thick brown lips.

Joanna nodded. She was surprised to hear him speak English but there was something comforting about knowing that she could communicate with him. The other sailor, taller, lighter-skinned, with almond-shaped green eyes, appeared at the door and cast his gaze around the room. He surveyed the women as though he was looking for something in particular until finally, seeing Jo, he pointed for her to come to him.

The smelly man stood in her way and the two men started to argue. Joanna wished that she could understand what they were saying but from their body language, it seemed that Smelly Guy didn't agree with whatever Green Eyes was planning. Finally, Green Eyes threw his hands up in disgust and sucked his teeth, pointing instead to one of the young Filipino girls. Joanna had noticed her already up on deck. She was pretty, with fine, delicate features and a good athletic figure, but when Green Eyes shouted at her, the girl began to cry, shaking her head, holding onto her friend. Green Eyes lurched forward and gripped her arm firmly before he dragged her out of the room. Smelly Guy turned back and faced the remaining women. After a couple of minutes, he backed out of the room and shut the door behind him. Joanna heard the key turn in the lock.

On the deck, Sergei and Vlad were sharing sideways looks. Neither of the ex-Spetsnaz soldiers had been happy about the order to reduce posture, nor how the Eritrean sailors had been invited to come aboard. The minute the Africans' boots landed on deck, both Russians realised that something was very wrong. They didn't like how the sailors were behaving nor how they had disengaged the safety catches on their rifles. The women getting taken down below was the final straw.

The Russians' job and their priority up until that point was to get Mr Chow, their client and principal, the man who was paying their wages, to safety. But now, their concerns ran only as far as preserving their own lives. Neither Sergei nor Vlad cared what happened to anyone else anymore. In any case, Mr Chow would only survive as long as they did.

The two soldiers had met during basic army training, having signed up for the National Guards after the Chechen hostage crisis when terrorists killed nearly two hundred innocent Russians. Both were well suited to the military and quickly worked their way up, earning their maroon berets and selection for special forces training. They were assigned to the 22nd Spetsnaz Brigade, Russia's elite counter-terrorism force, and sent to Crimea, where they operated as undercover civilians. Later, they served together in Armenia, Chechnya, and then Syria. More than once, Sergei, a tall, blond Muscovite had saved Vlad's life. Just as often, the muscular, bald man from Kaliningrad had repaid the favour.

Sergei had already done an appraisal of what they were up against on board the *Falcon*, knowing full well that his colleague and friend would be doing the same. They were initially being guarded by six men, but since two of the Eritreans had taken the women below deck, there were now only four men guarding the top deck. Sergei noted that two of the Eritreans' rifles still had their safety catches on and another, from the way he was holding his rifle, looked like he was carrying an empty magazine. The main threat was the officer, Kidane, who was sitting in the pilot's seat. As the boss, they had to assume he was fully loaded, both rifle and sidearm.

Vlad took the lead. He got to his feet, holding his hands up innocently as he fished out a packet of cigarettes from his breast pocket and approached the captain for a light. Kidane stood up immediately, holding his rifle square across his chest, blocking Vlad from getting any closer.

'Get back!' he ordered.

One of the young guards looked over, distracted by the sound of his boss shouting.

The bald-headed Russian flicked his cigarette into Kidane's face and his big, blond friend bounced forward and landed a heavy right uppercut under the distracted guard's chin, knocking him clean off his feet and onto the deck with a thud. He spun around and, as Vlad began to wrestle with Kidane for control of the rifle, Sergei sprinted across the beam towards the second guard on the starboard side.

The young sailor was lifting his rifle as Sergei ran at him, but before he could pull the trigger, the Russian special forces soldier dropped to the ground and threw himself feet first along the polished teak deck like a centre half performing a sliding tackle on an advancing centre forward. He skidded fast over the boards, raising his leading foot to hit the sailor mid-shin with his full weight. The sound of the young man's tibia fracturing made a satisfying crack and his body crumpled from under him. He landed on top of the Russian in a heap, screaming in agony as Sergei flipped him over and wrapped his arm around his neck. He snapped it with a solid wrench. *Good.* It was now two against two.

Unfortunately for Sergei, it was about to be two against one. He heard the sound of the shot just as he grabbed a firm hold of the last guard, the unfortunate lad whose rifle was carrying an empty magazine and who had frozen solid in the face of what was going on. As Sergei turned around, he expected to see that Vlad had disposed of the Eritrean officer, but he saw the exact opposite. In the struggle for the gun, the firearm had discharged just as the muzzle was pointed at Vlad's face and a round had taken out the back of his shiny, bald head. It was Kidane who was still standing, his face and uniform now covered in Russian brains.

Sergei spun the remaining guard around in front of him, holding his arm tight around the terrified young man's neck, using him as a shield.

'Drop your weapon or I'll kill him,' he ordered.

Kidane smiled as he wiped away a lump of Vlad's skull from above his left eye. He assessed his young subordinate, a young man from the south of the country near Assab. The boy looked pathetic, helpless in the Russian's iron grip, his eyes opened wide, beseeching the officer to save him. Instead, Kidane lifted his rifle and without a moment's hesitation, shot his own sailor in the head, splattering Sergei's face with bits of brain and bone. The boy's limp body slid to the deck. Sergei stood over him, now defenceless, and raised his hands. But before they even reached his shoulders, Kidane fired again. Another headshot, which took the Russian down.

The Eritrean sailor surveyed the damage. He'd lost two men and two hostages but he'd also dealt with the danger and still had control of the *Falcon*. He looked over to where the rest of the hostages sat cowering in the corner.

'Anyone else want to try mutiny?' he asked.

They shook their heads.

'Good.'

When they'd heard the sound of gunfire from the upper deck, several of the women in the cabin screamed. Others began to cry. Joanna Mason remained silent, knowing that whatever was happening up there was going to determine what happened next down below.

She reminded herself to remain calm and thought about her father. What would he do now? She thought about all the times that he'd taken her up on the Brecon Beacons where he'd shown her how to build a bivouac, shoot a rifle, skin a rabbit, find clean water; all kinds of skills that he'd said she might need one day. She could still hear his words, 'Sometimes you have to fight to survive, but first you have to survive to fight.'

She felt that this might be one of those times. Whatever happened, she had to survive.

Outside of the door, she heard the sound of Eritrean voices again and her heart sank. She figured that the gunfire must have been the Russians trying to take control, but whatever had occurred, the result hadn't gone their way. The Eritreans were still in control of the *Falcon*.

She heard the sound of a key in the lock and the door flew open again. Kidane walked into the room as everyone fell silent, watching him as he assessed them slowly, sinister, giving nothing away. Finally, his gaze settled on Joanna and he raised his hand, pointing his pistol directly at her. She froze, staring down the barrel into his dark, cold eyes. He seemed satisfied, happy with whatever thought had just passed into his head.

'Come now,' was all he said.

PART TWO

PART TWO

NINE

Jask, Iran

Two thousand years ago, the Iranian town of Jask was an important centre of Mithraism, the religion favoured by the Roman Legionnaires. The soldier's cult had much in common with Zoroastrianism, the religion once widely practised across Iran but which has now been almost eradicated. Today, Iran is the largest Shiite Muslim state in the world and General Ali Haddadi had dedicated his career to the fight to protect its people.

The two-star general was born into a poor family of Iranian Arabs in Khuzestan, the province that occupies the southwest corner of Iran next to the Iraqi border. His father, a simple fisherman, never lived long enough to see his son get selected for Iran's IRGCN – the Navy of the Islamic Revolutionary Guard Corps. He would have been proud of him. An illustrious twenty-year career had seen Haddadi win the Shoja'at Medal, the highest military decoration in Iran, before becoming Rear Admiral, then Minister of Defence and finally, Secretary of the Supreme National Security Council, the fifth most powerful position in Iran.

But in Haddadi's mind, his greatest achievement was undoubtedly going to be what he was planning for the town of Jask. The port had long since been an important strategic naval base, positioned as it was, on the mouth of the Strait of Hormuz, the narrow and crooked channel that divided Iran from its enemies across the Persian Gulf. Thanks to Haddadi's brilliant initiative, Jask was about to become so much more.

As Haddadi's limo pulled off the highway, he looked up at a bright red billboard, forty feet across, that towered over the city. At the centre of it was the face of his old comrade, General Ruak Shahlai. It was over a year since Shahlai had disappeared in Yemen and the Iranian government had erected billboards in his honour all over the country. Their intelligence suggested that Shahlai was being held by the British and Americans at a so-called black site, somewhere off-grid, untraceable, deniable to the outside world, from where it was unlikely that he would ever emerge. A British soldier called Matt Mason had led the mission to apprehend him, and Haddadi silently vowed revenge as the car whizzed by the billboard, shuddering at the prospect of what those Western pigs might be doing to his friend.

He put it out of his mind as the limo pulled up outside the airport convention centre and he made his way inside. The lobby entrance was adorned with Iranian and Chinese flags in preparation for today's meeting. Haddadi had deliberately intended to be late. He found the Chinese a little arrogant, so making them wait for him would remind them where they were and who they were doing business with.

An aide showed him to the meeting room on the second floor and as he entered, Haddadi nodded to his team of translators and lawyers. Finally, he turned his attention to the man he had come to meet, Xi Ming Bo. The Chinese foreign minister stood to shake the Iranian general's hand.

'General,' Xi said in English. He was also fluent in Japanese and French. 'It is an honour.'

'The honour belongs to the Islamic Republic of Iran,' the general said, equally comfortable speaking the world's lingua franca.

Xi had flown in on an unrecorded military flight from Beijing that morning. He knew that his Iranian counterpart was expecting the meeting to be a photo opportunity. He'd seen the flags in the lobby. Once the formalities were finalised, then Iran and China could make their historic announcement in front of the state-controlled press, who would syndicate it around the world. No doubt, Xi thought, the general was relishing the prospect of being on the front page of every newspaper in the world tomorrow morning.

No sooner had the UN agreement that prevented Chinese arms exports to Iran expired, than the two countries agreed an historic four-hundred-billlion-dollar trade deal. Haddadi wasted no time in capitalising on the opportunity and had proposed a programme of major arms transfers from Beijing to Tehran which would turn Jask into a vital part of Iran's security and surveillance operations for the next decade.

Xi smiled when he thought of the reaction the announcement would spark in Washington and London. China had played its cards well, and now nobody could ignore the fact that their influence was expanding significantly in the Horn of Africa. But before he gave the general what he wanted, Xi had a request. As they say in China, 'the negotiations only begin once the contract has been agreed.'

Haddadi's aide ceremonially produced two copies of the Jask contract, printed on thick weave paper, Iranian and Chinese insignias embossed at the top. The accord had been checked and double-checked by teams of lawyers on both sides, working late into the night to ensure that everything and *only* everything that had been agreed was included in the terms and conditions. The document had been fine-tuned to within an inch of its life. All that was required now were two signatures.

The aide placed a pen in front of each of the two esteemed men, an 18-carat gold fountain pen which had been ordered specially for the event. The Chinese foreign minister lifted it, impressed by its weight; but after a short moment, he laid it down on the table again.

'Maybe we could talk alone, General?' Xi said with a glance around the room.

There was an uncomfortable murmur among Haddadi's aides. No time had been allocated for a private talk between the two sides. It was entirely against protocol for Secretary Xi to ask for such a thing. The Iranian lawyers shot uneasy looks at each other. They were all thinking the same thing – in the circumstances, the most prudent course of action was to demand a recess to allow them to regroup. Haddadi, however, saw things differently. He waved away his aides with a shake of his hand and at once the room was cleared. As the door closed, the Chinese diplomat smiled to acknowledge his thanks.

'I realise this is unconventional,' he said.

'You are our guest,' Haddadi said as diplomatically as he could muster. 'In Iran, we never refuse a guest.'

'Thank you, General. May I?' Xi said, pulling a pack of cigarettes from his pocket before lighting one. 'There is something China values very highly. Something which has gone missing,' he said cryptically, blowing out a cloud of blue-grey smoke. 'I think you may be in a unique position to help us recover it.'

He produced a manila envelope from his briefcase and slid it across the table. The general opened it with a look of concern.

'I trust you know already about this?' Xi asked.

Haddadi tried to appear casual as he looked down and examined the envelope's contents. He thumbed through a series of satellite images, processing what he saw as fast as he could. The pictures had been taken very recently and showed a naval vessel intercepting a yacht, which judging from the coastline, was within Eritrean waters. The close-up images were a little grainy, but he could see people being moved onto the naval vessel before it returned to the coast.

The general looked up again and smiled at his guest. 'Of course.'

'Of course,' Xi repeated, trying to read Haddadi's face for clues, but the general gave nothing away. After a long pause, Xi waved at the contracts still sitting unsigned on the table between them. 'In which case, can we settle this matter?'

The quid pro quo was clear. Concede to Xi's request and the contract would proceed, refuse and it would not. Haddadi bristled but tried not to show it. He didn't like the Chinese habit of adding demands at the last minute and he wasn't in the practice of doing favours for anyone, not least a foreigner. What Xi was asking for was not impossible. It was well within his power to make it very possible. He nodded again to his guest and forced out another awkward smile.

'As I said, Secretary Xi. In Iran, we never refuse a guest.'

TEN

Poole, UK

The appearance of his boss, James Beeby in the office was always an experience that left Peter Hopkins feeling a little deflated. James was more often found drinking at his members' club in London or at his home in the New Forest, but every now and again he'd come in, just to stir things up a little. The man had a talent for finding exactly the wrong words, at the wrong time, and yet, somehow always came out of every situation smelling of roses.

'Any news on the *Falcon*?' he asked in a relaxed drawl that the most incredibly posh of public schoolboys seemed to have. Hopkins wondered if they practised it in their dorms. It suggested a state of mind that was entirely the opposite of the reality. There was certainly nothing relaxed about James. He was tightly wound at all times and the way he spoke reflected breeding, confidence and privilege, nothing more.

'Nothing since MTO in Dubai took the Mayday call and now all comms with the *Falcon* are down,' Hopkins explained. 'MTO called in CTF115 and USS *Mustin* was the nearest responder.'

'Really? A destroyer? Great.' James sounded impressed. 'Any ETA?'

'She was three hundred miles away,' he checked his watch, 'so another hour or so before they launch the Seahawks. We should have eyes on by 0900 hours, UK time.'

'Right and who do we have on board?'

'Sergei and Vlad.'

'Right,' James paused, he no longer looked impressed. 'Remind me why we used the Russians again?'

Hopkins bristled. They'd been over it at least twice at the time when the decision was made.

'Vlad speaks Chinese,' he said.

That was only part of the story, the part they'd agreed to use to sell the Russians to Wei Lun Chow. The truth was James had insisted on using the ex-Spetsnaz guys and not because of Vlad's Chinese.

'Of course, I remember now,' James said. 'You said they were cheaper.'

There it was. Classic James. Already shifting responsibility. Hopkins had mentioned the Russians' rate, but only in so far as he believed De Grasse should be paying them more. They did the same work, took the same risks as everyone else, so they should get the same wage. But James had disagreed. Margins were tight and he saw the Russians as a way to make more money. Hopkins wasn't in the mood to have that argument all over again now.

'Anyway, I'd better get onto the MoD,' James said. 'Other than the principal and our guys, do we know much about the crew?'

'Not yet,' said Hopkins, scanning the file. 'Sailing crew were all hired in, but I'm still waiting for a list of names and nationalities from the hire company. Catering was a Filipino outfit that the principal's used before. And four guests.'

'Family?'

'Uh, no,' said Hopkins, awkwardly fumbling for the right description, 'Personal friends.'

'Four of them?' James said, with the kind of lascivious grin that public schoolboys always did when sex was alluded to. 'Dirty old Chow.'

Hopkins couldn't find the right words to reply. It sickened him to hear James cackling when there was a boat full of people who may have been taken hostage by pirates.

'Right, well, I'm out to Hong Kong now. Chow's people are already freaking out over there and we need to get them organised. If this is what we think it is, then we should expect a call in the next twenty-four hours.'

'We should inform next of kin,' Hopkins said. 'As soon as I get those names.'

'No, let's find out what we're dealing with first,' James said, shaking his head. 'We don't want press all over this if we can help it.'

Hopkins nodded. He'd handled hostage situations before when he'd been in the Regiment, but that had included the full support that came with being part of the SAS, the country's elite fighting force. Now, he felt exposed, on his own, and not entirely sure of himself yet. As much as he hated to admit it, he was relying on James's experience to guide him. 'So, where do you want me?'

'Assuming the Yanks find the *Falcon*, my guess is there won't be anyone who's worth anything left on it. But they'll bring her into their base in Djibouti in any case. Head out there and see what we're dealing with. You got the short straw, I'm afraid,' James chuckled before he disappeared through the door again.

Hopkins sighed. This job was relentlessly stressful and some days he wondered if he'd made the right decision taking it. Leaving the SAS had been a tough call. He'd never wanted to be anything other than a special forces officer. He'd enjoyed almost every minute, living out his boyhood dream of being in the Regiment. He'd served his country in places that most of the people he'd grown up with had never heard of, let alone been to; Mali, the Central African Republic, and Yemen to name a few. His time in the Regiment had been the happiest of his life and the men he'd served with were the best he'd ever known. Leaving had been a bitter pill to swallow.

Hopkins's final operational duty had been a hostage rescue in Yemen the year before. The task had gone badly awry and the situation had developed into what had almost been an apocalyptic environmental disaster. Somehow, he and his team had pulled out all the stops to ensure that had not happened. What should have been a triumph, a proud day for British Special Forces, instead turned into a political shitshow. The politicians had twisted the facts to save their skins and in the fallout, one of the finest soldiers that Hopkins had ever served with, Staff Sergeant Matt Mason, had unjustly taken the blame. Mason had fallen on his sword to protect the reputation of the Regiment in what was an act of unparalleled selflessness. He'd shown a strength of character that the top brass could never emulate.

After Mason's departure, Hopkins had struggled on for a few more months, the whole time feeling guilty for allowing Mace to take the blame. Eventually, Hopkins rotated back to a desk job at the Directorate of Special Forces in London, but by then his heart had gone out of it. He requested to resign his commission which was accepted without question. Now he was working at De Grasse, a global leader in maritime security and intelligence. He'd taken over as the head of anti-piracy, responsible for putting security teams onto vessels operating in dangerous waters off the east coast of Africa, as well as taking the lead in any hostage negotiations that might result as and when things went wrong.

The explosion of piracy incidents off the Somali coast in the late 2000s had created a gold rush in the security industry, and the bolder the pirates became – taking superyachts, tankers, and even container ships for ransom – the more the companies that owned them needed help getting them back. James Beeby had been in the right place at the right time and De Grasse had gone from strength to strength, positioning itself as the number one company in the industry.

If your ship was passing along the east coast of Africa and around the Horn, then you needed De Grasse security. If you were unlucky enough to fall foul of pirates, then De Grasse were the gold standard in hostage negotiation. In all their time, De Grasse had never once failed to recover a ship and its crew in a kidnap situation they ran point on. Although recently, as the international community had strengthened its presence in the region, the hostage negotiation side of the business had been pretty quiet.

But that seemed like it might all be about to change because, right now, one of De Grasse's wealthiest clients was missing and everything suggested they could be looking at a kidnap. While James set up the negotiation team in Hong Kong, Hopkins's job was to prepare a fast response team so that if De Grasse needed boots on the ground, then they would be ready to hit it running. Until they had more information, there wasn't much he could action, but in Hopkins's experience it was always better to prepare for the worst. One of their top clients, two of their best men, and a whole crew of innocent people's lives could depend on it.

He scrolled through the contacts list on his phone, looking for a very particular number. He needed his best man on this, someone whom he could trust and someone who knew the lay of the land. When he found the name he was looking for, he dialled and waited for a reply.

'Hello?'

Hopkins smiled, recognising his old Regiment buddy's gruff West Midlands voice right away. 'Jack,' he replied. 'I need you in for briefing ASAP. We're on a flight for Djibouti in the morning.'

ELEVEN

The Golden Beach Hotel, Mozambique

'*Pop-pop, pop, pop-pop-pop.*' Mason woke to the sound of gunfire as though it was his 7 am alarm call. Afghanistan, Syria, Iraq, Yemen, Mali, it didn't matter where you were, it sounded the same. Eventually, you just got used to it. He'd grown so accustomed to it over the years, that he could turn over and go back to sleep if he needed to. But as he looked at his watch, and saw that it was 4 am, he heard another sound that made him spring to life. It was the unmistakable sound of a helicopter.

Before he'd found an empty room and lain down to rest, Mason had called Flossie to inform her about the previous day's events. She'd already heard about the dead elephants, but was understandably shocked and saddened to hear that Joseph was also dead and had been working against them. She told Mason that the Islamist attacks were all over the news and that reports suggested the insurgents had seized control of everything east of Mueda. They were slaughtering whole villages as they made their way south towards Pemba and there was now no safe way for Mason to get back to the reserve. She implored him to get out any way he could.

As soon as he'd put the phone down, Mason had convinced Maurice to let the local people outside the gates come into the hotel. A noisy crowd would only attract the jihadists and if they were on a brutal rampage, then everyone in their path was in danger. Mason had seen it before, seen how the cruelty of fanatics knew no limits, how they left a trail of destruction in their wake, murdering, beheading, and burning anyone who did not fit with their twisted ideal of how the world should be. With the crowd inside the gates, they could ensure they remained safe and also, crucially, that they remained quiet. That might buy them valuable time.

Once Maurice had conceded, Mason had found them an area where they could shelter around the hotel pool in the rear. With everyone safe, Mason and Maurice had used the hotel's satellite phone to make contact with the French oil company. The French hotelier had made it clear to his compatriots that everyone inside that hotel was going to die without immediate assistance. They had responded to Maurice's plea for emergency evacuation, and together they'd formulated a plan. The oil company chopper would arrive at dawn and take the women and children to a beach six miles down the coast, where small boats would carry them to safety on the nearby Quirimbas Islands. The men would hold off the Islamists until the chopper could come back for them.

To ensure that was possible, Mason had done a tour of the perimeter fence, briefing the security team on how to prepare for an attack. He'd split the men into two teams, assigning one to do patrols while the other reinforced strategic positions where Mason had seen they would have an advantage over anyone approaching. Finally, he'd assigned his ranger team to secure the rear of the building, ensuring that they couldn't be outflanked from the shore.

But now it seemed that the oil company's helicopter had arrived sooner than he'd expected and the sound of it had alerted the jihadists to their presence. Evacuation was always tricky, even more so when you were under fire. For a few crucial seconds, the choppers were vulnerable to attack from the ground and pilots got jumpy easily. Mason hurried down the stairs and out to the front gate. He was relieved to see the sentry posts were manned and holding their position. Keeping the Islamists back was essential to a successful EVAC.

Shots echoed out from the jungle beyond the gates again, a few tracer rounds scored through the darkness, disappearing again into the night sky beyond the hotel. For now, the plan was working, but it was only a matter of time before they would be overrun. In the meantime, he had to get the vulnerable out of there.

He ran back through the hotel, across the lobby, and out of the back door, past the pool to a clearing where they had decided it was best for the chopper to land. But something was wrong. The chopper was already taking off again, lifting into the air and banking away from the hotel. Mason looked around in confusion. The people had assembled just as he had planned, with the women and children lined up to leave first. Yet, the chopper was going without them.

'Where's Maurice?' he asked nobody in particular. 'Donde esta Maurice?' he shouted again to the crowd. Several of them raised their hands, eyes glued to the sky above, pointing forlornly at the chopper.

Mason sighed and his head fell into his hands. He thought for a second that he could hear the sound of a dog barking. He looked up again, into the sky, squinting to see in the darkness.

'He took his dog, boss,' said the man standing next to him. 'But he said he will come back for us.'

Mason looked into the man's eyes. The poor bastard actually believed what Maurice had said to him. But Mason knew that the chopper was leaving and that Maurice wasn't coming back.

Mason booted the dried out husk of a rotten coconut shell halfway down the beach. One day, he'd catch up with that French coward and do the same to his head, but in the meantime, he had to regroup. People were depending on him. Another dozen tracer rounds tore through the air over their heads and several of the children began to scream, their mothers covering them, trying to protect them from the horror. Mason did a headcount. In all, he estimated there were thirty people still inside the Golden Beach Hotel. Thirty people who needed him to get them out. The problem was that without Maurice, he had considerably less leverage. It had been hard enough to convince the oil company to come for a fellow Frenchman, he had no chance of getting them to come back for local Mozambicans.

The helicopter disappeared again in the darkness and the gunshots stopped. It would be a mistake to expect it to stay like that for long and there was also no way they would hold out for another night. Staying any longer in the hotel would be mass suicide. Their only option was to get out, and in the absence of a chopper that meant taking the road.

'Everyone out front,' he shouted over the crowd in a tone of voice that he hadn't used since he'd been in the forces. 'Now!'

It was enough to get everyone's attention.

The crowd followed Mason through the hotel to the front courtyard where he shouted to his men to prepare every vehicle they had. The Islamists would be preparing for their next assault. As the first light of dawn began to light up the sky to the east, Mason knew this was their last chance to escape.

He called the crowd together and laid out the plan. Outside of the gates was thirty feet of clear ground before you reached the tree-line. To the east was a single track that ran directly from the hotel to the coast. The jihadists would undoubtedly have taken up positions inside the trees, but there was nothing they could do about that. Their only chance was to take that track. Sitting in the hotel waiting to die was not an option. Making a run for it was.

The Nissan they'd recovered from the poachers would go first, driven by one of his own rangers, with two more armed rangers on the back and all the children loaded into the cab behind. The rest of the cars and one minibus would follow, while Mason brought up the rear. Someone had to stay back to open the gates and provide initial cover, so once everyone else was clear, he would follow in the last vehicle.

Nobody spoke. The people did just as they were told and, in total silence, they loaded themselves into the cars.

They were frightened. They looked to each other for reassurance but nobody was able to give any. They packed into the cars, sweating, their hearts racing, their mouths dry with fear. When the last person was loaded, Mason peered through the peephole in the gate. The clearing outside was empty. He could see no one. For now, the lane looked clear, even though he knew that they were out there, waiting for their chance. He walked back to the driver of the first vehicle.

'Don't stop. For anything. You hear me?'

The young man behind the wheel, whom Mason had recruited only weeks before, fidgeted nervously with the steering wheel, biting his bottom lip. He nodded to Mason that he had understood.

'This road goes for five miles,' Mason pointed in the direction he meant. 'You don't stop until you see a left turn. You know the old hotel? Good. Stop there. We'll go on foot to the beach.'

The driver looked back to Mason again. He could see the fear in the kid's eyes. 'It's gonna be the drive of your life, mate,' Mason said, laying a hand on his shoulder for a moment before he tapped on the top of the car. He ran back to the gate and checked the road outside one more time. He took a deep breath and threw the gates wide open.

The lead vehicle screeched out of the Golden Beach. The other vehicles in the convoy raced out after it. Seconds later they disappeared into the jungle, burning along the dirt road at nearly one hundred kilometres per hour, throwing up clouds of dust into the air behind. The last car stopped at the gate and Mason jumped into the passenger seat.

'Fucking go!' he shouted to the driver, the guard who had opened the gate for them the previous night. He put his foot down and sped off after the other cars. The dust was already so thick that neither of them could see the road through the windscreen.

But they could hear the bullets. Less than a mile down the lane, the convoy encountered the ambush that had been set for them. Bullets shot out from the trees, tracers firing across the road, hitting the cars. The sound of rounds ricocheting off the chassis sent Mason ducking for cover. A bullet hit the bottom of the car, tearing a hole in the floor below him. Another shattered the driver's window, showering Mason and everyone in it with fragments of glass.

'Don't stop!' Mason shouted. If they stopped here then they were fucked.

'I'm hit. I'm hit,' the driver cried out.

Mason looked across. A bullet had torn through the guy's right arm so that half his bicep was hanging off and blood was rushing out fast.

'Don't stop!' Mason said again. 'Keep going!'

'I can't drive. I can't drive,' he pleaded. His voice sounded weak, as though in a daze.

Mason looked down into the footwell and saw that the driver had also taken a hit to the leg. The space around the pedals was filling up with blood, while the vehicle was starting to lose speed. Another volley of bullets hit the car, shattering the rear windscreen. They couldn't stop here. If they stopped, they were all dead. Mason manoeuvred himself around, throwing his leg over the gear stick and into the puddle of blood in the footwell, feeling around until he found the accelerator pedal. He pushed down as hard as he could and took hold of the wheel, steering the car into the dust cloud, just barely managing to keep the wheels on the road.

'No good, boss,' the young man said before he passed out. Mason cursed under his breath. It never got any easier to watch a man die.

The shooting stopped and Mason realised that they were clear of the ambush. Still, he didn't want to stop. You never knew who was waiting in the trees. He continued to drive from the passenger side further up the dirt road until he saw that three SUVs had been positioned across the road. There was just a small gap between them, just wide enough for a car. He didn't like the feel of it.

Mason accelerated for the gap. It smacked of another ambush point. As they got closer, he saw that the bodies of the SUV drivers had been decapitated and dumped on the road next to them. The car clattered over their corpses with a bump. Mason shook his head. There was nothing he could do for them now. He had to protect the living. The dead were on their own.

The dust settled down as he approached the turning for the old hotel. He swung the car hard left and continued towards the old crumbling concrete building. The other cars had already arrived and he saw people piling out onto the tarmac. Mothers ran to the lead vehicle to check that their children were alright. A group of men carried a ranger down off the back of the Nissan. A bullet had taken out the back of his head. Two more men had died from gunshot wounds and several were injured. Mason gathered them all together, imploring them to keep moving. He led them around the back of the hotel and down a path that led between the trees towards the beach. They walked in stunned silence for twenty minutes until, finally, they stumbled out onto the sand.

True to their word, the oil company had sent the boats to rescue them. A small flotilla of fishing vessels was waiting to take them the short distance to the Quirimbas Islands. In a little over an hour, the survivors would be safe. Mason helped to load the children and the wounded on board. There was just enough space on the last boat for him. But he pushed the bow out into the water and waved for the driver to leave.

He wasn't getting on that boat. If he did, then there was no way back here. Within days, the whole region would be under the control of the insurgents and any chance he had to find out the truth about who had slaughtered those elephants on the reserve, and who had been responsible for the death of Joseph, would be gone.

Mason suddenly thought about Mwamba Kiba, the village headman, Joseph's father. What would he be feeling? By now, he would have heard the news of his son's death. He'd be crushed by it. Mason thanked his lucky stars that his own kids were somewhere else, safe, far away from this fucked up place.

'Go!' he shouted over the crashing waves.

'No boss,' the man replied. 'Al-Shabaab will be here soon.'

Mason shook his head. He'd come too far now to turn back. Maybe he was crazy. He'd nearly died twice already this week. And for what? To save a few elephants? It sounded ridiculous. He considered what he was doing for a moment but he knew he wasn't going to change his mind. He owed it to Joseph and his father. It was about more than just the elephants now.

The peace that he had found on the reserve was shattered. He was hard-wired to attack problems head-on. A lifetime in the world's most elite fighting force had seen to that. Matt Mason was not a man who retreated unless he absolutely had to. He knew now that he was in a real fight again and every sinew of his being was responding to that sensation at once. There was nothing he could do to stop it. He was staying to fight and that fight was about getting justice for something in this God-forsaken country. If he could stop even one bad thing from happening in this place, then maybe he could leave it better than he'd found it. That was the only way he was going to feel peace now and that was too important to walk away from.

'Go!' he repeated to the driver, pushing the boat further out into the sea, helping it over the breakwater. 'Look after them.'

TWELVE

Anrata Port, Eritrea

Nobody has ever heard of Anrata, a dusty coastal town perched on the end of a small peninsula along a sparsely populated stretch of Eritrea's Red Sea coast. Anrata boasts no famous alumni, has no historical significance and with a temperature reaching well into the forties most days, it's not a fun place to visit. All of which makes it the perfect spot to land a boatload of valuable hostages without attracting unwanted attention.

The naval gunboat had covered the short distance from the Zubair Islands to the mainland in a little over three hours. It had never reported hearing the *Falcon*'s mayday call, just quietly conducted its usual circuit, skirting the limits of Eritrean waters, reporting nothing unusual, remaining on schedule to return to base in Massawa by first light. That gave Captain Kidane just enough time to stop at Anrata without arousing suspicion.

Kidane was from, what in Eritrea at least, might be described as a well-off family. His father was a successful teff farmer in the highlands of central Eritrea, about as far from the sea as it was possible to get. The cereals that grew there were renowned for making the best injera, a local flatbread that was the staple of most Eritreans' diet, but the young Kidane hated farming and resented toiling for hours in the hot, sweaty fields, sowing seeds, threshing grasses, preparing bales for buyers who came from the cities of Asmara and Keren. As soon as he was old enough, he'd got as far away as possible. He signed up for the navy and persuaded his father to pay the necessary bribe to get him an officer's commission. But an Eritrean Navy captain's salary didn't afford a man the same lifestyle as Kidane had grown used to as a boy. So, gradually, he'd found other ways to supplement his income.

The gunboat slowed, damping down the engines as Kidane lifted his night-vision binoculars to scan the shore for signs of life. Like half of Eritreans, Kidane was Christian, but in the coastal towns like Anrata Islam was the predominant faith. He estimated it was two hours since the Muslims would have made their final prayer, so the houses near the water's edge were dark and silent. A single track led from the highway, through the centre of town to a small jetty that served a handful of fisherman's boats. He made out the silhouette of a minivan parked alongside and nodded, satisfied.

He gave the order for two of his men to follow as he stepped off the naval vessel along a roughly assembled gangway onto the shore. He saw two men step out of the van. It was still dark but he could just make out their faces enough to know that he didn't recognise either of them. The deal had been arranged through an intermediary in Massawa, a man who often called Kidane with requests for which he paid handsomely. It was usually to ensure a certain shipment passed unmolested either in or out of the country, across to Yemen or down the coast to Somalia. In this case, he'd offered triple the usual rate for the safe delivery of the high-worth passengers aboard the *Falcon*. It had been a little more complicated than he'd expected, but nothing he couldn't handle. Once he'd completed the handover, he'd have a tidy sum to add to his retirement pot.

'Hello, brother,' one of the men said in Arabic.

Arabic was studied in schools across the region but in the highlands of Eritrea, where Kidane was born, it was rarely spoken. Even in Asmara and Massawa, it was more common to hear English. The man spoke with an accent that suggested he was Somalian. Kidane had learned from his father to be wary of Somalians. His dad had taught him how they would always look for an angle, a way to get something more from the deal. Kidane wasn't surprised that they were involved in this. Kidnapping was the perfect business for Somalians.

'Peace be with you, brother,' he replied.

The man who had addressed him was shorter than his colleague, fatter too, with a big belly that protruded from under a Juventus football shirt that he wore with a set of ill-matching army fatigues. When the taller man stepped out from the shadows, his face caught a little of the moonlight. Kidane could see he was young, sixteen perhaps, light-skinned and lean, much better looking than his friend. The uniform hung loosely from his frame and looked incongruous with the bright pink pair of Crocs he wore on his feet. Both men carried AK-47s.

The younger man handed Kidane a small leather bag which he opened and counted the banknotes that were stuffed inside. Kidane looked unhappy. The purse was light. Of course.

'Where is the rest?' he said.

The man in the Italian football shirt ignored the question and simply replied, 'Passports?'

Kidane shook his head, sucking the night air through his teeth. Fucking Somalians. He spat onto the ground before he handed over five passports to the fat man. He had little leverage. It wasn't as though he could take the hostages with him. The best he could do now was complete the handover and take up the grievance with his contact in Massawa. He turned back to the boat and instructed his men to bring the hostages ashore.

Moments later, the five hostages appeared on the deck. Joanna Mason walked at the front, leading the others down the gangway to the dock. Guarding them was Green Eyes, the man who had taken the Filipino girl away when they had been on the *Falcon*. He pointed the muzzle of his rifle directly at Joanna, his teeth glowing with a maniacal smile. She didn't like the way that he looked at her one bit. She had no doubt that if they were left alone, he'd do something terrible to her. She turned her face away from him, putting him out of her mind, concentrating instead on where she was walking.

'Who the fuck are these guys?' she heard Jim say from behind her.

'Shut up,' Ben snapped in a loud whisper. 'Let's just see what they want.'

'Nah, man. This is bullshit.'

He sounded terrified. Joanna could tell that the bravado was only a cover.

When they reached Kidane and the Somalians, Green Eyes forced each of them down onto their knees. The guy in the Juventus shirt walked along the line, comparing each of their faces to the passport photographs.

'British?' he asked Joanna. She nodded silently.

'This is the one,' Kidane said to the fat man, pointing to Chow. The fat man studied Chow's passport and nodded.

'These guys are fucking jokers,' Jim said, eyeballing the younger of the two Somalians.

'What you say, English?' The fat man said, flicking through the passports, looking for Jim's photo.

'I'm not English, you prick,' Jim replied.

'Jim, just shut the fuck up!' Ben said firmly. The big Kiwi was going to get them all killed.

'I'm from New Zealand,' Jim continued, undeterred.

'New Zealand?' the fat man said, reading from Jim's passport. 'Where is this? Europe?'

'See?' Jim laughed, looking at Ben. 'Fucking amateurs.'

He turned back to the Somalian and eyed him with a look of pure defiance. 'No, it's not in fucking Europe, you idiot.'

Jo felt the fat man's tone shift immediately. He strode back over to the gunboat captain and began shouting in Arabic, pointing at Jim. The captain shouted back even louder. He was pointing to the contents of the bag. Both men seemed angry. She wished that she could understand what they were saying because their confrontation was ramping up her anxiety considerably.

'This is good,' Jim sneered. 'We got them fighting between themselves.'

Jo wasn't so sure that she agreed. It looked as though the captain's bag contained a sum of money and she guessed that he was asking for more. The fat guy kept shaking his head, as though he wasn't going to concede and somehow it all had something to do with Jim. The fat man kept waving Jim's passport at the captain but the captain just shrugged and pointed again to the bag.

'Can I get some water?' Jim said loudly over their discourse. 'When you two have finished with the foreplay.'

The two men stopped shouting and the fat man walked slowly over to Jim. 'Water?'

'Uh-huh,' Jim shrugged.

The fat man laughed. 'Of course,' he said. He waved to the younger guy to fetch some water. 'Please, drink.'

The young man held the bottle to Jim's lips, allowing the big Kiwi to take a generous gulp.

'Enough?' the fat man asked.

Jim nodded. 'Yeah, that'll do.'

'Yes,' the fat man said with a chuckle. 'That will do.'

The fat man lifted the AK-47 from his shoulder and, without hesitation, fired two rounds into Jim's chest, sending the big Kiwi reeling backwards. Jo, Chow, Woodsie, and Ben flung themselves to the ground, crying out in fear. Jo landed heavily on her side, knocking the wind out of herself. She fought to catch her breath, looking across the dirt at Jim, three feet away, dead still, the life already gone from him.

'Now, it is only four, so we are even,' the fat man said to Kidane.

Kidane cursed quietly under his breath before he stormed back to the boat. He didn't turn around once as he walked up the gangway and gave the order to cast off. His father had been right about Somalians. They couldn't be trusted. He vowed never to do business with them again and to never think again about what had happened on this night in Anrata.

Meanwhile, on the shore, the fat Somalian was dragging Jim's body to the dock. While he bundled him over the edge, the young guy gagged the hostages and wrapped strong electrical tape around their heads, covering their eyes and ears. Then he led them one by one over to the van and shoved them into the back. When the loading was done, the van pulled away and drove back to the highway.

THIRTEEN

Mocímboa da Praia Port, Mozambique

Wang Li Lan's go-fast boat slowed as they approached the Mocímboa da Praia jetty, closely watched by several heavily armed soldiers. An hour earlier she had supervised the port crane operator lowering her container – which carried a full quota of nearly two hundred and sixty containers – onto the deck of the *Sirrah*, the last ship due to sail out of Pemba for what might be a very long time. But the *Sirrah* was still in the dock because the rebels had blockaded the port and prevented it from leaving.

Organising her escape from Pemba had been no mean feat. The jihadists were already in the town, raping, looting, and chopping off heads, and the seas outside the harbour were jam-packed; a flotilla of hundreds of escaping vessels, boats of all shapes and sizes, filled to the gills with people fleeing in fear for their lives. Anyone who was anyone had got out by now and God help those who hadn't. Most were headed for Madagascar, Tanzania, or the Comoro Islands but Li Lan had taken a very different path. Her go-fast boat had turned north along the coast and she had escaped the danger of Pemba only to exchange it for an even greater one in Mocímboa.

Mocímboa da Praia was the province's second-largest port city and offered a few clues as to what was in store for its big brother, Pemba, two hundred and forty kilometres to the south. Two months earlier, the jihadists had run the Mozambique army out of Mocímboa after a sustained assault. Since then, the Al-Shabaab leadership had established their base in Mocímboa and were coordinating the terror that was taking hold throughout the province.

Li Lan stepped onto the jetty and nodded to the armed teenager waiting for her there. He stood upright, dressed in green army camouflage and sandals with a tell-tale Arabic kufiyah draped around his neck. He barely acknowledged her, using the muzzle of his rifle to usher her forward and a tilt of his head to make clear that she was to walk in front of him. At the end of the jetty, she saw that he was taking her to a bright yellow container which looked as though it had been converted into a bar. She could hear the sound of men shouting and laughing coming from inside. The door was painted with the symbol for Mozambique's best-selling beer, Impala, while its walls were splattered with posters advertising a half litre for the bargain price of thirty-five meticals.

She paused at the door but the soldier gave her a nudge, which sent her stumbling inside. As she regained her balance and adjusted her eyes to the gloom, she saw that the container was full of men in uniform. The air was heavy with smoke and there was a strong whiff of whisky. Gradually the laughter died down and every man in the room fixed his eyes on her.

She cast her eyes around, surprised to see so many foreigners. Sitting at a table in the middle of the room was the man she had come to see, a heavyset, middle-aged soldier in dark-green fatigues. Next to him was a rakish looking Arab, most likely Somalian, his eyes covered by a pair of mirrored aviator sunglasses in which she saw her own silhouette. On a tattered old sofa in the corner were two Tanzanians and behind them, in the shadows, sitting along the bar were a Ugandan and three Congolese. Above their heads, hung a black Islamist flag which looked rather incongruous next to all the beer posters. The big man lifted his head to look at her.

'Who is she?' He addressed his question to the soldier standing behind her.

'My name is Wang Li Lan, Colonel Lanya,' the young woman replied, able to answer for herself. 'I am here to discuss business.'

The colonel was well known in the province as the leader of Al-Shabaab. He had once been a colonel in the Mozambique Army but had long since defected to the other side. He was a notorious butcher and rapist, feared through-out the country. Just the name Colonel Lanya would strike fear into the heart of any citizen from the north.

'I do not discuss business with women,' the colonel replied, returning his attention to a pile of papers on the table. 'And I don't like Chinese.'

'You seem to like our money.'

A couple of the Congolese soldiers roared with laughter. They knew that such impudence could easily lead to the Chinese woman losing her head. But Li Lan did not smile. She had the old man's attention. He flashed a glare in the direction of the men at the bar and they instantly fell silent again. Finally, he looked past Li Lan to the young soldier for an explanation as to why he had made the foolish decision to allow this impudent woman into his office.

'She works for Kiba, boss,' the soldier stuttered, already deeply regretting the decision. 'The elephant man in Niassa.'

The colonel nodded and looked again at Li Lan. For the past three years, Mwamba Kiba, one of the headmen from Niassa, had been running elephant ivory through Al-Shabaab-controlled territory to Pemba. The Islamists had earned a healthy amount of 'tax' by permitting the consignments to pass. He had heard before of the Chinese woman who facilitated the onward shipping. Even so, he was still annoyed to see her now standing in his office.

'I don't work for anyone,' Li Lan said.

The colonel shook his head. 'So, what do you want?'

Colonel Lanya had a big round face on his broad shoulders. His skin was unlined and, in the shadow of the container, his lips looked black and full. He stared back at Li Lan and ran a hand casually over his bald scalp. She saw a bead of sweat drop onto his palm before he wiped it clean on his shirt.

Li Lan swallowed her distaste and continued. 'Your blockade in Pemba will put me out of business.'

'Not my problem,' he scoffed.

'I'm not here for problems,' she said. 'But I have connections to good trade routes. I want to keep them open.'

'How does that affect me?'

'The Mozambique Army will come soon.'

The old man laughed, the other men joined in. 'They are cowards,' he said with a dismissive flick of his hand.

'The West say that you are ISIS, they will send support.' Li Lan kept her voice level but her words only fuelled the laughter in the room. The men sitting at the bar almost fell off their stools.

'Let the Americans say what they want,' Lanya said.

'You will need weaponry.'

'Tsk,' he sucked through his teeth and looked at the Somalian sitting by his side. 'We have powerful allies.'

'We have the same allies,' Li Lan said, 'but not the same enemies.' She reached for a small pouch that hung by her side.

The young soldier twitched, raising his rifle a little but the colonel shooed him away and motioned for Li Lan to approach. She removed a chart and unfurled it on the desk. The old man looked closely at it. The map showed routes through the seaways from the southern tip of Africa to the Red Sea in the north and all the way east across the Indian Ocean to the Chinese eastern seaboard. Li Lan leaned across and traced invisible lines with her finger.

'I control routes from China to Saudi Arabia,' she said. 'And from there to Eritrea, Tanzania, and Pemba. I have my people in all the shipping companies, the ports, and customs. The government will try to shut down your supply routes but not mine. I am only a sea cucumber trader.'

The colonel could see what she was offering. He slid the map across so that the Somalian could see it. He removed his sunglasses to reveal that his left eye was entirely missing. In its place, a badly stitched scar ran most of the way down his cheek, disappearing behind his ear. Li Lan tried not to stare at the wound as he cast his eye over the map. Finally, he nodded his approval to the colonel.

Lanya re-evaluated the small woman standing before him. Maybe she could be useful after all. He looked again to the Somalian and shrugged as if to say that they were thinking the same thing. Then he stood and strode out of the container bar without checking to see if she was following. She was. Close behind him. And behind her, the Somalian.

The Mocímboa port had been entirely taken over by the jihadists. Black flags covered in Islamic text hung among an arsenal of weapons and military vehicles. Li Lan could see that whoever had been equipping these guys had spent some serious cash.

On the other side of the dock, Colonel Lanya stopped to address two soldiers standing guard over a group of containers marked with commercial logos that Li Lan recognised well. These were likely the ones they used to smuggle weapons. It wasn't as though they had anything to export in return, so now they lay empty. Or so she thought.

With a tilt of his head, Lanya instructed the soldier to unlock one of the containers. He pulled across the bolt, hoisted the door open and immediately Li Lan was struck by the sour smell of urine and body odour.

The second soldier produced a torch and handed it to the colonel.

'Come,' he said, disappearing inside the metal box.

Li Lan hesitated before she and the Somalian followed the colonel through the steel door. The heat inside was oppressive and the smell even more intense. The old man cast the torch around the box and Li Lan could make out the whites of human eyes looking back towards her.

In all, the container held seventeen young women. All young, lean, and attractive. Selected for their looks, she thought. The girls cowered silently together, their faces filled with angst. The light was dim, but as the beam drifted left and right, Li Lan was sure that she could make out bruises on several of their faces.

'You understand?' the colonel addressed her directly before he killed the light and shooed her back outside. The soldier locked the door behind them.

'Where?' Li Lan asked.

'My friend here, Colonel Razir Al-Haq, will receive the order in Mombasa,' he said, laying a hand on the Somalian's shoulder.

Al-Haq nodded his confirmation. Li Lan understood. Al-Shabaab had their dirty fingers deep in every criminal pie there was across the region. They taxed her for smuggling ivory. They were clearly importing weapons from the north. And now they were trading girls too. Not that Li Lan needed to pass judgement on any of that. She considered only the logistics. She was already thinking about how she could run the girls by small boat as far as Zanzibar and from there to Mombasa, Kenya. In the circumstances, it would be best if she was there in person to see it went smoothly. It would also allow her to ensure that her ivory shipment, also bound for Mombasa, passed through the port smoothly.

'Four hundred US for each girl. And you release the *Sirrah*,' she said.

Colonel Lanya's face didn't move. He showed her nothing until finally, he said, 'Three Hundred.'

Li Lan nodded her agreement. The money was immaterial. Barely enough to cover her costs. The important part was that he would give the order to allow her container to leave Pemba.

'Business over. Go, now!' he said finally.

The same soldier who'd led her in appeared to accompany her back to the dock but as she turned to leave, the Somalian, Razir Al-Haq, gripped her arm and stared at her with his one remaining eye.

'Do not disappoint us,' he said. 'You will not get a second chance.'

Li Lan nodded, controlling the urge to say any more. She had never needed a second chance at anything in her life. Weapons, girls, whatever they needed her to deliver was within her power. She didn't care. Her goal was simply to make money. To ensure that her father's business would be profitable for a good while longer. That was all that mattered.

FOURTEEN

Ten Kilometres West of Pemba, Mozambique

Matt Mason shifted awkwardly in the front seat of the Nissan. The air-con was turned up to full, but it was still sweaty on the 4x4's leather seats. He'd driven through the day, sticking to jungle roads, heading south towards Pemba. There was still nothing on the radio and his cell phone had been without signal for hours. He had no idea where the Islamists were or if they'd reached the regional capital or not.

He pulled out the phone he'd taken from the dead poacher in Niassa and scrolled through its contents again. As well as calls to and from Joseph, there were several calls to the number he knew from the voicemail to be the Wang Trading Company in Pemba.

It still annoyed him that he'd got Joseph so wrong. He was disappointed that the boy had betrayed him, that he'd betrayed his community to work with the poachers. But more than that, Mason was disappointed with himself. That he'd not spotted it earlier. Now Joseph was dead and Mason felt a responsibility to find out who was to blame, who had drawn the kid into the industry in the first place.

He knew that there would be more young men lining up to take Joseph's place and that trying to fight them all would be a losing battle. From bitter experience, he'd learned that to win the war you had to take out the people at the top and right now that meant getting into Pemba, because his hunch was that the Wang Trading Company was involved.

Mason slowed as he approached a junction up ahead. It looked as though the track forked with a larger road, which he guessed must be the main route into Pemba. He didn't want to risk driving on a major road right now so he pulled the Nissan into a gap in the trees from where it couldn't be seen from the road.

He continued on foot, keeping a steady five kilometres an hour, heading east until he saw what looked like a makeshift roadblock ahead. Two vehicles were turned nose to nose across the carriageway and standing in front of them, a couple of teenagers in soldiers' uniforms were waving around their AK47s. Mason suspected there was an 'officer' somewhere not far away.

He slipped quietly off the road and disappeared into the trees, climbing to higher ground, making his way to a hidden position from where he could get a good look at the situation below. It wasn't long before he heard another vehicle approach and saw the two teenagers wave for it to a stop. Moments later, another soldier appeared. He seemed older and angry as he shouted at the driver to go back. Whoever was in the car was not welcome in Pemba. Mason had seen enough. He continued around, moving quickly through the forest, keeping low, sliding deeper in among the trees.

Heading towards the setting sun, Mason kept moving until he was more than a kilometre clear of the checkpoint. The trees began to thin out a little and the ground became rockier underfoot, rising in front of him towards a low ridge. He kept his head low while he climbed, the gradient gradually increasing until he emerged, higher than the trees. Looking to his north, he could see that he was standing at the start of a peninsula, the sea on both sides, and what must be the town of Pemba perched at the end of the promontory, approximately eight kilometres away. He found some shade behind a rock and loosened his collar, taking a deep breath of the fresher, cooler air, and a sip from his water bottle while he considered the safest route into town.

He packed away his water bottle and began the descent. He didn't mind the heat and the stickiness that came with it. In fact, perversely, he quite enjoyed it because he knew he thrived where others struggled. During SAS selection, thirteen years before, he'd spent a gruelling month in the Brunei jungle and had been one of the rare individuals who found the terrain easier to operate in than the temperate climes of the Herefordshire Hills.

Fifteen minutes later, he paused again to take on water and withdrew the machete he'd been carrying since he'd arrived in Africa three months ago. He examined the blade, sharpened with a leather strap, the old-fashioned way. He was satisfied with the work. He still had the Vector pistol, but the knife would be his best weapon for what was to come – silent, fast, effective. He slid it back into its sheath and ran at a steady pace, continuing north along the cliffs at four kilometres an hour, just as he been trained to do.

An hour later, he saw the perimeter fence of Pemba airport and, beyond it, several thick black plumes of smoke rising high into the sky. The town had fallen and Mason knew that what was happening inside of it was going to be bad.

The time was now 3 pm and the sun, not so hot, was dropping in the west. He could detect the smell of the smoke now hanging in the air and recognised at once the bitter, unmistakable odour of war. It was a smell that Mason had encountered many times before. He had to move fast. Whatever horror was happening in Pemba during daylight would get infinitely worse once the sun went down. After another brief stop to rehydrate, he struck out again, continuing until the beach track turned into a path that led up past the town's petrol refinery. He'd finally reached civilisation and he knew that pretty soon he would be in the town. As he made his way up the hill, Mason could see the jetty of Pemba Port in the distance.

Upon reaching the main road, the carnage was clearer to see. A food truck had been stopped in the middle of the carriageway and the body of its driver lay on the tarmac next to it. The man had been crudely beheaded and the contents of his truck looted. On the other side of the road, Mason saw a row of large, gated houses, which he guessed belonged to the town's wealthier ex-pats. They were all on fire, plumes of black smoke rising into the clear blue sky.

As if oblivious to it all, a steady stream of people, mostly women and children, walked past in single file, silently making their way to the centre of town. The women carried what they could, balancing buckets and cloth bags precariously on their heads, all the while marshalling their young ones to keep up. Mason pitied them and not for the first time in his career, he felt lucky to know that his own family were safe and well, while so many others suffered so much. He fell into line, hiding among the crowd, pulling his cap down low over his head, stooping to point his face low to the ground.

With no way out by road, the people were walking to the port in the hope of finding a boat that could take them over the sea to Madagascar, Tanzania, anywhere but Pemba. They passed by the carcasses of dead animals, burnt-out cars, the occasional human corpse. Nobody said a word, they all ignored what they were seeing as much as the sound of sporadic gunfire coming from up ahead. To the east, Mason heard explosions, sounds of heavier artillery, possibly even mortars. *Where had these fuckers got mortars from?* He knew someone must be bankrolling all this destruction.

After thirty minutes of trudging along the main artery into town, Mason finally broke away and darted down a side street. It was too dangerous now to be out in the open, the sound of gunfire was very much closer. Mason hadn't witnessed anything like this since Iraq. To him, Pemba now looked a lot like Falluja.

At the end of the street, he ducked in behind an Italian restaurant, boarded up and long since abandoned. Its owners had probably had the means to flee in a hurry, unlike most of the poor wretches he'd seen back on the road. He pulled himself up onto its low corrugated roof to get a better look at what was going on. From a storey up, he had a better view of the road to the port. The street was already clogged with thousands of refugees, shouting, shoving, pushing their way to the gates, desperate to escape by any means possible. On the other side of the fence, inside the port, Mason could see a small armed security detail fighting to keep the crowd at bay.

He felt a sudden shift in the air and milliseconds later heard the crash of a mortar explosion. The force of it threw him flat onto his belly, knocking the wind out of him. He turned to see the melee that the bomb had caused. People were screaming, running in all directions. On the road below, the crowd surged forwards towards the gates. The throng grew louder, the desperation to escape felt even more electric. Mason knew he had no way back. One way or another, he had to get into that port.

FIFTEEN

SinoCheck Offices, Hong Kong

The fog on the bay was so thick that James Beeby could barely make out the outline of the skyscrapers as his taxi sped over the Tsing Ma Bridge from the airport to Kowloon. He could have stayed over there tonight, but he much preferred the drama of Hong Kong Island. Being in Central would allow him to make the most of time away from the wife and kids. Tonight, he'd check into his suite at the Mandarin Oriental, before heading out for some Wagyu beef and sautéed leopard coral groupa at Ming Court. On his way home he'd hit the Varga Lounge or the Ce La Vi club, maybe pick up a couple of expensive prostitutes to keep him company. But before the fun could begin, he had to sort out the situation that had developed with his client, Wei Lun Chow, at his offices.

James checked his emails and reflected on recent developments. During the twelve hours that he'd been in the air, the Americans had recovered the *Falcon*, drifting in the Red Sea. They'd found two dead Russians and a dead Eritrean sailor on board. It was less of a surprise to hear that Chow was now missing, along with four of his crew, whose details

James was scanning on his phone – two Brits, an Aussie, and a Kiwi. *Poor bastards.* There was little doubt now that they were dealing with a kidnap and ransom situation. In James's experience, which was considerable, a call from the kidnappers would be imminent and would be directed towards whoever had the most money, which in this case was Chow.

The taxi dropped him off at the SinoCheck building, where the receptionist checked his credentials before inviting him to take the lift directly to the executive offices on the forty-seventh floor. James was instantly pleased with the energy he found up there. People were running along corridors, phones were ringing, there was a palpable sense of doom in the air. That was good. He could work with that.

Since they'd received word that MTO in Dubai had taken the mayday call from the *Falcon*, De Grasse's corporate apparatus had kicked into gear. James had split the response team in two and deployed Hopkins to Djibouti, where he estimated the Americans would by now be docking the *Falcon*. Once Hopkins had taken statements from the survivors, his job was to set up the delivery team and make preparations on the ground for the hostage handover. In the meantime, James would head up the negotiation team in Hong Kong and iron out the details with the kidnappers.

Chow's executive assistant, Mandy, a prim, young Chinese woman met him at the executive reception and led him down the corridor to the boardroom. James took in the view. They were high up enough to see over the top of the fog bank, which covered the lower half of the city in gloom, while those who could get above it, were rewarded with uninterrupted blue, cloudless skies and views of Hong

Kong's imperial skyline. Not bad, he thought. Chow might have been a poor kid from the skids but he'd done alright for himself. His parents would be proud, if they ever got to see him again.

The boardroom had been assigned as the negotiation ops room and was already buzzing with activity. The room was sealed off from the rest of the floor and all the internal windows were blacked out. Access to what went on inside was on a strict 'need to know' basis and a list of people, which included a handful of senior in-house lawyers and accountants as well as the head of SinoCheck PR and Mandy, had all been briefed. Any other communication relating to Chow's disappearance was to be personally approved by James. Right now, information was all the leverage that he had and he wasn't going to give it away easily.

'Okay, gather round,' his voice projected around the room; clear, authoritative, commanding.

Everyone stopped what they were doing as James downed the last of his coffee and threw the empty cup directly into the bin. He looked to see if Mandy had noticed. She had. Good. Maybe he'd invite her to join him for dinner later. First, he had to lay out the strategy.

'So, we've been expecting first contact for a little while now, which means it's probably imminent. You should already know this, but let's run it through again for the slow learners. It's vital that we control the flow of information. Nothing goes beyond this room. The story we're telling must remain watertight.'

There was a murmur of agreement. James looked at them all. He'd made brief intros on Zoom while he'd been in the airline lounge in London, but there were still too many faces to remember. Some of them were pretty good looking too. He picked out a couple of particularly nice-looking girls. Then he saw a woman who really caught his eye. A tall, athletically built redhead, standing at the back, making notes. Mandy suddenly had some competition.

'I don't want anyone to get spooked when we get that call. They are going to ask for a silly number. I wouldn't be surprised to hear a hundred million dollars.'

There was a collective intake of breath and several of the accountants gave each other worried looks.

'But we're not going to pay that,' James continued. 'Our line is that SinoCheck is not as financially healthy as people believe it is. We'll pretend we're in debt. There's a pending lawsuit. We plead poverty. We're going to struggle to get the money together, etc., etc. Okay? I'll talk to each of you separately but first, I want to see the documents I asked for.'

The legal team had been working through the night to prepare a dossier showing that SinoCheck was facing a lawsuit from a rival. He'd ask them to concoct bogus correspondence from both sides, suggesting a settlement sum that would significantly dent the company's bank balance. In the past, he had used a similar tactic to good effect. Play the broke card and suddenly the guys on the other end of the line are a lot more willing to listen to a counter offer. A hundred million could quickly become ten if you could convince them that a realistic alternative could soon be zero.

'We believe that the group we are working with are just Somali fishermen. We've not had much activity in that region over the last couple of years, but before that, De Grasse dealt with several of these groups. Okay?'

Everyone nodded nervously. He continued.

'You're going to have to trust me. I've done this more times than you guys have had dim sum. They always follow a clear strategy, so as long as we keep to the plan, we'll get your boss back, safe and sound.'

He could feel the collective sigh of relief in the room. He was saying exactly what Chow's employees had needed to hear, but still, he was surprised to see several of them allow themselves a half-smile. The guy must be pretty popular. You didn't see that very often.

'What if they're not?' The question came from the back. He looked up to see it was from the redhead.

'Not what?' he asked.

'Fishermen,' she replied. 'What if they're not fishermen?'

'We've no reason—'

'Because there's no history of Somali piracy that far north.'

'Right, look . . . Let's just leave the thinking to the big boys, shall we?' Beeby said.

'And the captain of the USS *Mustin* reports that the *Falcon* was intercepted by an Eritrean Navy vessel,' she continued, before adding, 'Not fishermen.'

James forced out a chuckle, but he was scrambling to make sense of how this woman knew intel that hadn't even been shared with *him* yet. He looked more closely at her but drew a blank. He didn't recognise her at all. She was American, confident, and currently, extremely annoying.

'Sorry, I didn't catch your name?' he asked.

The woman pulled an ID from her pocket and flashed it over the heads of the rest of the room. James recognised the badge at once and tried to look calm, unflustered, both of which were pretty far from the truth. *What the fuck was the CIA doing here? He had cleared all this with MoD and they were happy for De Grasse to run point on it. There weren't even any fucking Americans on board for Christ's sake!*

'I'm sorry,' he said, squinting to see her badge a little better. 'It's still a bit far away to make out the name.'

'Redford,' she replied, putting the badge away again. 'Agent Redford.'

SIXTEEN

Pemba Port, Mozambique

Some cats like to climb, while others do not. The former may descend from ancestors, somewhere back in the mists of time, who hunted up in the trees like jaguars and leopards, while the latter more likely share their genes with bush cats like lions and cheetahs. The climbers do so because it gives them a sense of security, perspective on their surroundings, cover from would-be predators, and a chance to get closer to the pleasant warmth offered by the hot sun. If any lingering feline DNA was knocking around in Matt Mason's genetic makeup, then it definitely came from the tree cats.

The last drops of afternoon sun rained down on Mason's back as he skulked along the roofline of the buildings that surrounded Pemba harbour. He kept his head down so that he could not be seen by the crowd who packed into the streets below. He leapt silently from one roof to the next, landing softly, drawing no attention as he worked his way gradually closer to the port gates. When he was less than fifty metres away, he peered over the edge and noted how the barrier below was manned by six armed guards whose rifles were raised to keep the mob at bay. Either side of them, a two-metre-high metal fence topped with rolls of razor wire ran around the perimeter to the water. Even a cat would struggle to get in there any other way than through the official entrance.

Mason shuffled to the edge of the roof, away from the direct line of sight of the guards and leapt to the ground. He braced his knees and rolled to the side, just as he'd been trained to do a thousand times before, ensuring that he didn't sustain an injury. Once he was back on his feet, he dusted himself off and walked around the building, pushing his way into the crowd.

Around him, people seemed surprised to suddenly see a white man. The truth was that in many former European colonies in Africa whites still held sway by the nature of their skin colour alone, and the people moved aside to let him through. Mason knew that the guards would shoot any of these people if they dared try to breach the gates but they'd think twice before pointing a gun at him. So he confidently shoved his way forward until he was at the very front of the throng.

One of the guards saw him and instantly called for the barrier to be raised, raising a hand and ushering Mason towards him but as he stepped forward, the pole dropped again as quickly as it had risen.

'The port is closed now, sir,' said the guard, a slight note of apology in his voice.

'I have business in the port,' Mason replied. 'Let me speak to your OC.'

Another older guard was already moving quickly in his direction, looking Mason up and down. 'The port is closed, sir,' he said, shaking his head – the exact same words that Mason had heard moments before but more forthrightly delivered.

'Sergeant,' said Mason, noting the stripes on the man's sleeve. 'I have business with Wang Trading Company. Please, let me pass.'

The sergeant pointed to the container ship at the end of the jetty, already fully loaded, ready to leave. 'Miss Li Lan is the boss of Wang Company, sir. She loaded her last container onto the *Sirrah* this morning. Now she has gone.'

'Gone where?' asked Mason.

The sergeant shrugged and shook his head as the crowd surged forward again towards the gates. 'Please, sir. Move aside,' he said, edging Mason out of his way as he raised his rifle and fired two warning shots into the air. Mason took a step back, inside the barrier, as the other guards hurried to the sergeant's side, raising their rifles in defiance, pointing them at the crowd, warning them not to make another move.

Mason took another step back. Nobody was paying any attention to him now. All six guards were on high alert, looking directly at the angry mob. He stepped back again and sidled quietly to his left, disappearing behind a single-storey shack just inside the fence. Beyond the shack was a path that followed a line of low-rise prefabricated buildings to the dock. Each prefab had a small name card next to its door, none of which were familiar to him. They were most likely small-time shipping companies or seafood distributors. Mason hurried along, checking that he hadn't been followed, looking the whole time for the name Wang Trading Company.

Eventually, he saw it. The Wang company's name card was attached to the wall next to a black door. Of course, it was locked but Mason gave it a hard shove with his shoulder, forcing it open with ease. He slid through the gap, closing the broken door behind him and pushed a chair against it to keep it closed. He peered out of the window to check that he hadn't been followed before he lowered the blinds and hit the lights.

The office was pretty bare except for a few tacked up schedules on the walls and a filing cabinet in the corner next to a desk. Mason combed over it, looking for clues. What he needed was some connection from Wang Trading Company to the outside world. If they were using the place as a front from which to smuggle ivory, then there had to be a paper trail back to their legitimate business. Odds were that whoever was receiving the seafood that Wang Trading Company was shipping was more interested in the ivory smuggled with it.

The filing cabinets were full of dockets and bills of lading for the last couple of months. It looked to Mason as though the company was shipping a container of sea cucumbers out of Pemba pretty much weekly. According to the most recent paperwork, the ship in port was called the *Sirrah*, en route to Mombasa, and from a bill of lading Mason found in the wastepaper basket, it looked like the Wang Trading Company had a single container loaded on board. He pocketed the bill and decided to let himself out by the back door. Before he could do anything more with this information, he had to take a look at what was inside that container.

The shelves that lined the warehouse were empty, but judging by the pong, they'd been filled with drying sea cucumbers very recently. As he made his way to the far end of the space, Mason saw a thick, steel door, which had been left slightly ajar. He looked inside to see a small holding room, six-foot square, filthy blankets piled up in one corner. He bent down to take a closer look and spotted several dark bloodstains along their length and a shard of grey-white tusk encrusted to the fabric. It was just a fragment, but it was the evidence that he needed. He knew then that as many as a few hundred tusks had been laid out here very recently. Tusks that were now, in all likelihood, aboard the *Sirrah*, hidden among a load of stinky sea cucumbers, headed for Mombasa.

He backed out of the storeroom and took the door that lead out to the dockside. The *Sirrah* was already leaving, gangplanks pulled up, tug boat pulling its bow away from the key. Mason ran down to the jetty. Suddenly from behind, he heard the unmistakable sound of rapid gunfire. Things were now out of hand at the gate. The sight of the *Sirrah* pulling away had finally set the people into a panic and nothing would hold them back. Reaching the huge starboard side of the ship, he sprinted along its length, past the bow until he reached the side of the dock where the ship's tugboat had already cast away, towing the front of the ship out into the channel from where it could set its own course for the open sea.

Mason dived headlong into the water, emerging at the surface a few metres from the tug. He swam to the side of the boat and reached up, grabbing hold of one of the tyres that hung down, acting as a fender to protect the vessel from damage. Looping his leg out of the water and into the tyre, he contorted his body until he could lever himself high enough to get a hand over the edge. He hauled himself upright and dragged himself onto the deck.

Immediately, one of the tug's sailors came running towards him, waving his arms.

'Mister, you cannot—' he began but Mason interrupted him with a sharp jab to the solar plexus, crumpling him in two before he slumped onto the deck like a bag of spuds.

'I think I can,' Mason said, stepping over him and continuing towards the bow.

He placed one foot on the bow fender and launched himself from the back of the tug, getting just enough height to grab hold of the towline before he wrapped his feet around it. Moving like a monkey, he dragged himself up the fifteen-metre line until he reached the prow of the *Sirrah*. With one hand he took a firm hold of the ship's gantry and let go with the other, spinning himself around and using the momentum to pull his body up onto the deck.

Mason lay down on his back and breathed. Hundreds of people were now at the dockside, waving and screaming at the ship to come back, but the *Sirrah* was already too far out into the channel, the tug was disconnecting, and the ship's engines were fully engaged. In another couple of minutes, they'd be doing twenty knots on their way to Kenya. Mason didn't hold out much hope for the poor fuckers left behind. Their fate was now in the hands of the rebel jihadists who would flood the town and take the spoils.

He looked across the bay to where the sun was dropping like a stone behind the dark Mozambique rainforest. Somewhere out there, the bastards who had slaughtered those elephants were counting their money. He would be back to deal with them in good time, make no mistake about that, but first, he had to find the people who were bankrolling it all. The tusks of the elephants that he'd seen lying dead on the reserve only days ago were somewhere on this ship and they would lead him directly to the people who were responsible for the whole operation. When he found them, he would take them down and cut off the head of the snake. Only then could he ensure that it never happened again.

SEVENTEEN

Undisclosed Location, Ethiopia

Joanna Mason's hands were tied in front of her body. In that sense, she was better off than the others. Reaching out, she could feel that Ben, Woodsie, and Chow had all been tied together and their hands bound behind their backs. Everyone, including Joanna, had been gagged, which she resented not so much because she had anything she desperately needed to say but more that she wanted to close her mouth. The air temperature outside had been forty degrees for most of the day while inside the cramped space of the van it was considerably higher. She was feeling weak with dehydration.

Her father had described to her many times what a hostage should do in the event of a kidnapping. The most important thing, beyond staying alive, was to maintain a sense of where you were. Especially if you were moved by your captors. Doing that successfully was down to keeping a handle on two things – direction and speed. One trick that she'd learned from her dad was to feel for the heat of the sun on the vehicle, that way you could judge your direction of travel. The second was to listen carefully to the road surface below the vehicle because you could do sixty on a tarmacked road but no more than thirty on a dirt one.

Since the handover in Anrata, the vehicle hadn't stopped and hadn't left the tarmac. Jo had felt the first warm rays of the sun on her back, against the left-hand side of the truck, about two hours ago. From that, she reckoned they were driving south. When she had finally felt the vehicle turn, the heat had lessened for nearly an hour before it returned, which she judged meant it was mid-morning, the sun had moved around and the van was heading west.

Jo tried to conjure up a map of the region in her head. The gunboat had brought them to shore almost due west of the Zubair Group. After that, they'd driven south for two or three hours before turning west again, all of which would have brought them close to Djibouti. But the Djibouti/Eritrea border was closed, meaning the turn to the west must have been into Ethiopia. As she felt the van begin to cool again, she knew that it must be sundown, so they had been travelling for another six hours. Putting it all together, she'd say they were three hundred miles inside Ethiopia, heading west or maybe southwest, perhaps halfway to Addis Ababa.

If her father had been there to judge how accurate a guess that was, he'd have been proud of her. Her assessment was spot on. The van had indeed driven south from Anrata and taken the highway along the coast road until it turned west over the Ethiopian border. The National Route One was a good two-lane, tarmacked road that ran southwest, hugging the Djibouti border for three hundred miles before it turned west for Addis. But the two men driving the van had strict instructions to stop long before they ever reached the capital. As the sun set over the grasslands of the Yangudi Rassa National Park, they pulled over into a quiet clearing where they were no longer visible from the road.

Joanna Mason and her fellow captives lay silently inside the vehicle for another hour before their captors opened the doors. The space was instantly filled with a cool stream of fresh night air, but of course, with their eyes and ears still covered, none of them could be sure that it was night-time. Suddenly Joanna felt a firm grip take hold of her, yanking her out of the vehicle. She could smell burning wood and fresh coffee in the air and she realised that the men must have built a campfire. The hand forced her down until she was sitting on what felt like a fallen tree trunk and then removed her gag. She took a welcome full breath of air and flexed the muscles in her jaw. Then she felt the lip of a cup pressed to her mouth and she drank the cool water inside it greedily until the hand guided her fingers around what felt like a warm bowl. She cautiously explored its contents – it was filled with warm rice. Wasting no time, she began shovelling the rice into her mouth. It was the first food she'd eaten for over twenty-four hours.

As soon as they had finished eating, Joanna felt the gag again in her mouth and the mysterious person pulling her away again. Finally, they shoved her to the floor and bound her feet together. She lay in the dirt, bound, blind, and deaf and waited for something else to happen. An hour after that, she was fast asleep.

The fat man waited until everyone was asleep, not only Jo but his younger friend and all the other hostages. Joanna stirred slightly when she felt his footsteps on the dirt next to her, but a moment later she was wide awake as he grabbed a hold of the rope that bound her ankles and started dragging her across the dirt, further away from the rest of the group. She struggled to resist but had nothing with which to gain any purchase. Instead, her head bounced along off the hard floor. Her cries were muffled by the gag that was wedged deep in her mouth and with her eyes and ears still covered in tape, she could sense nothing but the pain from her own body scraping over the ground. A minute or so later, everything stopped and she felt the fat man cutting the rope that bound her feet.

Joanna tried to seize the opportunity, kicking out with her legs, trying to get herself free, but the fat man was too strong. He pushed her feet to the ground and sat down heavily on them. Every time she tried to move, the fat man was too quick for her and shoved her back down with a firm hand in the centre of her chest. He held her down for what seemed like an eternity, taking the opportunity to grope her breasts, cursing quietly under his breath. With his free hand, he began undoing her belt. Jo screamed silently into her gag, trying to wriggle out of his grasp, trying to squirm away, trying to flip herself over. But nothing worked. He was too strong, too heavy, too determined.

The fat man loosened his own belt, the buckle flapping limply to the side. He pulled down his trousers until they were around his knees and slumped forward so that his whole weight was pressing down on Jo's pelvis. Then she felt the cold steel press against her throat. Her breathing became shallow and dry while she wondered if this was how she was going to die. This wasn't how she'd ever imagined it, stabbed in the throat by the side of an African road. Suddenly, a wave of pain sliced across her face instead as the fat man tore off the electrical tape. The adhesive came away, taking chunks of Jo's eyebrows and eyelashes with it. A clump of her hair came away last and she screamed in agony into the gag.

She blinked as her eyes tried to focus for the first time in more than a day, but they were already filling with tears. The pain was unbearable. The fat man, still pressing the knife to her throat, leaned in close, removing the gag from her mouth, while pressing the blade against her neck. He was saying something in broken English. She fought back her tears to listen.

'You English bitch. Like Arab man. Yes?'

Jo glared at him, her gut aching from the pain that seemed now to be coming from every part of her body. She felt a trickle of blood running down the back of her neck, the tape having removed a patch of skin behind her ear. She fought the urge to throw up, while her eyes darted around, left and right, looking desperately for something that she could use to fight back. But there was nothing and, besides, her hands were still tied tight. She caught sight of the fat man's penis. He'd taken it out of his trousers and was holding it over her. Again he leaned down until she could feel his hot breath in her ear.

'Say it like this: "I English bitch. I like Arab man."'

Jo couldn't stop the tears. She felt them running down both cheeks along with a few drops of cooling rain. The edge of the blade pushed harder against her skin and she realised that there was nothing that she could do to stop what was happening. She had to give in if she was going to survive and that was the most important thing now. She would get her opportunity to fight in good time, but first she had to live because a dead person never got that chance. She nodded weakly and she focused on the fat man's face.

'I am an English bitch,' she said. 'And I love an Arab man.'

The fat man smiled before he glanced down and moved his leg over to push Jo's knees apart but she kept them stubbornly locked. He looked irked for a moment, clearly he was ready, having heard the words he wanted to hear. He slid his hand down Jo's body to force her legs open.

Jo watched him, concentrating hard. His breathing was shallow and fast, his eyes focused on getting what he so desperately wanted. She felt his hand force itself between her knees, pushing them apart. Another wave of nausea passed over her and she let her knees go limp. At once, she heard him let out a satisfied grunt, nodding enthusiastically, lowering himself a little, getting into position.

The knife scraped against her thigh and she realised that he was still using his knife hand to hold her knees apart. This was her chance. She clamped her knees shut again, locking them tightly around his wrist. She used all the strength in her thighs to hold him still like a bear caught in a trap and drew a breath, the deepest breath she'd ever drawn.

She rocked back just as the fat man looked up towards her, his face contorted in an angry snarl, and she released the breath, contracted her abdominal muscles, and rocked forward with all her worth, pulling her legs up sharply against his weight. Her body came shooting upright at speed, just as the fat man lost his balance and fell forwards. Their faces raced towards each other and Jo dropped her forehead, landing a solid head-butt squarely onto the bridge of his nose.

He let out a yelp and rolled off, trying to get away from the source of the pain, crawling onto his side, his hands trying to stem the blood now pouring freely from the centre of his face. Jo felt something drop between her knees. She thrust her hands, still bound at the wrist, into the darkness, feeling around until she found the knife. She gripped the handle and lifted the blade high above her head with both hands before thrusting it down again with everything she had. Five inches of cold steel slid into the space between his neck and left shoulder. The blade disappeared to the hilt with a solid thud and Jo saw his eyes bulge. His whole body contorted and twitched for a second before he gurgled out a lungful of blood and slumped lifelessly onto the dirt.

She fell back onto the ground, trying to catch her breath. She reached down and grabbed hold of her trousers, pulling them back up again. She wanted to cry. She wanted to scream. She wanted to be anywhere other than where she was. She'd fought off the filthy fucker, dead on the ground next to her, but she was still there. Still tied up in the middle of fuck knows where. The immediate threat was gone, but the whole nightmare was far from over.

She tried to catch her breath, tried to bring her attention back to the here and now, but she still couldn't quite believe what had just happened. Her brain was telling her that she should get up and run, that this was her chance to escape, but her body was telling her that she couldn't. She just didn't have the strength.

A shadow passed over her, blocking out the moonlight for a moment. She realised the other man, the younger, skinny guy was awake. He walked over to the fat man and checked his pulse. Then he looked back to Joanna with a look of almost respect.

'I don't like this guy,' he said.

'That makes two of us,' she replied. She was still panting heavily.

The skinny guy smiled. 'Okay,' he said, helping her back to her feet. 'Time to go.'

He pushed Joanna back into the van before he woke the others and shoved them in next to her.

'Are you okay?' Ben asked as he tumbled into the space. He could hear from Joanna's breathing that something was wrong.

Joanna didn't answer. She didn't want to talk about it. The van turned back to the main road and again she began to count. This time, she was sure they were heading south, driving faster than before.

EIGHTEEN

On Board the Sirrah, Indian Ocean

Far away, off the port side of the *Sirrah*, Mason could see tiny dots of light blinking along the coast. The fourteen-cylinder diesel engine rolled over and over and over, churning the waters below, pushing fifty thousand tonnes of steel and cargo along at a steady twenty-four knots. The whole ship stank of oil and Reldan, a toxic chemical sprayed liberally over the decks to keep the cockroaches at bay. Although the only thing that Mason could smell was the odour of tobacco drifting up from a rolled-up cigarette that perched on the edge of his bottom lip. Again, in vain, he tried to find some signal on his phone.

He gave up and put the phone away, figuring that he might as well enjoy the smoke and the time he had to think about what he was going to do next. Since he'd climbed aboard the *Sirrah*, Mason had been prepared to face some resistance from the crew, but his appearance on the ship had so far gone undetected. Not that anyone seemed to be actively looking for him. There are strict rules governing stowaways and, ultimately, the company that owns the ship is on the hook for the costs. In practice, that means nobody looks for what they don't want to find. Just to be sure, Mason had found a quiet spot near the bow, in a space behind the anchor chain and as far from the bridge as he could get, where he could hold up and shelter from the spray and the wind.

Mombasa was six hundred miles north of Pemba, which meant that he had another eighteen hours on board before they made landfall. In the meantime, he might as well put that time to good use. Somewhere among the hundreds of containers on the *Sirrah*, there was one that contained a shipment of ivory. If he could find it, then he could follow it when they landed in Mombasa and was, almost certainly, loaded onto another ship. Right now, his priority was to work out where its final destination was. He flicked the cigarette butt overboard and took out the paperwork he'd recovered from the Wang Trading Company office in Pemba. The bill of lading showed that container number WANU114655 had been loaded onto the Sirrah the day before. According to the docket, it should hold four tonnes of sea cucumbers, but Mason suspected a good chunk of that was elephant tusks.

He checked that nobody was around before he walked along the port side towards the stern. He looked up at the towers of containers, scanning each box for the serial number of the Wang container. They were laid end to end, four or five high and six rows across the beam. He reckoned at least a hundred in total on the deck, maybe two or three times that below. He edged his way along a row, trying to read off each serial number, but he quickly realised that it was a futile endeavour: he couldn't make out the numbers near the top of the pile. In any case, unless WANU114655 was on the bottom of a row, he was going to struggle to access it.

'I hope you don't mind rats.'

It came from behind him and Mason span around in time to see the man who'd said it stepping out of the shadows into a patch of light. He was black, six-four, with a handsome face that suited his tidy moustache. He was smoking a cigarette and held up the packet to offer one to Mason.

'They're alright with a bit of chilli sauce,' Mason said, politely declining the offer of more nicotine with a shake of his head.

The man laughed. A little too hard. It wasn't that funny. He put the packet away and pointed to the tower of containers looming over them.

'You can't steal anything. They're all locked and sealed.'

'I'm looking for something that belongs to me,' Mason said before correcting himself. 'Well not me exactly but … it's a long story.'

The big man's eyes narrowed. He was used to stowaways on board the *Sirrah,* but the unofficial company policy was if someone wasn't causing trouble then they weren't worth worrying over. Anyhow, most were picked up by the customs officials in-port. But the guy standing in front of him didn't look like a stowaway. For a start, he was white.

'Come,' he said after a long pause. 'You look like you could use a drink. Then we'll find your container.'

Mason followed him back along the port side towards the light that shone down from the bridge. The control room was perched on top of a forty-foot tower. It had to be that high to see over all the boxes on the deck. The big guy led them through a heavy metal door and up a steel staircase, four floors up and onto the galley where two other men were driving the boat. They looked a little surprised to see they had company.

'Alright?' Mason said.

'This one is Aku and the one over there is Sherry,' the big man said, pointing first to a short Indian man and then to a taller Filipino one. 'We are the four o'clock watch. I'm Dahir.'

'Mason,' Mason said, shaking each man by the hand. 'Nice boat.'

'Ship,' Aku corrected.

'Right,' said Mason. 'Nice ship.'

Dahir returned with a bottle of rum and two glasses. Everyone aboard a container ship deals with the monotony and solitude in different ways, and for Dahir it was drink. He filled both glasses to the brim and handed one to Mason before knocking back his own in one. Figuring that he had eighteen hours to kill, Mason did the same. It had the desired effect. Dahir looked pleased. He laughed a little too hard again before he threw open a side door that led to a small platform with two chairs. He offered Mason a seat while he poured two more large rums.

By the time they were halfway through the bottle of rum, Mason and Dahir had traded war stories. Literally. Dahir was from Somaliland, along the northwestern shore of Somalia. He had fought against the Somali government during the civil war in the late 1980s, helping his countrymen to victory. The next day Somaliland declared its territories independent, an act that has still never been recognised by any other country, but Dahir had already decided he'd done his bit for his fledgling nation and left for Djibouti to find work. He found it on the container ships and now, twenty years later, he was first mate.

By the time they were halfway through the second bottle of rum, Mason had told his own story, recounting to Dahir how he too had fought for his country, in far-flung places all over the Arab world. He told about how his career had come to an abrupt end in Yemen and how he now found himself working in a game reserve in Mozambique. He explained why his mission was to find whoever was behind the smuggling operations in Niassa and why he was on the *Sirrah* looking for container WANU114655.

'What was the number?' Dahir asked, slurring a little. He stood and stumbled back into the control room, collecting a large red book from one of the shelves.

'WANU114655,' Mason repeated. It was etched into his brain.

Dahir thumbed through the book, running his finger down a list of handwritten entries, closing one eye to help him focus. 'WANU114655?' he asked, finally.

Mason sat upright. 'Yeah, that's it.'

'No,' Dahir said, slamming the book shut. 'Not on this ship.'

Mason got to his feet, suddenly sobered by Dahir's words. He took the book and scanned the list for himself. There were hundreds of container numbers, written into the ledger at the time of loading. One by one, he checked them carefully, looking for the Wang container.

'It must have been missed,' he said, looking back to Dahir for agreement.

'Not possible,' Dahir shook his head, 'Aku supervises all the loading himself and trust me that guy doesn't miss anything. The container you're looking for isn't on this ship, my friend.'

Mason slumped back into his chair as his heart sank. He was in the Indian Ocean, heading to Kenya, in pursuit of a container that wasn't even on the ship. It could be anywhere. He'd followed a total dead end and now he had no passport, no money, and a lot more explaining to do to his employer. He poured himself another shot of rum and decided to work it out in the morning.

NINETEEN

Hong Kong

Seven people sat around the boardroom on the forty-seventh floor of the SinoCheck building, waiting for the phone to ring. It was nearly 4 am and the room was littered with take-out boxes and empty soda cans. There had been some argument about who needed to be there and even more about who would take the call when it eventually came. SinoCheck's lead lawyer, Charles Xi, had wanted to handle the negotiation but James Beeby had convinced him otherwise. This was James's forte, he argued. If they wanted their boss back alive and didn't want to go bankrupt in the process, then they had better leave it to the professional. Charles had eventually backed down; the Englishman had a point, this was his business.

Nevertheless, Charles insisted on several key personnel being present – Chow's second in command, Tony Cheung, head of legal affairs, Kelly Lam, and Anita Fu, Chow's EA who'd point blank refused to go with James for a drink, despite his persistence. James was still pretty annoyed about that. The last person at the table was Agent Redford from the CIA. He was even more annoyed about that. The woman had still offered him no explanation of why she was there, and while Charles maintained that she was his personal guest, there was no way he could get her to leave.

All the hostages' contacts were being identified and tomorrow morning James would begin contacting them to inform them of the situation, but for now they wanted to keep as close a lid on this as possible. It was vital that any incoming calls from unknown numbers be channelled through the central SinoCheck number in Hong Kong. Although, nobody was anticipating that would happen yet. The first call was always made to the company that owned the boat. If you were after money, then why waste your time speaking to anyone other than the richest guy in the room?

There were four large whiteboards on the walls, each filled with details that made up the central plan which had been formulated during a long discussion held over the previous twenty-four hours. In the middle was a dollar amount, ringed in red felt-tip pen. '$10,000,000' was the target ransom they'd eventually agreed upon. Tony had expressed his concern with putting a value on his boss's life, but James had reassured him that this was the only way to conduct the negotiation. If they agreed to the kidnapper's first demand then they would simply double it. They expected some push back and James was the man to give it to them. Sure, they might end up paying more than ten million but it was a good ballpark figure. Of course, James had said, that if he could keep the negotiation to anything below that, then Chow should be pleased. He'd joked that maybe Chow might even bung him a bonus for it.

The previous day, the US Navy had recovered the *Falcon*, drifting in the Red Sea. James had been relieved to hear that the five-hundred-million-dollar boat wasn't damaged beyond a couple of bullet holes in the furniture. The insurance company would be happy about that. What was more of a problem were the three corpses they'd found on board, which included two of his employees and meant a mountain of paperwork for him to get through. Below deck, they'd found a traumatised Filipino crew, huddled together in the master suite. A few of the women had been sexually assaulted, which was another headache for him, not to mention that repatriating them to Manila wasn't going to be cheap. He decided to add it to Chow's bill.

The *Falcon* had been taken to Djibouti, where it was being held at the American base. It would mean more paperwork still to get it back but the costs would be minimal compared to what they could have been. James reassured Charles that in similar situations in the past, the principal's boat had formed a large part of the ransom collateral. They could have been looking at several more million on top to get it back, but the fact that they had simply abandoned it suggested that they weren't seasoned pros. With any luck, he'd laughed, these guys were amateurs and he could drive the price down even further.

The phone rang at 4.15 am and Redford nodded to Anita to begin the recording device which was set to tape the call.

James stretched out a little tension in his neck, craning his head from one side to the other and then, on the fourth ring, pushed the green button and laid the handset down so that everyone could hear. This was it. This was the call. It was showtime.

'Hello. This is James Beeby. I'll be your contact,' he said in a confident, public school-educated voice.

There was a pause on the other end of the line. James smiled. The caller would have been expecting someone else. The confusion gave him a slight advantage.

'What's your name?'

'Fifteen million dollars,' the reply came over the speaker in heavily accented English. James saw the others around the table shift uneasily in their seats.

'That's rather a mouthful,' he joked. 'Is there something else I can call you?'

Tony and Charles gave Redford an uncomfortable look. James was seriously getting on everyone's nerves. Joking with kidnappers who were holding Chow's life in their hands wasn't the agreed strategy and Charles felt a pang of regret that he'd conceded to letting the Englishman take the lead. After a few long painful moments of silence, the voice spoke again.

'Raghe.'

James relaxed a little, nodding reassuringly to the rest of the group. He'd already told everyone, more than once, how he'd been in these situations many times before and how the most important thing was to establish a rapport quickly. Which was ironic as he hadn't established rapport with any of them.

He replied to Raghe, speaking slowly and calmly, showing that he would set the tone. From experience, he knew that if he adopted a standard of mature, adult conversation from the outset, then Raghe was likely to follow. People's speech patterns often mirror the tone of the dominant conversations, so it was essential not to let Raghe hear any frustration, irritation, or provocation in his voice.

'Okay, Raghe. Let's be clear that my priority is to make sure that the people you are holding get home safely,' James said. 'I'm hoping that you help me with that.'

'I already told you the price,' Raghe said, his voice was flat and emotionless.

'You did and you were very clear,' James said. 'But before we get into that, I need to check everyone is okay? Is anyone injured? Does anyone need medical attention? Is everybody safe for now?'

'Yes, they are safe,' Raghe said before he added, 'for now.'

'Right, that's good. Thank you. I know we can solve this together, Raghe.'

'You bring the money, I bring your friends, mother-fucker.'

'Right. Okay. Good. Now, can I confirm that US dollars is what we're talking about? Because we can also operate in bitcoin, if that suits you better.'

'No bitcoin,' Raghe said. 'Only dollar.'

'Fine. Dollar is fine,' James replied. 'And what about location, Raghe? Where would you like the handover to happen?'

'Somalia,' Raghe offered. 'Details later.'

James gave Redford a smug 'told you so' look. Just as he'd said, the kidnappers were Somalians, probably opportunistic fishermen who were looking to make a fast couple of million.

'Okay, Raghe, so I'm hearing that you want US dollars. But you know none of the people you're holding have that kind of money?'

'We know who the Chinese man is,' Raghe said.

'Don't believe everything you read, Raghe. Mr Wei's company is facing a major lawsuit from one of their competitors. There simply isn't the money in the company to pay what you're asking for.'

'You want to talk to your boss ever again?'

'Of course, and I could maybe find five million dollars to prove that to you, Raghe.'

There was a long silence.

'Fifteen million dollars,' Raghe said.

'Now listen, Raghe—'

'No more listening, motherfucker. Fifteen million. We will tell you where tomorrow. Get the money ready.'

'I need to hear Mr Wei's voice before I agree to anything,' James said.

Raghe shouted something in Somali away from the phone. There was another noise in the background. Someone was being dragged across the floor. Then they heard a new voice on the line.

'Hello? Who is this?' It was Wei Lun Chow.

'Mr Wei? This is James Beeby from De Grasse, sir. Are you okay?'

'Where's Tony?'

'I'm here, Chow.' Tony leaned in closer to the phone.

'Tony? Don't give these cocksuckers one kuài of my money. You fucking hear—'

The phone went dead.

PART THREE

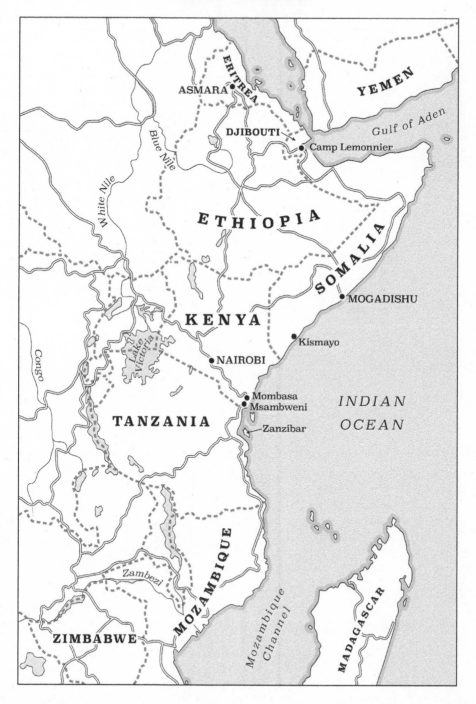

PART THREE

TWENTY

Hereford, England

Kerry Mason stood as if in a daze and walked to the fridge. Before she knew it, she was sitting back down at the kitchen table with a large glass of white wine in her hand. She took a generous gulp and looked at the clock on the wall. It was 10 am, which meant that it was 11 am in Mozambique. Matt would be at work on the game reserve. She picked up the phone and called his number, but it made no connection, only a recorded message in a language she didn't understand. *Was it Portuguese they spoke over there?* She wasn't sure.

She took another gulp and tried to replay the conversation that she'd just had with the woman from HR at a company called SinoCheck. She'd said on the phone that her name was Candy, or Mandy? She wasn't sure. It was one of those made-up English names that Chinese people usually had because their real name was too hard to pronounce. In any case, the whole conversation now felt like a bad dream. She'd said that she was working with a security company in Hereford. She remembered thinking how unusual it was. Matt would probably know them. If they were using ex-Regiment guys. They all knew each other. It was partly why they ended up living in Hereford even after they'd left the special forces. There was safety in numbers. Matt never spoke much about the details of his trips away, but she was sure that he'd made enemies. They all had. Sticking together in Hereford near camp was the safest place for them all and she couldn't imagine they'd ever feel safe living anywhere else.

At least, she'd thought that they were safe. How wrong she was. She felt a rush of nausea, but as she fought to control it another emotion took hold of her and she started to cry. Seconds later she was wailing, tears streaming down her face, falling into her glass. The reality of what Candy or Mandy had just told her was beginning to sink in and, other than calling Matt, she didn't know what to do. Joanna, her only daughter, and along with her son, Sam, one of the two people she loved and cherished more than anyone else in the whole world, was missing.

What did 'missing' even mean? The woman had said it so casually like she was talking about her car keys. 'Don't worry,' she'd said. 'We need you remain calm for Jo,' she'd said. 'SinoCheck will pay for everything,' she'd said. 'We'll find her and bring her back,' she'd said.

Kerry wiped her face and fetched a framed picture from the shelf. The kids were pulling silly faces, she and Matt had big grins. They'd been happy then. In Pembrokeshire, on holiday, six years ago. She looked closely at Joanna's face, her angel, and cried again.

Eight days ago, she'd waved her daughter off as her bus left from the Commercial Road coach station for London. After seven months away in Devon doing her naval training,

Joanna had been so excited to get back on the water with Ben and the rest of the gang. 'You're gonna be so jealous of my tan,' was the last thing Joanna had said before she'd boarded the bus. Another wave of tears burst out at the thought that they might have been the last words she would ever hear her daughter say. And that she'd not get a chance to say back 'I love you' or 'I'm so proud of you' or any of the other things she wished that she could tell her now.

She realised that she'd hit redial on the phone again without even thinking to, but again she only heard the foreign message. She'd heard so many messages in so many languages she couldn't speak over the years that she was more used to hearing them than the sound of her husband, sorry, ex-husband's voice. She still couldn't get used to that. *Ex-husband.* As though their life together was now an ex-life, rubbed out, cancelled, consigned to the past. Except for the kids.

Matt Mason might have been an absent husband but he'd always been an excellent father. He loved his children and had provided for them since they'd married at just eighteen and Joanna was born shortly after, Sam a year later. Since then, Kerry had led a conflicted life, raising two beautiful children, all the while worrying that their father might not come home.

The job required Mason to travel often and although he always kept the details to himself, Kerry only had to watch the news to work out if he was in Syrian or Libya or Mali or God knows where else there were people who wanted to kill him. Her whole adult life she'd felt a mixture of pride and pain at what her husband did for a living. Being a soldier's wife was no picnic, but at least you knew what you'd signed up for. Nobody could say that you hadn't been warned. *But this?* This was different. The deal was that Mason would be the one in the firing line, she'd never imagined that the danger would come for her children.

The Chinese woman had said that the man who owned the boat, another Chinese name she hadn't quite caught, was her boss. That he was rich and that the people who'd taken Joanna most likely wanted his company to pay a ransom. She said this was how things usually worked and that the security company had lots of experience dealing with 'situations like this'. *Situations like this.* There was no situation that she could imagine that could be even close to this. Her heart was physically hurting. *What would they be doing to Joanna?* She tried to put the thought out of her mind as she drained the glass.

Matt would know more than her. Part of the Regiment's work involved rescuing people. People who'd been kidnapped in Iraq or Afghanistan or Yemen. The last place he'd been posted before he left the Regiment. She'd seen the story of course. It was all over the news. A man had been tortured in Yemen for information about the whereabouts of a hostage and the integrity of the Regiment had been called into question. The papers said that the 'bad apple' had been identified and dealt with. Matt had left at the same time. She knew it was no coincidence. He'd said nothing as usual, but she knew all the same. *Could Matt have tortured people?* She didn't want to think about it.

People often asked her husband, usually after they'd had too much to drink, how many people he'd killed. Matt always gave them the same answer. 'I prefer to talk about how many people I've saved.' She liked that answer. She preferred to think of him saving people than killing people. People needed saving, didn't they? And if he was to be believed then he was good at saving people. Very good at it. Right now, she needed him to be good at saving their daughter. She didn't know Mandy or Candy from Adam. She didn't trust her, or anyone else for that matter, to find her daughter and bring her home safely. She only trusted her husband to do that. She trusted Matt Mason to save Joanna Mason.

She put down the phone and walked back to the fridge. One more glass of wine and she'd call Matt again. He'd know what to do. He'd find their daughter. He'd bring her home.

TWENTY-ONE

Mombasa Port, Kenya

Mason felt a hand grab him by the shoulder almost before he realised that he was awake. His instincts kicked in and his left hand shot up, gripping his assailant's wrist, while his right reached for the knife on his belt. It was as if both hands had minds of their own, working independently of each other. He opened his eyes and a rush of pain shot directly to his brain. He struggled to adjust to the bright daylight and winced, realising that he was feeling the effects of last night's rum. The second bottle had left its mark. As he focused, he saw that he needn't have worried. He was not being attacked.

'Ssshh!' Dahir whispered, deep and low, cautionary but reassuring. Mason loosened his grip on the big man's wrist and let go of the blade.

Dahir helped him upright, while Mason took in a lungful of air and let it out again slowly, hoping that it would take a chunk of his hangover with it. Dahir was looking back along the starboard side, his face riven with concern. He raised a finger to his lips to tell Mason to be quiet.

'We have reached Mombasa,' he whispered. 'The pilot is coming aboard to take us in. Better if you stay hidden until the time is right. I will come back.'

Mason nodded silently. He was more than happy to keep his head down for a while. It would give him some time to prepare for getting off the ship. He'd crossed an international border with no paperwork and he didn't want to be explaining that to Kenyan customs officials.

As he tucked himself into the space behind the anchor chain, Dahir hurried off to the stern to begin the business of bringing the ship into port. Mason found a spot from where he could see their course. The *Sirrah* was still over half a mile from Kilindini, the largest container port on Africa's eastern seaboard. In front, Mason could see a line of ships, queuing in the narrow channel, waiting their turn to get into the harbour. Below, there were scores of dhows, buzzing around, heading in and out to sea.

Slowly, the *Sirrah* made its way through the mouth of the harbour. Overlooking them was a crumbling sandstone castle, perched high up on the cliff. Fort Jesus, built by the Portuguese in the sixteenth century was the fortress that determined who dominated trade in the Indian Ocean for over four hundred years. After the Portuguese, it fell to the Arabs of Oman, who in turn lost it to the British at the end of the nineteenth century. How little the world had changed, Mason thought – countries fighting for an advantage, trying to gain an edge in the pursuit of greater wealth.

The *Sirrah*'s crew brought the ship in slowly, shadowed fore and aft by a pair of tugs, guiding it into the berth that had been assigned to it for unloading. There were already twenty other container ships being serviced along the same dockside, cranes working tirelessly, moving heavy containers on and off the decks, preparing loads for transit to the rest of Africa or onward to the super-ports of Asia. On the other side of the bay, a brand-new second terminal had been constructed with three deep-water berths which could cope with the enormous Panamax ships capable of carrying thousands of containers at a time to China and the Far East.

Mason heard the hydraulic winches kicking into gear on the deck above, feeding thick ropes off the bow and down to where the port workmen looped them over solid steel cleats to keep the ship from falling off the dock. Peering out of the gap, he saw the gantry crane operator climbing into his glass cabin, firing up the motor that propelled the multi-storey structure along its rail, the boom looming overhead. In less than six hours, the *Sirrah*'s cargo would be land-side, replaced by a new cargo, destined for another journey elsewhere.

A vehicle pulled alongside the ship and Mason watched a group of men in hard hats, carrying clipboards step out and begin the admin of landing a new ship. Meanwhile, a group of stevedores appeared and, after raising a long wooden gantry to the port side, began running carts of food and fresh water on board. Several more officials appeared and Mason saw Aku, the Indian guy from the previous night, walking down the gangway to hand over the crew's passports. As the man in the hardhat checked the documents, Mason sensed that something was off. A commotion began to stir among the customs officials and their voices grew louder. He was too far away to make out what they were saying, but it was clear that whatever the Indian had told them had given them a sense of urgency. When Aku pointed back up the gangway, directly to the place where Mason was hiding, he quickly pulled his head away, ducking down before anyone could spot him. He cursed Aku. The Indian had given him up. Mason had to move.

He crawled out from behind the anchor chain and pulled himself back to the deck, peering over the edge. For a brief moment, he considered the jump but discounted it again immediately. The splash would make too much noise and, besides, the fall would probably break his legs. He needed another way off the ship. He saw Dahir running towards him, waving frantically for him to hurry. The huge Somalilander was pointing to a stack of containers.

'Quickly,' he said. 'Inside here.'

Mason followed, seeing that Dahir had broken the seal on one of the containers. The law required that every box be sealed at the port of the loading to ensure that nothing inside a container had been tampered with. A broken seal would be a red flag to customs. It guaranteed that the box would be investigated on the shore.

'The box will be impounded,' Dahir said. 'But I will come and find you. Now go.'

Dahir saw the hesitation in Mason's face. He was asking the Englishman to trust him. To get inside a locked box, that would be impounded by the very people he was trying to avoid. The crane swung overhead and nudged itself into place. Any second it would begin unloading the cargo and the first container would be port side. Mason heard the sound of the customs boss shouting instructions to his men, telling them to search the ship. He looked again at Dahir.

'Do not worry, my friend. I will come,' Dahir said. 'But better you go now.'

Mason opened the door to the container. Inside, the space was packed full. Rows of timber logs from floor to ceiling with just enough space for him to slide inside. Mason cursed his luck. But what choice did he have? He nodded to Dahir before he stepped in.

'Don't leave me to die in this box,' Mason said.

Dahir smiled. Both men knew the risk that they were taking. Mason was putting his trust in a man whom he had only met twenty-four hours before and the first mate was putting his job on the line to save a total stranger.

Dahir quietly shut the container door and Mason was cast into total darkness. He heard his phone ring and grabbed for it, cursing himself for not putting it on silent earlier. The sound would give him away. He saw the caller name flash up on the screen as he rejected the call. It was Kerry calling. *What the fuck did Kerry want?* They hadn't spoken in months and she was calling him now? She was probably drunk. Wanting to talk about getting back together again. He wasn't in the mood for that. Now was definitely not the time for that conversation.

He put the phone on silent mode and slid it back into his pocket. Outside, he could hear Dahir sliding the bolt across and he knew that he was now locked in a cell from which he could not escape. One way or another that door would open again and on the other side of it might be an angry customs official ready to cart him off to a cell. In the meantime, all he could do was trust his new friend and hope he came back.

TWENTY-TWO

Camp Lemonnier Base, Djibouti

The French Foreign Legion was founded in the mid-nineteenth century from an elite force of highly trained infantry soldiers, tasked with defending France's colonial interests in Africa. What made the Legion unique was that its soldiers were recruited from all over the world. You didn't have to be French to join the Legion. If you were up to the job and you survived long enough, retired Legionnaires were rewarded with a French passport.

One of the Legion's many missions was to protect the French colony of Djibouti, over which they ruled for nearly one hundred years. The small Islamic country, perched on the Horn of Africa between Eritrea to the north and Somalia to the south was of enormous strategic importance to the control of the Red Sea and Suez Canal. That is why twenty years ago, long after Djibouti became a republic, the US agreed to pay the Djibouti government an undisclosed fee to lease the old French Foreign Legion base at Camp Lemonnier. Today Lemonnier holds thousands of servicemen from the US Navy, Special Forces, Marines and Air Force.

From the seat of their Gazelle helicopter, Peter Hopkins had a good view of the base. The ninety-acre site took up a sizeable chunk of coastline south of Djibouti City, running parallel to the city's airport to the sea. In his headphones, he heard the Americans give them permission to land and the chopper set them down on the hot asphalt alongside three enormous Reaper drones.

Hopkins led Jack down the steps and immediately looked for their contact. Their communication with James had been brief, to say the least. The *Falcon* had been discovered drifting fifty miles south of the Zubair Group by the American SH-60 Seahawk helicopter launched from USS *Mustin*. The pilots had realised that there was nobody on board capable of piloting the boat, which was a time bomb given the amount of sea traffic in the strait, and had immediately airlifted three men on board to regain control. With the *Falcon* secured, it was agreed that the best plan of action was to deliver the survivors to the nearest safe port – the base at Lemonnier.

Hopkins was initially relieved to hear that the *Falcon* had been found. Recovering a half-billion-dollar asset was a good start. But he'd been less thrilled to hear that Sergei and Vlad had been killed, while the *Falcon*'s owner, Wei Lun Chow, and his crew had been last seen by the remaining people on board, boarding a naval boat carrying the Eritrean flag. The four Chinese nationals and twelve Filipinos were being debriefed, and at least one was being treated for serious sexual assault. Hopkins had wanted to get to Lemonnier asap because once they were processed into the system, he'd lose his chance to speak to them.

'Captain Hopkins.'

Hopkins span around at the sound of his name. Nobody had called him Captain in a long while and while he recognised the voice, he couldn't quite place where from.

'Well, fuck me,' Jack said, beating Hopkins to the punch. His face lit up with a broad smile because walking towards them across the landing zone was someone neither of them had ever imagined seeing again.

The tall red-haired woman smiled as she reached out and shook both British men by the hand. She took a step back and made a show of looking them both up and down. 'Civvie street looks good on you guys,' she said.

'Wow. It's good to see you, Agent Redford,' said Hopkins.

'Yeah, nice one, bab,' said Jack. 'Eh, where can someone take a shit round here?'

Redford sighed. 'Follow me, boys. The briefing room has facilities.'

They climbed into a military jeep and sped off past the drones and a line of aircraft hangars, taking a turn into a side street lined with familiar-looking signage. The base had a Pizza Hut, Subway, and a Green Beans Coffee. Jack smiled ruefully. The Yanks always had to make everywhere look like home, so that this strip of desert along the Red Sea felt more like Arizona than Africa. Like that was any better.

They pulled up outside a two-storey concrete building and followed Redford inside, passing through security where they turned in their phones and firearms. While Jack relieved himself, Redford took Hopkins into an office on the second floor and offered him a seat. He stayed standing.

'I met your boss in Hong Kong, yesterday,' she said.

'James?' Hopkins replied.

'Yeah. He's a real piece of work.'

Hopkins shrugged. 'I can only apologise.'

From his reaction, she could tell he didn't want to get into it.

'I'd like to interview the survivors,' he said.

'Not possible,' she replied.

'Two of my men are dead, Redford.'

'Sergei Antonov and Vladamir Krotov.'

She handed him a file. Hopkins opened it and scanned the contents. It contained full background profiles on Sergei and Vlad, everything from where they'd gone to kindergarten to all their known associates. Not something the Americans could have pulled together this fast. She was telling him that the CIA had been covering the Russians for some time.

'I don't understand why the CIA is involved in this. My understanding is that there were no Americans on board. And I heard you'd taken a desk in China,' he said. 'I thought you were done with this place after what happened in Yemen.'

'Uh-huh. I've been based out of Beijing since August.'

'So …' he tried to connect the dots for himself. What was she doing back in the Horn of Africa? Of course, it could only be one thing. 'CIA are interested in Wei Lun Chow?'

Redford allowed herself a half-smile. 'Chow's been cooperating with us since before I joined the desk. Let's just say that he's no fanboy of the CCP but after what happened to Jack Ma, he knows better than to say that in public.'

Hopkins had heard all about Jack Ma. The third richest guy in China had suddenly disappeared last year after daring to suggest how the Chinese Communist Party might improve a few things. The rumour was that Ma had been taken in for some heavy reprogramming, the reality was that he reappeared three months later, apologising for everything he'd said. In the meantime, his company's planned multi-billion-dollar IPO was indefinitely shelved.

'You think the Chinese are behind this?' Hopkins asked.

'We don't know for sure yet, but it seems possible. Either way, it is vital that Chow is not returned to China. We can't protect him there and losing his intel to Beijing would be ... Well, let's say it would be a problem.'

Hopkins suddenly realised why it had been so easy to get access to Lemonnier. He'd hoped to be the one asking the questions, but in fact, he was there to answer them.

'The *Falcon* was planning to travel to the Dahlak Islands but then changed course for the Zubair Group. Who knew about the new itinerary?' she asked.

'No one. We don't share that information.'

'Well someone did.' She placed a series of satellite images onto the desk for him to see. They showed the pirates' skiff approaching the *Falcon* the day before.

'Pretty much anyone could have tracked the *Falcon*.'

'And reacted that fast?' she said incredulously. 'Look at the times.'

Hopkins looked again at the photographs. There was less than an hour from when the *Falcon* took its new course to when the first skiff appeared. Redford was right. Unless they'd been really unlucky, it looked as though the pirates had known exactly where to find them.

'That intel could only have come from on board,' he said.

'We've already debriefed the catering staff and Chow's hookers, we're pretty sure none of them knew.'

'So it was crew?' Hopkins couldn't believe what he was saying.

'That's where things get interesting,' she said. 'You seen this?'

She handed him another piece of paper, which Hopkins immediately recognised as the *Falcon*'s manifest. This was the first time that he'd seen a full list of everyone who'd been on board, listed by name and passport number. He scanned down the row of names, checking off the ones he recognised – Chow, Sergei, Vlad. Below that was a bunch of Filipino names and then the Chinese women. Finally, he saw the names of the crew and his jaw dropped so hard it almost dislocated itself.

Redford studied his reaction carefully. 'You didn't know?'

Hopkins shook his head, looking so shellshocked that she believed him.

'Yeah,' she sighed. 'Like I said, real interesting.'

Just then the door opened and Jack came walking in. He furrowed his brow, sensing something had happened while he'd been otherwise engaged. He looked to Hopkins for an explanation but Redford beat him to it.

'Jack,' she said, 'when did you last hear from Mace?'

As Jack caught up with what he'd missed, Hopkins turned to Redford. 'We have to tell him.'

Jack was already shaking his head. 'That's a bad idea.'

'Yeah? And what about when he finds out we kept this a secret?' Hopkins protested.

'He'd only turn up here like some kinda loose cannon,' Jack said, tossing the papers onto the desk.

'Well, the next of kin have been informed, so whether you like it or not, he probably already knows,' Redford interjected.

Jack sighed and looked at his watch. It was 6 am, but his body clock told him it was earlier. Or later. He didn't know any more. He'd covered so many air miles since leaving the Regiment, that time had long since ceased to mean anything. His internal sense of time was broken. He slept when he was tired, ate when he was hungry, and shat when he needed to shit.

Hopkins had offered him the job at De Grasse as soon as he left the Regiment and he hadn't fancied looking for work elsewhere. The pay was a lot better than what he'd ever got in the forces too. Some of the lads had gone into bodyguarding famous celebs and billionaires. Mace had gone off to save some elephants. But for Jack, jumping out of helicopters and kicking in doors was what he enjoyed best. Even better if something needed blowing up.

What he hadn't anticipated was that he'd be back in the Horn, having to rescue his best mate's daughter from a bunch of jihadis. If he'd known that, he'd have thought twice. At the same time, if it was what he had to do, then he was going to make sure it got done properly.

'There's more,' Redford said, picking up the remote from the desk and booting up a screen on the video wall, while Jack poured himself a coffee. Moments later she was pulling up an image on the screen. 'We have pictures.'

Both men looked closely at the image. Jack produced a packet of rolling tobacco and knocked out a cigarette in seconds. He sparked it up and took a deep drag, letting out a dense cloud of smoke, followed by a deep raspy cough.

'Right,' he said, clearing his throat, 'where's that?'

'Anrata,' Redford replied. 'It's a small fishing village in Eritrea, five hundred miles north of here.'

She scrolled through a series of grainy images that showed the gunboat docking in port, the group meeting at the dockside, and the last image showed the minivan leaving, heading south along the coast road towards Djibouti.

'They're in Djibouti?' Hopkins asked.

'If only,' Redford replied. 'The border is still closed.'

She pulled up a CCTV video taken at the Ethiopian border. It showed the same minivan crossing into Ethiopia. The footage showed the time as 6.43 am.

'I had Langley redirect some satellites for me. Some of the coverage is patchy because of last night's storms but we picked up the vehicle again along the national road a hundred miles from Addis.'

She pulled up another satellite image onto the screen. It showed the vehicle turning onto a track that led to a clearing half a mile from the main road close to the Aledeghi Wildlife Park in central Ethiopia. The quality was poor. The time showed 17.56 and the daylight had already begun to fade.

'The resolution here gets real patchy,' Redford said, 'but then we get a little luck. It looks like they built a fire.'

The next image she pulled up showed a group of people sitting around a campfire. Jack struggled to make out Joanna

Mason from the others. The resolution was too poor, glitching from the electrical storms that had passed across the skies the previous evening. What did strike him was the number of bodies.

'I count six.'

'We're missing someone,' Hopkins said.

'Somebody got dropped.' Jack lit another cigarette. He didn't like how this was going.

'What have we got after this?' Hopkins asked.

Redford shook her head. 'Our coverage went out totally when it started raining. After that, we have a hiatus for nearly five hours. By the time the cloud cover cleared, the vehicle was gone.'

'Gone where?' asked Jack.

'We're still working on that,' she had one more image in her file, 'But we do have this.'

She pulled up another image on the screen. It was good enough to see the remains of the campfire. The rest of the site had been cleared but lying face down on the ground was a dead body.

Jack felt nauseous. For all he knew right then, that could be Joanna lying dead on the dirt. He and Matt Mason had passed Selection together nearly fifteen years ago and since then, they'd fought side by side all over the world. They'd saved each other's lives more than a few times and there wasn't another man that Jack respected more than his friend from Walsall. If that was his little girl in the picture on the screen, then Hopkins was right and Mason needed to know, but on the other hand, if it wasn't Joanna, then he didn't need to know it might be.

'Oh fuck,' he said.

'I'll be in Addis within the hour. We have an asset there who I trust.'

'We need to tell Mason,' Hopkins said again.

'Tell him what?' Jack snapped. 'Your daughter might be lying dead in a field but we're not sure? Shut up, Pete.'

Hopkins decided to bite his tongue. 'Thanks,' he said to Redford. He appreciated what she was doing.

'I'm guessing De Grasse haven't heard anything more from the kidnappers?' she asked.

'Nothing,' Hopkins replied.

'Right, well we need to share intel as soon as they do . . .' Redford paused, looking at the screen, pulling up the original image of the Eritrean gunboat. 'We picked up something on Tempora. Since the *Falcon* was taken, GTE's been scanning the metadata that's flying around on our intercept partners within the region.'

Jack and Hopkins nodded. They knew about the Tempora system. US and British spooks used it to sift through internet and telephone traffic, listening out for pre-programmed key phrases that raised red flags for national security. Nobody could hide from a program that could listen in on billions of interactions around the world every day, so it wasn't a great surprise that Redford had accessed it for something like this.

'Someone on board that naval vessel made a call to this number in Eritrea,' she said, pulling up the metadata on the screen. 'The registered user name is bogus but we've tracked its location to an address within Eritrea. We'll look into that. More concerning is that the last few calls from that number have been to a number within Al-Shabaab territory in Somalia.'

'Oh Christ,' Hopkins said. 'This gets worse and worse.'

'And you better call your boss, because his "opportunistic fishermen" theory,' she did the finger quotes, '. . . is now officially bullshit, so De Grasse is in danger of aiding and abetting terrorism, which as you know, is a bit of a "no-no". Even in the UK.'

Hopkins looked crushed. He knew the rules. While it was fine to pass ransoms to fishermen who were classed simply as criminals, the second you had evidence that a terrorist organisation was involved, the rules forbid you from handing over as much as a penny. To do so was to risk De Grasse being shut down.

'You still don't think it's time to share all this with Mason?' Hopkins asked.

Redford considered it. 'We should have a positive ID on that body within two hours.'

If it was Joanna Mason lying there then, of course, Mason had a right to know, but there was another outcome that was troubling Redford just as much. If that was the Chinese tech billionaire's corpse they were looking at, then the US had just lost one of the most important assets they'd had in China for a generation. She said a quiet prayer that it would turn out to be neither.

'Two hours. Let's get something solid first, and then we should talk again about bringing Mason in.'

'Fine,' Jack relented. 'Two hours.'

TWENTY-THREE

Mombasa, Kenya

Six hours locked inside a metal box had given Matt Mason time to think. For the first two hours alone in the darkness, he'd thought about what he was going to do if he was discovered by customs officials. He heard voices come and go on the other side of the door. He heard someone shouting instructions to search the lifeboats, turn over the crew's quarters, look in the engine rooms below deck. While he stood silently inside the container, he listened to them searching for him outside. But luck was on his side and the container door remained shut, the moment of discovery never came.

Instead, he was saved by the huge dockside gantry crane. Its spidery spreader came sliding along its rails, dropping down and plucking the five-tonne container from the deck as though it weighed no more than a box of matches. Of course, the crane driver did not expect that there was a human being inside, so the transition from ship to dockside had been pretty rough. Mason had tried to steady himself but, with nothing to hang onto, he'd been thrown around like a T-shirt in a tumble drier. The experience reminded him of the first time he'd jumped into a hot zone in Iraq, fifteen years before. Mason's patrol had been inserted at night into Al-Qaeda-controlled territory, under the cover of an electrical storm.

He wouldn't have admitted it then, but he didn't mind admitting now that he'd felt petrified that night. He wasn't scared of the jihadis, wasn't scared of jumping either. In fact, he loved jumping. For Mason, the fear always came from being in the aircraft. There was something unsettling about giving over control to someone else. That, and an unhealthy disposition for motion sickness. He'd puked all over himself that first time. Some of the other lads had been so disgusted that they'd puked over themselves too, and it started a chain reaction of vomiting. Not that it mattered. You dried off pretty quickly once you jumped. The sick fell right off you when you were falling at two thousand kilometres an hour. The piss-taking he'd suffered afterwards though had lasted a lot longer.

The crane set him down again on the dock and soon after, someone had spotted the door seal had been compromised. Mason heard more shouting – an order for the container to be taken away. Again, he was lifted, this time by a forklift truck, and moved to a quarantine area to await further investigation. By now, Mason calculated it was late, maybe 7 pm. The office staff had finished for the day and so nothing more would happen until morning.

His legs were beginning to ache. There was nowhere to sit, nowhere to stretch. It was forty degrees inside the steel box and he had no water and no food. His eyes had adjusted to the darkness, but there was nothing to see. Piles of timber rose from floor to ceiling and the air was filled with the smell of sap. He tried to start his phone again even though he knew it was now dead. He sighed. Three days ago, he'd been at work on the reserve in Mozambique, happier than he'd been in years and now, somehow, he was locked up in a metal box in Mombasa, hundreds of miles away. This was exactly the sort of shit that he was supposed to have left behind in the Regiment. He was starting to wonder if it wasn't just him.

He ran through everything in his head again. After being discovered on the *Sirrah* by Dahir, he'd seen nobody. After he'd left Dahir, he'd gone directly to his hiding place behind the anchor chain. He'd slept off the booze there until Dahir had come to wake him. In total, three people had known that he was on board. Protocols on big ships required that stowaways be reported immediately to the next port. If the big guy from Somaliland was going to give him up, then he'd have done it right away. Besides, Dahir had been the one to help Mason escape. On balance, he was sure that he could discount Dahir as the one who'd betrayed him.

The two men on the bridge were different. The tall guy had kept himself to himself, but the short Indian guy, Aku, had been edgy, suspicious of Mason from the off. Then Mason had seen Aku talking to the customs officials on the dock, pointing towards his hiding place on the ship. He wasn't being paranoid. There was no doubt in Mason's mind. Aku had to be the one who tipped off the customs guys in the port. But why? What was he getting out of it? If Mason had been discovered, it would amount to a pile of paperwork for the officer on deck. It would have been Dahir who would cop the blame.

Mason remembered the conversation he'd had with Dahir about the Wang Trading Company container. It was fuzzy because they'd been so drunk, but Dahir had shown him the ship manifest, shown him that container number WANU114655 hadn't been loaded onto the ship in Pemba. But he'd also said that Aku had been the one responsible for logging all the boxes. What if Aku had deliberately not logged the Wang box? What if Aku was somehow involved with Wang Trading and when Mason started asking difficult questions, he'd seen an opportunity to get rid of him?

Mason was interrupted by a noise from outside of the door. Someone was out there. He froze, standing statue-still, holding his breath, making as little noise as possible. It was likely that the quarantine area was patrolled by security at night and he'd come too far to get caught now. He really didn't want to be thrown in a Kenyan jail cell. But there was nothing he could do about it because whoever was out there was already unlocking the bolt.

Mason readied himself, turning his body square, lifting his fists into a boxing stance. If he got the chance and could strike first, then he might get lucky. If the guard was alone, then he could take him out and make a run for it. He braced himself as the heavy metal doors swung open.

Mason sprang out, both feet landing squarely, knees bent like a coiled spring. His eyes darted around, assessing what he was dealing with, looking for where he could land a strategic blow. As he laid eyes on his target, his fists tightened and he lurched forward with full power. But just before he released the trigger, he realised that he knew his opponent.

'Fuck me!' Mason cried as he pulled out of the punch just in time.

'Mace, it is me, Dahir.' The big man was stumbling backwards, holding his hands up over his head.

'I can fucking see that,' Mason said, blowing off a little of the adrenaline. 'Where have you been?'

'Hey, *you* came onto *my* ship, my friend,' Dahir snapped, before lowering his voice again. 'I take a big risk to come here.'

'Okay, okay, sorry,' Mason held up his hands. 'It's just hotter than a Brummy curry in there.'

Dahir looked blankly at him. 'Doesn't matter,' Mason said, sucking in the fresh air. He'd been breathing tree sap for six hours. He spotted the bottle of water in Dahir's hand and reached for it.

'Yes, take it.' Dahir handed it over and looked around while Mason hydrated. He was beginning to wonder if helping this stranger was such a good idea. The quarantine area contained around twenty containers, cordoned off behind a ten-foot-high, chain-link fence topped with razor wire. The silhouettes of the boxes were visible only because the moon was nearly full. 'Come, we must go.'

Dahir scampered into the darkness, running behind the containers, while Mason followed close behind. On the far side of the yard, Mason saw where the sailor had thrown a heavy blanket over the razor wire. For a big guy, Dahir scaled the fence easily, swinging his leg over the blanket before lowering himself safely onto the other side. Mason copied his route and when both men were on the other side, he followed him between the sheds, staying in the shadows until they reached Dahir's car, parked back on the main road.

Once they were under the streetlights of the city, and he was sure that they were safe, Dahir breathed a sigh of relief and allowed himself a wry chuckle. 'You are a lot of trouble for me, Mr Mason,' he said.

'I appreciate it, mate,' Mason raised his hand and the two men fist-bumped. 'But I have another favour to ask.'

Dahir's smile slid quickly from his face. 'What is it now?'

'I need to find your friend,' he said. 'Where's Aku?'

TWENTY-FOUR

Msambweni, Kenya

Long before the giant container ships ever criss-crossed the world's oceans, sea trade was conducted almost exclusively by dhow. The traditional Arabian sailboats with their distinctive slanting, triangular sails and sharp upward bows that protruded proudly above the waves were the cargo ships of their day, carrying spices and timber, ivory and slaves across the Arabian Gulf to faraway lands in Iran, India, and beyond. Eventually, the supertankers replaced the wooden boats when it became impossible to make a living carrying small cargoes over thousands of miles, but still, the dhow didn't die out. Many were repurposed for fishing, tourism or serving local trade routes instead, kitted out with diesel motors that meant a good one could cover two hundred and fifty miles in a single day. Or Macímboa to Kenya in less than two.

The second that Wang Li Lan had realised what she had to do, she called Abrahim, an old Arab who knew her father well. As a little girl, she'd watched the two old men drink their strong coffee while playing backgammon under the shade of the palm trees on the Zanzibar shore. Abrahim always had a glint in his eye and occasionally some candy in his pocket. Now the old man ran weekly trips back and forth along the coast from Kenya to Mozambique in his dhow. Since Li Lan had taken over the business, she'd used Abrahim often, whether to bring down fishing equipment from Mombasa or to send up a consignment of crab to Zanzibar. More than once, he'd proven himself useful in a tight spot. And right then, Li Lan knew she was in a tight spot.

They'd loaded the seventeen girls into the hull of Abrahim's dhow and set sail for Zanzibar, stopping there only briefly to refuel the tanks and stock up with fresh water. Under the cover of darkness, they'd resumed their journey, striking out for the southeast coast of Kenya and a small fishing village known in Swahili as Msambweni. Li Lan had a contact in the port there who sometimes supplied her with additional sea cucumbers when she needed to make up a larger order. Over the years, Kassim had become a loyal friend and when she'd asked him to arrange for a truck large enough to convey a special cargo from Msambweni to Mombasa, he'd done so without asking any difficult questions.

She'd watched from the shore as Abrahim's dhow began the return journey to the islands of her birth before she and Kassim hit the road, driving north towards Mombasa. Kassim said very little, while the radio played a local talk show, the guests discussing the latest corruption allegations made against a local politician by the press.

Li Lan hadn't slept in nearly twenty-four hours, but when she closed her eyes, she was too wired with adrenaline.

Her mind was racing with thoughts that skittered through her brain. How had she moved from selling sea cucumbers to human trafficking in the space of a week? What would her father and brothers think of what she was doing? Her brothers still pushed her around. Even now, though she ran the whole African side of the business, they took her for granted and didn't appreciate her contribution. She didn't think that they would understand that now she was making a sacrifice for them. She was doing what needed to be done to keep the family business alive. Which was more than she could say of them, living it up in Hong Kong, spending the family's money. They'd have nothing if it weren't for her.

Beyond her sense of duty, she also felt something else. Something stronger even. She felt excited. She rubbed her tired eyes and glanced sideways to Kassim, concentrating hard on the dark road ahead. A faint smile crept across her lips. She couldn't deny it. Li Lan had spent her whole life packing and loading smelly fish into boxes or wading through fisheries, inspecting and quality controlling product. She had spent years chasing customer payments, rearranging schedules, booking transport routes. Yes, she'd been successful, made her family money, but never before had she felt what she did now. Excitement. She was out of her comfort zone and she liked how that made her feel. She looked at Kassim again and this time she allowed herself to smile wider. This was fucking cool. Some might disagree. Some might argue with the morality of what she was doing, but she didn't care. Business in Africa was tough and only the toughest survived. Her brothers would never have had the balls to do this and if it played out the way she hoped, then she was going to forge a new and very profitable relationship for the family business.

An hour and a half after leaving Msambweni, Li Lan saw the light pollution in the sky over Mombasa and forty minutes later they took the Likoni ferry over to Mombasa island. She knew the city well, having overseen the loading of high-value shipments on several occasions. Sometimes, even when her presence wasn't required in the port, she took the opportunity to visit the big city and to enjoy the luxuries on offer. She would check in to one of Mombasa's tourist hotels and book herself a massage before she took a walk around the pretty whitewashed buildings of the old town or picked herself up a treat in one of its huge shopping malls.

Even though it was nearly 9 pm, the crowds were still on the streets, children playing football on the side of the road while their parents sat at food stalls, enjoying fried fish and a bottle of Tusker. Kassim weaved through the evening traffic, beeping his horn often, shouting occasionally at someone driving on the wrong side of the road, fighting their way towards the rendezvous in the industrial district of Changamwe to the northwest of the harbour. Finally, they reached their destination, a rundown, three-storey, concrete tenement block which looked as though it had seen better days. Kassim said nothing, just looked at his client to check they were in the right place. When Li Lan nodded silently, he shrugged and pulled the van into a parking space outside the front door.

A light came on inside the block and a fat woman appeared at the door. Li Lan stepped down onto the dirt and walked directly to the rear of the van where Kassim was already unlocking the back door. The girls piled out, one by one, and the fat lady shooed them into the building and down a barely lit corridor to a cramped dormitory where ten sets of bunk beds had been laid out. On the floor was a bucket of water for washing and a hole in the floor as a latrine for everything else. Li Lan didn't like the smell in the room. She was glad she wouldn't have to smell it when she woke tomorrow morning.

When the girls were all inside, the fat lady locked the door and motioned for Li Lan to follow her up the staircase to the first floor. She paused at a large wooden door and knocked before she opened it and waved for Li Lan to go inside.

Razir Al-Haq, the one-eyed Somalian, who she'd first met only days before in Mozambique, now sat alone at a desk in the dimly lit room. Li Lan approached him, looking around for clues as to what this place might be. It looked like a classroom, with a chalkboard on the wall and desks lined up on either side. Some of the writing on the board was in English, other words were in Arabic and there was a book-shelf in one corner containing textbooks she recognised from her own school days.

Al-Haq stood and came around the central desk, peering at her with his one eye.

'You read Arabic?' he asked.

'Yes,' Li Lan replied.

'Then you can read the Koran.'

'I am not religious.'

'Neither are they,' he said, 'yet.'

Li Lan looked confused. She had anticipated that the girls were being brought to Mombasa as prostitutes. She didn't imagine for a moment that the Somalian with one eye was an educator.

'Follow me,' he said.

Again Li Lan found herself walking up the stairs and along the dim corridors of the building until she faced another locked door. The one-eyed Somalian took a key from his pocket and opened it, casting a little light inside with his torch. Inside, she could see more bunks. More girls.

'These are the ones who are ready,' he said before he stepped inside.

He pointed the torch at a girl, no older than seventeen, thin, bright-eyed, fearful, lying on the top bunk. 'Say hello to our guest,' he said in Arabic.

'Hello, Miss,' the terrified girl stuttered. 'Nice to meet you.'

'Very good,' Al-Haq laughed. 'Very good.'

He led Li Lan outside and locked the door behind him.

'They are to be transported to my customer in the Middle East,' he said.

Li Lan realised that he meant that she would be the one to do the transporting.

'That is not possible,' she replied before she added, 'Not for the price.'

'As long as the girls arrive next week, then everything will be paid double,' he said. 'And your ivory will be released for delivery to Hong Kong.'

Li Lan considered the offer. More money. More excitement. The ivory released. It would be a new challenge but
of course, she could transport the girls. It would require
some time to get ready but it was possible.

'I need a few days,' she said finally.

'Very well,' replied Al-Haq. 'You have two days to prepare. I will tell the customer to expect his cargo at the end
of next week. We have a deal?'

Li Lan nodded. Preparations would have to be made.

TWENTY-FIVE

Aledeghi Wildlife Park, Ethiopia

Abel Ahmed parked the Toyota Auris next to the burned-out remains of a campfire and killed the engine. He checked the rear-view mirror to reassure himself that nobody had followed them down the track from the national road. He caught sight of his face in the reflection. He looked tired and old. His hair was receding and the glaucoma in his left eye was getting worse. He'd go back to the doctor when he returned to Addis.

'You can take it off now, ma'am,' he said to the passenger sitting next to him before he stepped out of the vehicle.

Abel scanned the area, checking for signs of life. There was nobody to be seen. He lit a cigarette, savouring that first drag and allowed himself to relax a little. Since he'd received an encrypted message from his CIA handler six hours earlier, he hadn't stopped moving. First, he'd arranged a private vehicle that wouldn't attract attention, then he'd collected her from the airport and driven them a hundred miles east of Addis to this exact spot. Now, as he enjoyed a minute's peace, while she removed her head covering in the car, he understood why. Lying face down on the ground, ten metres in front of the car was a dead body.

Agent Redford got out and walked directly to the corpse. Abel sensed that she was already less stressed than she had seemed during the drive. He didn't know that was because she'd already clocked that the cadaver was neither Joanna Mason nor Wei Lun Chow.

'Give me a hand with this, would you, Abel?' she said, folding one leg over the other so that she could turn the guy over.

Abel flicked his cigarette away and moved alongside her. He lifted the shoulders, while she took the hips and together they flipped the body over so that it was lying on its back. Abel noted how it felt cold, the muscles already soft and loose, suggesting that rigor mortis had been and gone. He reckoned the guy must have been dead for at least a day but not much longer or else the animals would already have found him.

Redford took pictures with her phone. As a matter of course, she'd send the images to Langley and have them run facial recognition software to see if he showed up on any of their databases. But in truth, she didn't hold out much hope. The US had neglected East Africa for such a long time, that compared to what they knew about the Middle East, the region was a total blackout.

'Somalian,' Abel said. 'Al-Shabaab.'

'How can you tell?'

'This is how they look,' Abel said with a shrug.

Abel himself was not Somalian. He was Oromo. Like his half-brother, Abiy, the prime minister of Ethiopia. Although they had the same father (they were his thirteenth and fourteenth sons respectively) they were born to different mothers. Their father, a farmer in the hills north of Agoro, having taken four wives as is tradition among the Oromo people, had had nineteen children in total, so even though Abel and his half-brother were close in age, barely six months between them, they had never been close in life. Abiy had joined the military and gone to study engineering overseas in London and Ohio, while Abel had taken the bus to Djibouti and studied medicine at the public university.

The world had watched Abel's brother's rise with interest as he'd gone from child soldier to prime minister, picking up the Nobel Peace Prize along the way. Nobody had been more pleased to see it than Redford. During her stint in the Horn, first in Djibouti and later in Yemen, her job was to recruit a network of potential agents and informants, a role that she had performed with some aplomb. Abel, the half-brother of a prime minister, had been the jewel in the crown.

Often potential leads didn't amount to anything but when she encountered Abel, whose brother was already a senior member of the Ethiopian military, he had proven to be quite an asset, even more so when he made a career move into politics. At first, she'd pursued the usual CIA strategy – money – but gradually Abel had proven himself to have his brother's nose for the game. One day, the doctor had plans to run for office himself and the CIA could help with that.

Redford looked down at the dead guy again. 'When did Al-Shabaab start operating out of Eritrea?'

'Al-Shabaab care only about money,' Abel replied. 'Piracy was a good business for them. But since three years, there is no chance to do this business in Somalia.'

'Because every navy in the world is patrolling that stretch of coast,' she said.

It was true. Thanks to the efforts of the international community, there hadn't been a significant piracy incident off Somalia's coast now for over three years. And until now, Eritrean waters were considered too far north for the pirates to operate.

Not only that but Al-Shabaab had recently lost control of two major income generators – the port in Kismayo and the massive Bakara Market in Mogadishu, which together meant lost revenues of close to one hundred million dollars annually. They'd also lost out to Syria for international donations from those nefarious donors who sought to fund jihad. Increasingly, they had become dependent on their illegal activities, from extortion to smuggling – ivory, girls, charcoal, narcotics. It wasn't surprising that a return to kidnapping could form a part of that strategy.

'What would you do?' Abel asked the question like it was the most obvious thing in the world. 'Do you give up? Of course not. You just move.'

'And the Eritrean Navy?' Redford still sounded a little incredulous. 'What, they just cut them in on the deal?'

'Why not?' Abel said. 'Before, Al-Shabaab paid the fishermen to do their dirty work. Even a small fishing boat can kidnap a big ship, you know? They pay a little to the fishermen and with the hostages, they take them and make big money from the West. So now they pay the sailors instead. So what? What's the difference?'

Redford let it sink in. Al-Shabaab was undeniably an evil terrorist organisation. They had links to both Al-Qaeda and ISIS and they'd been responsible for attacks all over East Africa including the devastating Westgate shopping mall attack in Nairobi that cost hundreds of innocent people their lives. But they also controlled half of Somalia, running the local economy with coordinated taxation and social security systems for their people. You could condemn them for their morals, but you had to credit them for their efficiency. They were certainly no idiots.

Until recently, piracy, kidnap and ransom in Somalia had been an important income stream for Al-Shabaab and so it wasn't impossible that what Abel was suggesting was correct. Any organisation would miss lost revenues that ran to millions of dollars. It was logical for them to seek out ways to reboot the enterprise elsewhere.

The level of corruption in the Eritrean Navy was no secret either. While the idea of paying a US naval officer to facilitate a kidnapping was unthinkable, things were a little different in a country that was run by an evil despot. Corruption bred corruption and she didn't doubt for a second that the right guy could be found for the right price. However, there was still one thing that she couldn't explain.

'So how'd this guy wind up dead?' she said.

Abel shook his head. He didn't have an answer for that one, but whatever the reason, it didn't bode well. The most successful kidnap situations were the ones that went smoothly and the dead guy lying at her feet didn't scream 'smooth' to her.

'If Al-Shabaab really did plan this, then someone in Eritrea was working with them.'

'Nothing is simple in that country,' Abel sighed. 'But anything is possible.'

'I need you to go to Asmara,' she said. 'Someone knows who ordered this.'

Abel nodded. Being the brother of the Ethiopian prime minister bought him a certain cache in the Eritrean capital. There were people there who he could trust to be discrete.

'And you? Where will you go?' he asked.

Redford sighed. Her most important asset in China and the daughter of the man who had saved her life in Yemen were in the back of a van heading east into Al-Shabaab territory. One of the hostages was dead and there was no certainty that others wouldn't follow. There was only one place she could go.

'Somalia,' she said. 'Call me in Mogadishu when you have the intel. In the meantime, I better make a phone call.'

TWENTY-SIX

Undisclosed Location, Somalia

Time had lost all meaning for Joanna Mason. Night had become indistinguishable from day, and sometimes she couldn't tell if she was awake or asleep. Her eyes stung from the electrical tape still wrapped around her head. Her wrists burned from the plasticuffs. They'd moved her several times since the van had delivered them all to the first house. Was that yesterday? Or the day before? It was hard to be sure. Sometimes she'd been left alone for hours. Sometimes they put her with one or more of the others. But they were never left together for long. Someone always got moved again.

They were moving them around to confuse them. To keep them complicit. The bastards. Make sure you never knew where you were. Who you were with. It was designed to be distressing. It was all designed to be distressing.

The heat inside the new house was constant. She was always too hot. Always sweating. She couldn't remember the last time she'd washed. It must have been back on the *Falcon*. The times she'd asked to go to the toilet, they'd mostly allowed it. But not always so she'd soiled herself more than once. The stink of it clung to her and flies were everywhere. Buzzing around. Resting on her skin. Crawling through her hair. She'd given up trying to shake them off.

She received food and water infrequently so she was always hungry. Always thirsty. And tired. And sad. She missed home. She wanted to cry every minute of the day. She wanted to let it all out and weep for what was happening to her. To all of them. But she wouldn't. She wouldn't give the fuckers the satisfaction of seeing her do that.

She could sense when the guards were there. Even when they tried to be quiet. She felt them come and go. Sometimes they lingered. Watching her. She could hear their breathing. There was one guard who said a little. The one who had delivered them here. The one who spoke the best English. There were new guards now too, who said nothing at all. From the sounds of their feet on the concrete floor and the rhythm of their breathing, she'd worked out there were four in total.

The one who spoke was gentle with her. The others handled her roughly. One of them had thrown her to the floor when they'd arrived at the new house. When she'd tried to get up again, he'd shoved her against the wall. Ben had spoken up for her but they'd beaten him for it. Excessively. She'd heard him cry out with pain, begged him to be quiet. The guard had shouted something in Arabic. His voice stern. She hadn't understood the words. Then they took Ben away.

She'd asked them what they wanted. Where she was. Where were they taking her. Where they had been. But nobody ever answered her questions. She asked them to remove the tape. To loosen her hands. To give them more water. Food. Sleep. She argued. She reasoned. She bargained. But she never begged. She knew that she had to keep strong. Had to be resolved. Remain impenetrable to their mind games.

She thought about her father often. How he would find her. Come for her. How he would rescue her. He would rescue them all. And punish the men who had brought her here.

She wondered if he knew already. Whether he was out there looking for her right then. At that minute. Surely, the security company would know by now. The Russians had worked for them. Poor bastards. And Jim. All dead now. She played what had happened over and over. How Ben had told Jim to be quiet. Told him to leave it. But Jim was Jim. Big. Bold. Made him who he was. Made him a good sailor. But also made him dead.

She knew she had to keep the others alive. It felt like they were her responsibility now. Ben was in pain. Constantly. And riddled with guilt for taking the *Falcon* south. Mumbling to himself about how he should have listened to his instincts. Should have put his foot down. Should have saved Jim.

Woods was broken. Crying all the time. Hysterical about dying. He went on and on about how they were all going to die. How it was inevitable. The kidnappers wanted money and he had none. His parents were skint. Their farm was bust. Nothing she said to him would change his mind. She felt guilty about it, but she actually began to look forward to the times when they were separated.

She woke. Or at least she thought she'd woken. She was definitely moving again. Driving. She could hear cars beeping their horns. And a crowd. Music blaring out of a speaker. She noted everything. It might be valuable when she got out of here.

Was she alone? They'd all been together but then they'd taken the others away again. But now she could hear a voice. Whispering in the darkness next to her

'Di-Fin-Do. Di-Fin-Do.' It was Wei Lun Chow. He hadn't said much since they'd left the *Falcon* and she hadn't really known what to say to him either. In fact, this was the first time she'd been alone with him.

'Mr Wei?' she whispered. Chow fell silent. Suddenly, Jo thought she recognised what he'd been saying. '"Diffindo?" Is that from Harry Potter? Were you doing a Harry Potter spell?'

The question was met with silence but she could hear him moving in the darkness next to her. Finally, he spoke, 'You know Harry Potter?'

'I'm a British teenager, Mr Wei. Of course I know Harry Potter,' Joanna couldn't hide the irony in her voice. 'Hang on, wasn't "Diffindo" the spell Hermione used to free Ron when he was tied up by one of the Death Eaters?'

'Antonin Dolohov,' Chow replied.

Joanna snorted with laughter. The first time she'd laughed for days. 'That's it,' she said. 'But wouldn't it be better to use the spell Antonin used to tie Ron up in the first place? So we could get away?'

'Oh, In-Car-Cer-Ous?' Chow replied. 'Yeah. Good idea. Tie up those bastards and make a run for it.'

Joanna felt a tear well up in her eye, but the tape around her face meant that there was nowhere for it to go. For a second, she'd forgotten where she was but, just as fast, it had all come rushing back. She was, still kidnapped by terrorists. She was still tied up and locked in a boot with a Chinese billionaire. Even if they were talking about Harry Potter.

'Mr Wei?' she said. 'I'm scared.'

Wei Lun Chow shuffled his body around. His hands were tied behind his back, but with a little contortion, he made just enough room to feel for Joanna's arm. With his fingertips, he squeezed as gently as he could. He knew that the girl was in this situation because of him. He also knew that right then, he'd have done anything, given anything to change that. But he didn't have that power. He was Ron Weasley in the Deathly Hallows, tied up, helplessly waiting for someone to rescue him.

'It's okay,' he said with as much conviction as he could. 'It's going to be okay.'

The vehicle stopped abruptly and Joanna heard the boot open before she was dragged out again. Someone pushed her from behind, shoving her head down, forcing her forwards. They were moving inside a building. She heard the street sounds become muffled and muted. They were walking upstairs. She heard a door open. It felt cooler inside. Then came a sharp pain behind the knee. She was falling.

Pain came again as she hit a hard floor of cold stone. Then the sound of a key turning.

'Hello?' she said.

She waited for a reply.

'Mr Wei?'

But there was only silence.

TWENTY-SEVEN

Mombasa, Kenya

The women in his native city of Mangalore rarely gave Aku Agarwal a second look. Even the low-caste girls from the poor areas across the Gurupura River averted their eyes when he would smile at them. He had long since given up any hope of finding a wife in his home town. On the other hand, he had high expectations of his visits to foreign cities, where the women considered him exotic. Aku liked to try new things, explore different cultures to his own and when he travelled, he considered the local women to be part of that experience.

This was his third or maybe fourth time visiting Mombasa and he had worked out the best way to meet girls. The first time he'd been in town, he'd stumbled around Mtwapa, a tourist strip of bars and clubs along the north shore. He'd met many girls there. But they had wanted money in exchange for sex. He didn't like that. Paying for sex wasn't sexy.

Some of the guys from the ship had encouraged him to use dating apps instead. By paying a small fee, he could set his location to the next port, so that by the time they arrived, he could already have dates arranged with local girls. It was a strategy that proved much more successful and now, when he landed on shore, he usually had three or four girls lined up. One for each night of his shore leave. If he got lucky even once, then he considered the trip a success as it gave him something to brag about to the guys back on board.

Sitting at a stool along the bar in the much more salubrious Nyali district of Mombasa, he opened his phone and checked the app for the fiftieth time that day. Estelle looked good in her photos. She was light-skinned with long straight black hair and although her nose was a little big for Aku's taste, she had a good body, which more than compensated for it. Most guys would consider her a seven out of ten. The guys on board would be jealous. He stood up to smooth out his linen trousers and straighten his shirt. He thought he looked good. Hopefully, Estelle would too.

On the other side of the bar, sitting just adjacent to a crowd of British tourists on their fifth beer of the day, was a dark-skinned, long-haired man wearing a short-sleeved shirt and sunglasses. A casual observer would assume that he was sitting with his countrymen, but other than a couple of exchanged comments about the time and the location of the bathrooms, the man kept his own company. As Aku's date arrived and took a seat next to him, the man casually glanced their way for half a second before returning his attention to the newspaper on the table in front of him.

Matt Mason scanned the headlines. A humanitarian project in Dubai had recently completed distributing a million meals to underprivileged Kenyans, the price of tea had hit a five-year low, and Kenya's top marathon runner was feeling positive about the upcoming Olympic Games. He took a sip of his beer and ignored the Indian crewman's feeble attempts to charm the girl sitting next to him.

Mason had worked undercover many times before during his days in the Regiment. As an Arabic speaker, with such a dark complexion, he was perfect for this work in the Arab world. In Syria, he'd once adopted a legend as a visiting Islamic scholar and secured access to areas behind Assad's lines, where he gathered intel on the dictator's chemical weapons operations. Thanks to Mason, the RAF had been able to destroy several locations where the substances were being produced. Now he was on a considerably less risky assignment but one which he still felt very strongly about – sitting in a bar in Kenya watching Aku crash and burn with a local girl who no doubt was expecting Hornblower only to find Donald Duck.

Dahir had known where to find Aku right away, so after freshening up, and refuelling his stomach and phone, Mason had taken a taxi across town and skulked into the bar unnoticed a few minutes after the Indian sailor. Mason was sure that Aku played an important role in smuggling containers of ivory out of Pemba for the Wang Trading Company but there was no point in confronting him yet. The container that he'd followed from Pemba with the serial number WANU114655 may still be in port, may still contain the ivory, or may have been transferred to another container for onward shipping to China. There was only one way to be sure and that was to follow Aku until he led Mason to it. For now, he needed to stay close to Aku and ensure that he wasn't spotted.

Mason kept watch of what was happening across the bar, careful not to make eye contact with either of the people sitting at it. From their body language alone, he could see that the couple were engaging in small talk. The young woman was sitting back, eyes glazed over, nodding politely, smile wide, if a little forced. Not that Aku seemed to notice. Even over the music, Mason could catch enough to get the gist. He was monologuing about his travels, his experiences on the high seas. The poor girl was being talked at, not with. Mason would bet a million dollars that Aku still didn't know the first thing about her.

When he and Kerry had started dating, they'd been teenagers. Mason was already in the Paras and Kerry was training to be a nurse. He'd loved listening to her talk as much as she loved regaling him with stories about life on the wards. She always had a way of making every day sound like a scene from the funniest movie he'd ever seen without making anyone the butt of the joke. She was beautiful and funny and kind and he'd loved her from the first moment he'd ever heard her voice.

But he'd never been able to fulfil his side of the bargain. Truth be told, he'd never felt comfortable in the relationship. Five minutes with a shrink would probably be all you'd need to explain why. His father died when he was still very young, leaving his mother with five hungry mouths to feed. She'd worked two jobs to do that, which didn't leave a lot of time for parenting. Mason had to learn quickly how to fend for himself, rely on himself, fight for himself. Unfortunately, he'd proven to be a little too good at the fighting side of things. By the time he was seventeen, he faced a crossroads.

One way led to more violence and eventually prison, the other to the army and the chance to make something of himself. He'd made the right choice.

But the man was still a product of the boy and Mason couldn't shake the inherent lack of trust that he felt in people. That didn't really make for good husband material. He had to be honest with himself and with Kerry. One day, maybe he'd make peace with his past and find someone else but in the meantime, he wanted only to channel everything into the two things he loved more than anything – the job and his kids. They were far more important to him than finding a girlfriend.

As Aku launched into another story about how he'd singlehandedly saved his ship from running aground in the northwest passage, Mason remembered the missed call he'd received from Kerry the day before. He should send her a text. Just to check in and see that everything was okay. But as he fished his phone from his pocket, he was interrupted by the sound of another phone ringing across the bar.

Aku looked annoyed as he stood up, apologising to his date and gesturing that he had to take the call. He walked to the front door, his voice rising in clear irritation as he stepped out onto the terrace. Mason put his phone away again and called the waiter over to settle his bill.

Five minutes later, Aku was on the move. His date looked relieved when he called the evening to a premature end and a little irked when he suggested they go halves on the bill. Aku barely made eye contact with her as he said goodbye and walked out onto the street.

Mason was already waiting, positioned fifty metres further down in the road in a tuk-tuk. He watched Aku flag down a taxi and instructed his driver to follow. The two vehicles joined the traffic, heading north along the paved streets of Nyali, past the big houses with swimming pools out front, driveways lined with palm trees and stone walls covered in bougainvillaea. They turned into the Nyali Road, swerving a little to avoid a flock of goats, grazing along the grass verge. Everywhere, half-completed tower blocks and even larger mansions were being thrown up in preparation for cash-rich buyers who were flooding into the city from the East. At the top of Links Road, the taxi turned west and crossed the bridge onto Mombasa Island before eventually pulling over in the Shimanzi region. As Aku continued on foot, Mason threw a ten-dollar bill into the tuk-tuk driver's lap and leapt out, careful to remain a safe distance behind.

Aku walked fast, turning into Shimanzi Road towards the port, past rows of nondescript, dirty-white concrete warehouses. The roadside was littered with the carcasses of clapped-out flatbed lorries and, overhead, a web of power lines criss-crossed a magenta sky. In the distance, Mason could see the oil refinery's huge storage tanks looming like alien spacecraft, but he saw little sign of human life, other than a solitary forklift driver loading bags of maize onto the back of an old eight-wheeler. Finally, Aku reached a tall iron gate on top of which sat a corporate logo – WellBox. He tapped a security code into the keypad and immediately the gate buzzed to let him in.

Matt Mason watched him vanish into the WellBox complex. Mason would bet ten to one that whatever was beyond that gate offered an important clue as to where the ivory from the reserve was heading next. He decided to wait and see what happened next, withdrawing to a hiding place next to a disused warehouse across the street from the Well-Box gate. He'd sit tight until Aku moved again. But before that, he saw something even more interesting.

Greentea Peng filled the space inside Li Lan's head as she turned into the road towards the port. She loved English urban music, the heavy R&B beats fused with soulful, psychedelic melody. It seemed to suit this place. It also suited the new noise-cancelling JBL headphones that she'd found in the mall. Since Li Lan had arrived in town, she'd been out shopping, eating, treating herself to all the things that she couldn't buy in Pemba. Expensive headphones were a particular favourite. She loved nothing more than to make a playlist and walk the streets of a city while music, cranked up to maximum volume, blocked out the sounds. Her own soundtrack was always preferable, allowing her to replace a part of the world with her own, improved version of it.

She approached the WellBox gates, passing the same rows of nondescript, dirty-white concrete warehouses, the same flatbed lorries and, overhead, the same web of power lines that Mason had seen ten minutes earlier. She saw the gas storage tanks and the forklift driver loading the old eight-wheeler. But she did not see the former British Special Forces soldier hiding behind the warehouse that lay adjacent to it.

Matt Mason watched the diminutive Chinese woman walk past his hiding place. Li Lan stopped at the tall iron gate below the corporate logo – WellBox – and tapped a security code into the keypad. The gate buzzed to let her in.

She took off her headphones and killed the music before she made her way to the company's workshops around back. She paused for a moment to look at her route, mentally retracing her steps, imagining how it could be repeated with twenty women in tow. The offices would be busy in the daytime, so to be safe, she should allow another hour or two to be sure that everyone had gone home. But not too late – most of the port's companies engaged security during the night-time.

She found the workshop where she had arranged to meet her contact and slid the heavy corrugated metal door to one side. Inside was dimly lit, full of old containers, brought in for repairs. Containers were always getting damaged in the course of business. Sometimes they were punctured by forklifts, other times they dropped from cranes. When they fell, they dented, and without repair, they corroded and rusted. Cleaning, repairing, and fixing up damaged containers was par for the course in the shipping business and WellBox were one of many companies that provided the service. During the daytime, these workshops were abuzz with men working hard, welding patches, repairing broken locks, repainting logos.

Li Lan spotted her company logo, Wang Trading Company, on a container tucked away in a far corner of the space. As she approached it, she saw no sign of the man she'd arranged to meet. There were various tools scattered across the concrete floor: an acetylene torch, a protective mask, a collection of saws and spanners – the only evidence that he had been there recently.

She assessed his work. The container had a thirty-six-inch by twenty-four-inch hole cut into one side. Just large enough for her to step through. Using the light from her phone, she looked around inside, a false wall had been created in the container so that the hole opened up into a small space on the other side. It was just large enough to accommodate a dozen women. Li Lan smiled. She was pleased with what she saw.

Li Lan had requested that the container be adapted for smuggling human beings. The changes had been made exactly as she had specified. A pair of car batteries were wired up to an electric light and fan. She flicked the switch and the light blinked on, illuminating the whole space, allowing her to see in more detail. There were sixty litres of bottled water stacked up at one end and a similar volume of canned fruit juice as well as four empty thirty-gallon barrels for the collection of excrement and urine. It wasn't exactly first class, but it would do.

Ordinarily, a forty-foot-long sealed steel box wouldn't give its occupants much chance of surviving an ocean crossing. Especially, if something went wrong. Li Lan had read reports of people dying while using containers to get themselves over borders illegally. She wasn't prepared to take that risk. She didn't need a multiple manslaughter charge hanging over her. That was the kind of thing that Interpol or the CIA came looking for you for. Even a Chinese passport couldn't save you from that one.

She'd also heard rumours of people using soft-top shipping containers, which have a canvas roof that lets fresh air seep in, but she deemed them too risky, too prone to investigation and, besides, few of them were used in the route to UAE. Instead, she had come up with this ingenious plan.

The hole in the side of the container would be filled back in with the missing piece, hinged on the inside so that it could only be opened from within. Once the girls were loaded, the cracks would be fully concealed from the outside with an epoxy resin and then painted to match the container's exterior. The women should be able to survive inside the box for as long as ten days, three longer than the time needed to reach the Middle East. They could open up again as soon as they were deposited on terra firma.

She heard a noise and cut the lights. What she was planning was against every international law and if she were caught she'd end up in jail.

She listened carefully until she heard the unmistakable sound of footsteps. Someone was coming. She backed quietly into a shadow and froze, listening to the steps growing louder until, finally, they turned the corner and she saw who they belonged to. She breathed out a sigh of relief. It was only Aku. The Indian man was carrying a tube of epoxy resin which he'd gone to get from another of the workshops. He looked quizzically at her and gave a casual wave.

'Only me,' he said.

Li Lan liked Aku. He'd been useful to her ever since she'd brought him into the operation two years ago. He'd proven to be a reliable insider within the shipping company and she'd used him on the last half dozen ivory shipments to Hong Kong. As the man responsible for logging containers onto the manifest, he was in the perfect position to make a box totally disappear, which is exactly what he'd done with the container that she'd sent from Pemba last week.

'We will be ready?' she asked.

He rolled his head from side to side in the way Indians did, looking as though they meant 'no' when in fact they meant 'yes.'

'Bring them here tomorrow,' he said. 'The next morning, this box will be loaded onto the *Neptune*.'

'What about air?' she asked.

'There will be enough to breathe,' he said confidently. 'The smell gonna be pretty bad though. Rotten food? All that piss and shit? Glad it ain't gonna be me in there.'

Li Lan didn't care about any of that. It didn't matter how comfortable it was for the people who ended up in this box. All she had to ensure was that as many of them arrived intact as possible. Of course, it was possible that a couple of them would perish. She'd made that clear to the one-eyed man when they'd spoken on the phone. But she'd also explained that using this method was the best way to ensure the greatest number of them made it. He'd accepted her terms.

'Okay,' she said. 'Let's clear up. We come back tomorrow night.'

TWENTY-EIGHT
Mombasa, Kenya

Razir Al-Haq took off his sunglasses and dolloped a scoop of coconut oil onto the wound that stretched from his forehead to his cheek. Rubbing in the soothing balm had become part of a daily routine that offered a little relief from the pain that he still felt. Despite having lost his left eye more than seven years ago, he still often imagined that he could see out of it, but the truth was that he had a blind spot that covered more than one hundred and eighty degrees of his field of vision.

The incident had occurred just outside of Barawe in Southern Somalia when a US drone strike had launched a Hellfire missile that ripped through the vehicle Al-Haq was driving. Everyone else inside, including the Emir, Ahmed Abdi Godane, had been killed instantly when red-hot shrapnel tore through the glass and steel. For a reason that was known only to Allah, peace be upon him, Al-Haq had been spared, required only to sacrifice an eye.

That day marked the start of a dark period for Al-Shabaab. The Americans had launched a sustained attack on their positions across the country and where once the organisation had controlled over half of Somalia's economy, including that of the capital, now their control had been reduced to patches of countryside.

It was Al-Haq who had advocated a change of strategy to the new emir. He had agreed that they could no longer rely on handouts from Saudi Arabia and Dubai to conduct their campaign. Wealthy Sunnis around the world were sending their donations to Syria, Libya, even Mali. If Al-Shabaab sat around and waited in the queue with their begging bowl then nothing would progress.

Initially, there had been resistance when Al-Haq suggested that Al-Shabaab speak with envoys from Iran. For many of the old guard, Iran was still the enemy, nothing more than Shiite infidels waiting to be eradicated for their heresy. But Al-Haq had counselled them to listen and urged the new leadership to remember that the true enemy lay not to the east but to the west. The Americans and the British were also the adversaries of Iran and the Iranians had given a lot of money to others who could prove that they were the enemy of their enemy.

So the money had piled in. Iran had proven to be a very good customer for the Somalian uranium that flowed freely from the Al-Shabaab-controlled mines. Al-Haq had supervised the smuggling operation personally – uranium in one direction, arms in the other. As the relationship had grown, so too had the opportunities, until pretty soon, Al-Shabaab was acting as the conduit for Iranian arms to every anti-Western terrorist organisation in Africa. He had funnelled Chinese and Iranian weapons to Libya, Tigray, Yemen, and Mozambique. Pretty soon, he was confident that Al-Shabaab would be back to full strength and ready to seize back control of their country again.

But of course, nothing was ever straightforward. He put his sunglasses back on and sat down, lighting up a Marlboro. He had to hand it to the Americans, they still made the best tobacco in the world. As he enjoyed his cigarette, he considered the request he'd received from Iran. It had been made personally by a very senior general – General Haddadi. The general had impressed upon Al-Haq the sensitivity of what he was asking for and had promised to make it worth his while. Ordinarily, Al-Haq would have acquiesced immediately to such an important friend of the cause, but in this case, things were a little more complicated. What Haddadi was asking for had already been promised to someone else.

Last night, the hostages had been brought over the border into Somalia and secured at a location within Al-Shabaab territory. Since then, his men had moved them several times to ensure that nobody who might be tempted to betray them would have sufficient information to do so. Only he and his four most trusted men knew where the hostages were now. Nonetheless, another move would be sensible, but first it was time to call the Englishman back.

Al-Haq called his tribesman Raghe into the room. The two men were clansmen and people had often commented how similar they looked. Before the accident. Now, while Al-Haq was scarred to an extent that even his own mother would struggle to look at, his cousin retained his fine features, a large, defined nose and proud chin gave him a regal air. Raghe was not and would never be part of Al-Shabaab, he was more valuable to Al-Haq as long as he remained nothing more than an opportunistic criminal.

Most countries in the West had now passed laws forbidding payments to known terrorists. Al-Haq laughed at the suggestion that Al-Shabaab was anything of the kind. Terrorist was a judgement-laden label. Freedom fighters would be more appropriate in his opinion. Nevertheless, he had to remain pragmatic and the fact was that the second his own name was linked to the hostages then the ransom payment would become considerably harder to settle. It was better to leave it to his cousin as he had done many times before.

Raghe dialled the number on his Thuraya mobile sat phone. Networks weren't always reliable in the rural areas of Somalia, but the satellite phone guaranteed reception wherever he was by bouncing the signal off one of the company's half dozen satellites. After three rings, the number picked up and Raghe nodded to let him know all was well. He recognised the voice as the same one he had spoken to two days before.

'Hello, this is James Beeby speaking.'

'I have location for you, motherfucker,' Raghe said.

'Raghe?' James replied.

'Kismayo. We do like last time. Remember?'

'I remember. At the old fish market?'

'Yes,' Raghe replied. Al-Haq nodded in agreement. 'Same.'

Four years ago, one of Al-Haq's teams had captured a Greek oil tanker and brought it into dock in Kismayo. They'd wired it with explosives and threatened to blow it to pieces with the hostages on board unless the owners paid them ten million dollars. The Englishman, Beeby, had conducted the negotiation on behalf of the Greeks and the handover had gone smoothly. The Greeks got their ship back after settling on seven million dollars, ransom in return.

'We'll need a couple of days to get that kind of money to Kismayo, Raghe.'

'You have forty-eight hours. We do not want to hurt anyone but if we must, we will do it. 1600 hours, the day after tomorrow. Kismayo. Do you understand?'

'Yes, I understand,' James replied.

'Or we will kill one hostage.' Raghe hung up.

Al-Haq sucked his teeth and considered his options. The ransom on offer was a significant sum and he was looking forward to his cut of it.

'Move them to Kismayo tonight,' he said to his cousin. 'Then move them again in the morning. You understand?'

Raghe nodded. 'And what about the girls?'

'I will travel to Mombasa tonight to make the necessary preparations.'

'Very well,' Raghe replied. 'Travel well, cousin. And do not worry. I will prepare everything in Kismayo.'

The two men stood and embraced before Al-Haq watched his cousin leave again. He knew that he was taking a risk with this new strategy, but it was vital that he kept his paymasters in Iran happy. They were an important source of business and everything must be done to meet their needs. They would be expecting a shipment of women the day after tomorrow and Al-Haq was going to make sure that they were not disappointed.

He threw a few things into a bag and made ready to leave. Tomorrow he would be back in Mombasa to make sure things ran smoothly.

TWENTY-NINE

Mombasa, Kenya

Matt Mason heard his stomach rumble in the darkness and realised that he was hungry. He'd been sitting in the shadows, keeping an eye on the WellBox gates for over two hours now and before that he'd spent most of the day locked in a container or chasing around Mombasa after Aku. He'd missed breakfast, lunch, and dinner. Even so, he knew he wasn't going anywhere near food anytime soon. As soon as he had the chance, he wanted to see what was inside that compound.

He considered himself a patient man. Or at least he did now. As a lad, he'd hated waiting for things. If he saw something that he wanted, then he took it. If he had to fight for it, then he fought for it. Delayed gratification wasn't exactly something that poor kids like him understood. But the army had taught him the benefit of patience. Soldiering involved a lot of waiting around. Waiting for things to happen. 'Hurry up and wait' was what they often called it. You didn't always know when things were going to kick off but you sure as dammit better be ready when they did. Your life depended on it.

He heard their voices before he saw them. Li Lan and Aku appeared together, the big security light clicked on as they passed it, and let themselves out through the gate. There was no doubt that they were together. Working together. Mason watched them walk back up the Shimanzi Road until they were out of sight. Now that he had seen them together with his own eyes, he was positive of the connection between them. The Chinese woman must be connected to the Wang Trading Company and Aku was working for her. The question was where were they sending the ivory to. There was only one way to find out.

He made light work of the WellBox perimeter fence, having already worked out where best to avoid the security light. He had expected the inside of the compound to be covered by CCTV and no doubt security would patrol the area, but so far he'd seen neither. Nonetheless, he took no chances, moving carefully in and out of the darkest spots, picking his way deeper into the compound in the direction from where he'd see the Chinese woman and Aku appear minutes before. Finally, he reached the workshops and waited again until he was sure that he was alone. Somewhere inside one of those outbuildings was a clue.

He worked his way from building to building, careful not to make a sound, checking every crate for a sign of the serial number WANU114655. He knew that the Wang woman had loaded the crate in Pemba and now he was sure that Aku made sure not to log it, which meant that it must have been unloaded in Mombasa, possibly intended for China. But he needed to find that crate if he was going to work out where it was going to. As he worked methodically from workshop to workshop, crate to crate, he could feel that he was getting closer to the truth.

He'd been searching for over twenty minutes by the time he found what he'd been looking for. In the final workshop, tucked into a far corner, he saw a forty-foot container with a familiar marking on its side – 'Wang Trading Company'. Bingo. Mason checked that he was still alone before he crept around to the front of the box and looked for a seal. Relieved not to find one, he unhinged the bolt and opened the steel doors. His face fell when he saw what was inside.

Nothing. The container was empty. It smelled exactly like the Wang warehouse had back in Pemba – bitter and foul – but, save for a few cracked and broken fragments of sea cucumbers on the floor, it contained no cargo. He stood in the doorway, deflated by what he could see. It didn't make any sense. He'd searched all the other workshops already and this was the only one that belonged to Wang Trading. In any case, most of the other containers were smashed, broken, unusable.

He closed the doors again, hooking the first one shut and then swinging the other door round to lock it back up. But as the door closed, something caught his eye. He opened it again and looked inside. Something didn't look right. He stepped back and moved to his right-hand side from where he could look along the container and still see inside of it. They didn't match. The outside of the box looked longer than the space inside the box. Someone had built a false wall.

Mason went around to the other side, running his fingers up and down the corrugated steel to feel for any flaws in the metal. In the bottom left corner, he felt it. A very thin seam of epoxy resin had been applied to a small patch of the outer container in a square. He took out his phone and used the light to take a closer look. It was just visible. A coat of paint and you'd never see it. It was approximately three feet by two feet. Big enough to get a person through. Big enough to get an elephant's tusk through too.

Mason stopped to consider. If he were to break into it now, then there was no way to disguise it again. Not without tools and fresh epoxy. If the ivory was inside, he had his proof. But then what? The goal was to catch the people responsible, there was nothing he could do now for the elephants who'd died to give up the tusks that might be inside that box.

He noted down the number of the container – WANU997653. If his hunch was right then this container would be loaded onto a ship bound for China in the next couple of days. With Dahir's help, he could track it on board and then be there on the other side when it arrived. Finally, he was making some progress.

He jumped when the phone in his hand started vibrating and went to turn it off. He had no desire to speak to anyone right now. He had to get back out of the compound before WellBox's security team started their patrols. But as his thumb moved to hit the Decline Call button, he stopped when he saw the name of the caller. The name Captain Peter Hopkins. That was a surprise. Hopkins had been his last OC, the Rupert he'd served with on his final SAS task in Yemen and who had, surprisingly for an officer at least, turned out to be a half-decent bloke. Out of curiosity, Mason took the call.

'Hopkins,' he said in a half-whisper.

'Mace,' the voice was just as he remembered it, 'you alright?'

'Been better, Pete.'

'Oh, shit. I'm sorry, Mace.'

'I'm kind of in the middle of something right now, mate.'

'Right, I'll be ...' Hopkins paused. 'This isn't a social call, Mace.'

'Go on.' Mason sounded concerned.

'It's about Joanna.'

PART FOUR

THIRTY

Mogadishu, Somalia

Ordinarily, the only way to fly from Mombasa to Mogadishu is to divert through Ethiopia or Uganda, which
turns a ninety-minute, six-hundred-mile, straight shot up
the coast into a fourteen-hour meandering journey. To save
Matt Mason that hardship, Agent Redford had organised
for him to hitch a ride on a transport flight landing in Aden
Adde International Airport and sent an armoured SUV to
deliver him directly to the Sahafi Hotel.

The Sahafi is regarded as the safest place to stay in what
has long been known as the most dangerous city in the
world. In theory, Mogadishu has been under the control of
the Somali government ever since Al-Shabaab were driven
out in 2011. But the terrorist's enduring influence on the
ground remains palpable and their attacks on strategic
targets are frequent. The city remains an incredibly dangerous place to live, particularly for foreigners. Journalists, UN
staff, NGO workers and any other foreigner is considered
by Al-Shabaab to be the enemy. It was a group of journalists who were the intended target of the car bomb placed

outside the Sahafi in 2015, which killed twenty people and injured dozens more.

Not that Mason was worried about Al-Shabaab. Ever since he'd heard the news that they had kidnapped his daughter, the only thing that had stopped him from being physically sick was thinking about what he was going to do to the bastards once he'd found her and made sure she was safe. One thing was sure, it was going to be so brutal that whoever was responsible would regret what they'd done for the rest of their short lives.

He had put Mozambique and Wang Trading entirely out of his mind. What had seemed like the most important thing in his life less than a day ago, now seemed a total irrelevance. Mason's children were his whole world and his daughter in particular was his pride and joy. Sam was a great kid too, but Joanna was more like him. She was the one who always wanted to come hiking or camping with him in the Brecons, the one who craved adventure, who listened to his stories over and over again as though she'd never heard them before. Joanna was the love of Mason's life and as he sat in the back seat watching the SUV pass through the Sahafi Hotel security checks, he knew that nothing in his whole life mattered more than seeing her again.

One question kept running through his mind. *Why had he not known sooner?* From what Peter Hopkins had said, Joanna's boat was intercepted by an Eritrean naval vessel two days ago. Two days when he'd been locked in a dark container on a ship at sea and then running around Mombasa looking for Aku. He'd never forgive himself if anything happened to Joanna now. While he was thinking about elephants, his daughter had been transported over the Ethiopian border and the CIA had tracked the vehicle into southern Al-Shabaab controlled Somalia. The situation was a fucking shitshow. The only glimmer of hope that Hopkins had offered him was that contact had already been made with the kidnappers and another of the hostages, the rich Chinese bloke who owned the Falcon was going to stump up the ransom. The logistics of the handover were still being worked out.

Hopkins was waiting for him at the hotel door. Mason could see right away how uncomfortable he looked. The guy was shitting his pants. Again.

Indeed, Hopkins was shitting his pants. Mason looked pale, his hands clenched in fists, his eyes pin-sharp. Hopkins had worked with Mason in the most dangerous situations imaginable, but he'd never seen him like this before.

'Mace, I'm so sorry,' he said, shaking his old staff sergeant's hand.

'Never mind that, Pete,' Mason replied. 'Where are we going?'

Hopkins led the way, taking Mason through the hotel lobby to the room that had been assigned to them in the rear. Most of the Sahafi's four hundred rooms were empty, demand for rooms in a bombed-out hotel not being what it was. Still, Hopkins had chosen it as the best place to establish their Ops room while they waited for the next call from the kidnappers. The fact was, there simply wasn't a better option in Mogadishu. The Sahafi was as safe from Al-Shabaab as everywhere else and, in any case, it was the only hotel that had twenty-four-hour air-con and Wi-Fi, both of which were rare in a city where electricity was considered a luxury item.

They entered the Ops room, a crappy hotel meeting room laid out with Formica tables in a square on top of which were several laptops. A big screen hung on the wall next to the whiteboard covered with names and phone numbers. It was low rent, but it was the best they'd been able to pull together in the circumstances. Mason recognised nearly everyone who was there.

He shook his head in dismay when he saw his best friend look up to acknowledge his arrival. 'What the fuck are you doing here?'

'Don't go giving it Billy Big Balls,' Jack replied.

'It's my fucking daughter,' Mason barked.

'See?' Jack sighed, looking around the room. 'I said this would happen.'

'Okay, gentlemen,' Redford interrupted. 'It's good to see you again, Mace. I'm sorry it's not under better circumstances.'

Mason grunted. His back was up and he wasn't in the mood for reunions. He pointed to James Beeby, sitting quietly in a plastic chair. 'Who's he?'

James stood up and held out a hand. 'James Beeby, Mace. I'm in charge of the hostage negotiation.'

'Not any fucking more, you're not,' Mason replied, declining the handshake.

He walked over to the whiteboard and scanned what was written on it. He tried to remind himself to remain objective, but it was hard. Thoughts of his daughter locked up in a cell somewhere by a group of jihadis raced through his mind. He punched the board so hard that it toppled over. Everyone in the room winced as it crashed to the ground, but Mason didn't give a shit. He could only think about Joanna, how he should have been told. Should have found out as soon as this whole thing happened. He'd have gone straight to Eritrea and found her before she ever made it as far as the Somali border. He'd have acted while these people were fucking around, doing what exactly? He looked around the room again. Something seemed strange. If a Chinese billionaire was being held hostage with Joanna, then why were they running the op from inside a shitty hotel in Mogadishu? It didn't add up.

'Someone want to tell me what the fuck is going on?' He directed the question to Redford.

'The game has changed, Mace.' She crossed the room and picked the whiteboard up, putting it back where they could see it. 'Since we found out that Al-Shabaab are directly involved, the whole operation has to be hush-hush.'

'We could have NCA come down on us like a tonne of bricks if they even knew we were talking with terrorists. I mean, I shouldn't even be here,' James pitched in.

Mason glared at him so hard, he decided not to say any more.

'The good news is that Chow's people still want to put up the cash,' Redford said. "They're wiring it from Hong Kong via an account in Switzerland and a broker in Germany to a bank in Nairobi. We're just working out how to get fifteen million dollars into Somalia.'

Mason shrugged. 'Why not just wire it here?'

'There isn't a bank in Somalia that we can trust to handle that amount of cash,' Redford answered.

'So, fly it in. Same way as I came.'

'Negative,' Redford said, shaking her head. 'No way I can swing that with Langley. Officially, this is still a civilian matter.'

'Why are you here then?'

'For the rich Chinese bloke,' Jack said with just a note of scorn.

'That's another story, Mace. Joanna's safe return is absolutely my priority,' Redford said.

'I don't care about that now,' Mason said. 'Let's just get that money up here.'

'We discussed using a civilian plane but we feel the risk of getting stopped is high. If we lost that money, Mason, then …' She saw that Mason followed her train of thought, 'Flying it out is too risky.'

'So, we drive it over the border,' Jack said. Mason could tell from his tone that it wasn't the first time he'd said it either.

'How long have we got?'

'On the last call they told James to be ready within forty-eight hours,' she checked her watch. 'That was four hours ago. They haven't given us more beyond that.'

Mason considered the options. It didn't take him long because there weren't any.

'And the money's been wired to Nairobi, you said?'

Redford nodded.

'Looks like I'm going to Nairobi then, don't it?'

THIRTY-ONE

Asmara, Eritrea

Coffee is a key ingredient of Eritrean social life. Making a good cup, Eritreans say, requires patience and skill. First, the beans must be roasted in a skillet and pounded with a mortar and pestle, then poured into a pot of cold water and ginger root. The mixture is brought to the boil over a gentle flame and poured through an oxtail filter, into a small porcelain cup.

'You want sugar?' Abel asked the man sitting opposite him.

'Of course,' he answered. 'Four.'

Abel Ahmed, the half-brother of the Ethiopian prime minister, chuckled as he piled four sugar cubes into his old friend's cup. He always enjoyed coming to Eritrea and to Asmara in particular. Eritrea's capital was a prettier city than Addis. He particularly enjoyed the Italian colonial architecture and the coffee house Ammin had chosen for their meeting, with its high vaulted ceilings and whitewashed stone walls, was no exception. All around them, well-heeled Eritreans and Ethiopians chatted. Citizens of both nations were happy to be able to visit each other again, happy to

217

share coffee and make up for years of fighting and lack of communication.

Abel and Ammin had met at university in Djibouti during the bad old days of the war. After the two men graduated, Ammin had been ordered back home and conscripted into Eritrea's secret police. In the intervening years, he had risen to a position of considerable influence. Drinking coffee in a beautiful coffee hall, it was easy to forget that Eritrea was still a one-party state, whose ruling party maintained an iron grip on political control by ensuring the people had no freedom of speech, no parliament, and no elections. It would be fair to say that, despite their great coffee, Eritrea was Africa's North Korea.

Nonetheless, some people dreamed of the day when the regime would falter. Private conversations happened in the shadows all over Asmara and Addis, concerning how the two countries could one day reunify and bring democracy and prosperity to their nation. Ammin and Abel were joined in their passionate belief that Ethiopia and Eritrea could be stronger together than they had ever been apart.

Ammin appreciated how Abel's work with the American CIA could become an important asset one day in further-ing their cause, so when his friend had asked him for a favour, he'd cautiously looked into who might have given the order to intercept the *Falcon*. Now, he took another sip from his cup before he licked his big brown lips and fixed his old friend with a serious look.

'The thing of which you ask is settled,' he said.

'Already?' Abel sounded surprised.

'Not by us,' Ammin replied. 'The navy did it for themselves.'

'They sanctioned this?' Abel asked.

'A captain by the name of Kidane confirmed what you believed – the Somalians.'

'He has "confirmed"?'

Ammin took another sip of his coffee and considered how to phrase his answer. 'It took a little persuasion. But yes. He says he was supplied with the intelligence thirty minutes before and that it came from our friends in Somalia.'

'How can that be?' Abel said. There was no way that Al-Shabaab could have known that the *Falcon* had changed its route and passed that knowledge to Kidane.

'That, I cannot answer,' Ammin sighed. 'The captain says only that the caller was a man named Razir Al-Haq.'

Abel noted it down. Razir Al-Haq was not a name he knew.

'Be very careful my friend,' Ammin said.

Abel considered his friend's advice as he bid him farewell. He thanked Ammin with a close embrace and hurried into the street outside, already reaching for his phone. He had to contact Agent Redford to confirm that this man Razir Al-Haq had ordered the kidnap.

Redford's phone picked up on the second ring. 'I have confirmation that the order was placed by our friends across the border,' Abel said.

'Do you have a name for me?' Redford replied.

'Razir Al-Haq.'

Redford was already typing the name into her screen. She was relieved to see that Al-Haq was known to the CIA. According to their intel, Al-Haq was head of pirate relations, heavily involved in smuggling arms as well as several well-known kidnappings and ransoms over the past five years. He came from the Hawiye clan, an old and powerful family in southern Somalia with deep connections to senior Al-Shabaab leadership. In fact, he was rumoured to have been present when the US had taken out the old emir with a drone strike seven years ago.

She enlarged the most recent photo they had on file and winced. Al-Haq was no looker that was for sure. He had a deep scar that ran from his forehead to his chin through where his left eye had once been.

Redford thanked Abel for his work and hung up the call. It wasn't surprising that the Somalians had been involved in the kidnapping but it still wasn't clear how they'd known where to find the *Falcon* in the first place. There had to be a leak coming from the boat. She was now more convinced than ever that someone aboard the Falcon had ratted them out. She looked back to the face on the screen and picked up the phone to Langley. Now that she had an ID on Razir Al-Haq, she at least had somewhere to start looking for who that person could be.

THIRTY-TWO

Nairobi, Kenya

Fifteen million dollars doesn't fit in a briefcase. No matter how many movies you've seen. It just doesn't. Even if you took brand new, one hundred dollar bills and vacuum packed them, that amount of cash still weighs over one hundred and fifty kilograms, the weight of two grown men, and takes up nearly two hundred litres, the volume of eight briefcases. Between the three of them, Matt Mason, Peter Hopkins, and Mad Jack only had six hands.

The larger problem was that there's no easy way to get fifteen million dollars in cash into Africa. There aren't many banks, money exchanges, or Western Unions that can handle that amount of money and all the places that can are in Nairobi, East Africa's commercial hub. The three British ex-SAS soldiers had been in town for less than two hours and already they'd made what was, even by I&M Bank's standards, a considerable withdrawal.

The ransom that had been negotiated by James Beeby in Hong Kong, had been wired by SinoCheck's lawyers to an anonymous account in Zurich, from where it was transferred via a broker in Frankfurt to I&M in Nairobi's central commercial district. In a private office on the bank's sixteenth floor, Peter Hopkins had signed for the cash and a bewildered young cashier had watched as Mace and Jack transferred the stacks of money into three seventy-litre duffel bags which they slung over their shoulders before they left.

With the weight shared out evenly, each bag contained five million dollars or fifty kilos of paper, which felt even heavier as they made their way through the city's ninety per cent humidity to where they'd parked the vehicle. All three men were sweating buckets long before they'd even reached the car park.

The challenge now was to get the cash across the border. Mason had decided that they would take the most direct route, following the road east, past the refugee camps along the border between Somalia and Kenya before reaching the crossing at Liboi. The constant stream of refugees meant that NGO vehicles often crossed at Liboi and so their presence there should attract less scrutiny from customs than the bigger crossing to the north.

After leaving Nairobi, they'd taken it in turns to drive the five hundred kilometres to the border, rotating the wheel, catching short bursts of sleep. Peter Hopkins was at the wheel when he first caught sight of the frontier. He nudged Jack awake. Mason was already sitting up in the middle, eyes darting around as always, assessing every angle. Their progress slowed as they fell into a queue of four pickup trucks up ahead. Mace immediately saw the reason why.

Each of the vehicles was loaded with bundles of miraa, or khat as it is often known, a local plant containing a powerful stimulant that is chewed by people all over the region. While khat is legal in Kenya, it is banned in Somalia. So the huge piles of it, wrapped up in banana leaves, loaded onto the back of the pickup trucks, were being smuggled over the frontier. Not that the people smuggling it had made any attempt to hide it.

The queue slowly edged forward as they passed through an unmanned Kenyan checkpoint into the no-man's-land between the two countries. They drove along a fifty-metre-long dirt strip. Pedestrians walked on either side carrying plastic sacks of rice and maize on top of their heads. At the Somalian border, access wasn't so easy. The road was blocked by a length of bamboo that had been fashioned into a barrier and lowered to halt their progress.

Mason shifted uneasily, reaching below his seat for the Browning 9mm he'd taped there. Joining a convoy of smugglers hadn't been part of the plan and there was no predicting how things would go down. On one hand, the smugglers might distract the Somalian border guards from the three white guys and the fifteen million dollars hidden in their luggage, but on the other hand, it could raise the alert level to where they started stopping and searching everyone. One way or another, Mace wasn't going to let that happen.

A young Somali soldier raised his hand to stop the first pickup and immediately a man stepped out and followed him into a small hut to one side of the barrier. A couple of minutes later both men appeared again and the young soldier waved the vehicles through. Mace had no doubt that money had changed hands. Wheels had been greased. It was reassuring. The soldier continued to wave all the vehicles through, giving the British men's Hilux a perplexed look as they reached him.

He waved for them to stop and Mason released the safety on his pistol, preparing for the worst. Meanwhile, Hopkins kept his eyes firmly on the soldier, handing over their documents, all the while scanning activity in his peripheral vision. Nobody inside the Hilux said a word.

The soldier took the paperwork back to the hut before he reappeared with another soldier, older, half-dressed, his shirt flapping open revealing a broad bare chest. The older guy was now holding the documents and he walked around the vehicle, checking everything like he was at a dealership considering whether or not to buy it. He appeared again at Hopkins's window and handed back the documents with a polite smile before he waved for the young soldier to raise the barrier. Hopkins put the car in drive and they edged slowly into Somalia.

Twenty minutes later they passed their first sign for Kismayo. The old metal marker was so riddled with bullet holes that although the port town was still over two hundred kilometres away, it looks like it said twenty. Jack checked his phone for reception again.

'We've got company,' Hopkins said, looking in the mirror.

Jack and Mason turned around to look out the back window. One of the pickups they'd seen at the border was following close behind.

'He's been on us since we came over the border,' Hopkins said.

'Lose him then.' Jack had seen Hopkins drive before. For an ex-officer, he had some decent skills.

'I'll do my best.'

Hopkins floored the accelerator, powering the SUV along the bumpy single track road. Either side of them patchy scrubland whizzed by and the pickup disappeared in a cloud of their dust. Mason eased back in his seat, Hopkins stepping on it a little was no bad thing. They'd get to Kismayo sooner.

The pickup may have disappeared from view but it was most certainly still there. The driver, born not far away, knew the road from Nairobi to Kismayo like the back of his hand, so that even when he couldn't see the road, he knew where the bumps and turns were.

Hopkins checked his mirrors again. Suddenly the shape of the pickup appeared out of the fog and rammed his rear bumper. He felt the SUV's back end slide out of his control for a moment until he wrestled back control again.

'Fuck!' he screamed.

Jack sat bolt upright again, looking in his mirror. 'Little, fuckers,' he said.

Hopkins slid the SUV back and forth across the track, changing his line, making them a harder target. His foot was flat to the floor, the speedometer teasing ninety km/h. He checked his mirrors, but the dust behind had masked the pickup entirely. They were a sitting duck, waiting to get rammed again from behind.

The pickup's speed was much faster than the SUV. The vehicle was built for this terrain, taking the potholes and puddles in its stride far better than the luxury 4x4. It was quickly back on the British men's tail and the passenger, his face wrapped in a cloth scarf, eased himself out of the window and took aim with his AK47.

Jack saw him first. 'Down!' he shouted and all three men slid lower in their seats just as the AK's rounds sprayed at the SUV. One round took out Jack's mirror, while another exploded the back window, sending small squares of glass all over Mason. Again, Hopkins changed the line, making it harder for their assailant to get a line of sight.

'Fuck this,' Jack said turning around and pointing to a bag on the back seat. 'Pass us that, Mace.'

Everyone in the Regiment was trained in demolitions but few took it the level that Jack had done. He'd always loved blowing shit up, ever since he'd been a kid, so when they'd given him the chance to make a career out of it, he'd relished it. Twelve years in the Regiment gave him ample opportunity to blow up more shit than he could even remember and old habits died hard. Mason handed him the bag and immediately Jack found what he was looking for – an RKG-3 anti-tank grenade.

The RKG-3 was Jack's grenade of choice. Its Russian design allowed for it to be thrown so that, mid-air, it automatically deployed a parachute that ensured the charge landed face-down. But Jack always modified his RKGs, removing the parachute, so that it could be thrown directly at a target. As long as you got your throw right, the grenade would explode on impact, and it didn't matter if it hit a tank, an armoured vehicle or a concrete wall, it made a big hole and killed everyone inside.

'Keep it straight, Pete,' Jack said, crawling back over his seat into the back.

The pickup appeared again from the dust cloud and Jack saw the passenger side window opening. The shooter was getting ready to have another go at them. As Hopkins straightened the SUV, he was fancying his chances of hitting the target this time.

But he'd never get that chance. Jack crawled back over the back seat so that he was facing directly out of the shattered rear window. He grabbed the grenade in his good right hand and eased the fuse out with his left. It weighed just over a kilogram so he knew to aim a little higher than the roof to allow for a little drop. He pulled his hand back and as though he was casting a dart at the bullseye, he released the grenade into the air.

At over eighty kilometres per hour, the grenade hit the windscreen of the pickup in less than a tenth of a second. Jack's shot had been perfect, the charge landing squarely so that the fuse ignited the warhead containing over three hundred grams of TNT. The explosion was instant, lifting the front axle of the pickup clean off the road and flipping it into the air as it disappeared in a fireball of flame and smoke. The shockwave caught up with the Hilux, throwing Jack and Mason forward against the front seats while Hopkins fought to control the lurch sideways when the wave passed underneath.

'Whoaaaa,' he shouted as he struggled to keep control.

'That'll fuckin learn' 'em,' Jack laughed. The pickup had landed in a ditch to the side of the road and was already engulfed in flames. Whoever had been inside it was well and truly cooked.

'Good work, mate,' Mace said while Jack climbed back into the front seat. 'What do you reckon? The kid in the bank?'

Jack considered for a moment. Getting attacked on the road when you happened to be carrying fifteen million dollars was a little too much of a coincidence. Someone must have tipped someone off and there weren't too many candidates. Assuming they could trust their own people, the handover in the bank was the one time they'd exposed themselves.

'This is why I bank with Barclays,' he said, finally.

Hopkins and Mason looked at the gruff Brummie and laughed. Mad Jack was as consistent as time itself. He never looked happier than when he'd just blown something to pieces and, right now, sitting in the passenger seat moments after they'd almost been shot to shit, he looked the happiest they'd seen him in ages.

'Okay, lads,' Hopkins smiled. 'Let's crack on. It's another three hours to Kismayo.'

THIRTY-THREE

Mogadishu, Somalia

James Beeby pulled back the yellow Dralon curtain and peered past the reinforced steel bars to the street outside. Nothing was happening out there but he was looking anyway. Anything to kill some time, to distract him from the waiting. Behind him, his phone lay on an old antique rosewood desk, a legacy from when people with money used to come to Somalia to do business. The last time it had rung was a call from the kidnappers that morning telling them to be prepared for a handover of the hostages at 3 pm. Mason and the others had arrived from Nairobi, armed themselves, and headed back out again. They were in position, waiting for the second call. It was already nearly four.

Next to him, Redford lifted a cup to her lips and cursed. It was still empty. It had been empty the last three times that she'd tried to drink from it. Since she'd received the intel from Abel, she'd been mainlining the stuff. The Sahafi Hotel's coffee was pretty ordinary, but the quality didn't matter right now. All that mattered was that she stayed alert while they waited for confirmation of the handover.

In the meantime, she had upped their efforts to track down the location of Razir Al-Haq. Once Chow and his crew were safe, she would find the man responsible and bring him to justice.

Abel's intelligence on Al-Haq had been a game-changer for her bosses in Langley. Al-Haq's connections to Al-Shabaab was the difference between cooperation and assistance. Langley's priority had been the War on Terror now for more than two decades and Al-Shabaab were near the top of the list of organisations they wanted to shut down.

Redford had been gathering proof for some time that America's enemies were using insurgency as a way of desta-bilising Western interests in Africa. Wei Lun Chow had been instrumental because his software could track and trace suspicious shipments of cargo crossing the world's oceans. Over the past year, they had worked together to compile evidence of arms shipments diverting to Al-Shabaab in Somalia. But his disappearance now, at such a crucial stage threatened the whole project.

The order from Langley was exactly what she'd needed to hear; do whatever it takes. She put down the cup again and checked her screen for updates. The team were work-ing overtime back in Virginia where it was still the middle of the night.

James Beeby began pacing the room. Again. He'd been driving her nuts ever since he'd flown in from Hong Kong that morning. He had an irritating habit of con-tributing nothing but tension to the situation without adding anything that might help relieve it. If she hadn't already done a thorough background check on him, then she'd never have believed that the guy was a professional hostage negotiator. Apart from anything else, and despite all the big talk, he'd pretty much rolled over and agreed to everything the kidnappers had asked for. It wasn't her money that they were spending, but she was pretty sure that if it had been, she'd have got them down from fifteen million dollars.

'James, why don't you go and ask at the front desk for some fresh coffee?'

She waved her empty mug in the air as James snapped out of whatever fresh anxiety loop he seemed to be stuck in.

'Ugh?' he said before he realised what she'd just said. 'Oh yes, of course.'

He seemed relieved to have something to do as he left the room but not as relieved as she was to see him go. She took the opportunity to check in again with Langley.

The eavesdropping assets were working overtime. Every mobile phone network in Eritrea, Ethiopia, and Somalia was being tapped. Most of the world's biggest cell phone networks paid three major encryption companies hundreds of millions of dollars every year to keep their customers' data private. What none of those networks realised was that the CIA owned two of those companies and had enough leverage over the third to be granted full access. Unless you were in China or North Korea, the CIA could listen in to your calls or read your texts without your knowledge.

Langley had also sanctioned Redford to tap into their satellites circling over the Horn. Their geo-synchronised orbits were busy snapping images and recording video all over southern and central Somalia, sucking up every potential signal from the air like giant data hoovers.

Meanwhile, two MQ-9 remote-controlled Reaper drones were standing by for launch from Lemonnier. When she needed them, she would call for their deployment. Within thirty minutes they could be circling, high overhead, unseen from the ground, providing real-time video images with high enough resolution to read a number plate as well as crystal clear radio intercepts and, if needed, eighty pounds of Hellfire air-to-ground missiles.

But first, she had to find the target, and the problem remained that doing that meant processing an enormous amount of data. The challenge was to sift through the 99.9% of it that was irrelevant, which usually required teams of people to filter, decipher and analyse the reports generated from listening into millions of conversations passing through their algorithms. You could fast-track the process if you were able to pick up keywords, names, or phrases. Anything that narrowed the search helped. The gold standard was a voice signature. With that, Langley could engage voice recognition software to refine the search.

Redford had started by trying to piece together Kidane's network. By scanning his historic phone records, Langley had unlocked recordings of all his previous calls. The analysts had immediately set about translating every call that he'd made in the two weeks before the *Falcon*'s interception. This had been no mean feat as Kidane frequently spoke in not only English and Arabic but also Tigrinya, Tigre,

Dahalik, and his own tribal language Bilen, which initially nobody at Langley had even been able to identify let alone understand. Eventually, they'd found someone who could and by eliminating certain numbers, they'd zeroed in on the number of his contact in Massawa.

Kidane had called his Massawa contact four times in the previous fortnight. Redford reviewed the transcripts again, looking for anything she might have missed. The first call was a discussion of what she assumed was a previous job, in which it seemed like Kidane had been paid to ensure a dhow from Iran didn't attract any attention on its way into Eritrean waters. The next two calls, three days apart, confirmed that Kidane was being paid to intercept the *Falcon*. In the final call, made twenty-two minutes before the *Falcon* was intercepted, Kidane's contact in Massawa provided him with the exact GPS coordinates of the *Falcon*.

At no point during any of the four calls did Kidane's contact reveal his identity, but crucially, now that Langley had his voice signature, they could start to build up a profile of his network. Redford wanted details of any calls he'd received from Somalia in the hour before the *Falcon* was captured because if her hunch was right, then Razir Al-Haq had been the one making that call.

Redford's phone rang as James returned, holding a fresh flask of hot coffee. She pointed to her cup and gave him a thumbs-up as she answered the call. She could already see that it was Langley on the line.

'This is Redford.'

'Agent Redford.' She recognised the Texan drawl right away. Shotton was one of the best analysts on the team.

'Shotton. What've you got for me?'

'So we're still trying to figure out who this guy in Massawa is, but his call history makes for pretty interesting reading. You should have the report now.'

Redford saw the email land in her inbox and opened it. 'Any calls from Somalia last week?'

'Affirmative. This could be your guy, Al-Haq. You'll see more details in my report, but the guy in Massawa got a call from Somalia four minutes before he made the call to Captain Kidane. You think that's a coincidence?'

'The Somalia number has gotta be Razir Al-Haq,' Redford said, speed-reading the report on her screen. 'Do we have ears on what was said?'

'Afraid not. Military-grade encryption. We got geolocations. Still working on content.'

'Keep on it.'

'Sure. One thing . . .'

'Shoot.'

'This is pretty weird. And again, the encryption software is pretty good so all we got is geodata, but the Somalia number, that we think is Al-Haq, took a call two minutes before he called Massawa.'

'Go on.'

James was topping up her coffee, his eyes fixed on her expression. She realised that her face must be giving away the way she felt about what she just heard. If Razir Al-Haq was the caller from Somalia who had relayed the *Falcon*'s whereabouts to Kidane via the unknown Massawa number, then the call *he'd* received immediately before that must have been from whoever knew what those whereabouts were. It had to be the leak from the *Falcon*.

'It came from the UK,' Shotton said.

'What came from the UK?' Redford asked.

'The call. The incoming call to Al-Haq came from Hereford, England. A phone registered to a security company called De Grasse? You heard of them?'

Redford was stunned. Her brain felt like it was going to explode.

She had to warn Mason.

THIRTY-FOUR

Kismayo, Somalia

Jack extinguished another cigarette in the debris of this afternoon's meal. A plate of half-eaten kebabs and flat-breads was now covered in butts and flies. Hopkins didn't smoke and Jack's constant chuffing got on his nerves. But he wasn't going to say anything, he needed the big guy to be relaxed for what was about to happen. He checked his phone again before he poured himself another cup of mint tea.

'You want one?' he asked.

'Nah,' Jack said, lighting another cigarette.

After crossing the border into Somalia, they'd driven directly to Kismayo and after a brief turnaround, redeployed to their location half a kilometre from the central fish market near to the port. The terms had been clear. The hostage release was dependent on the kidnappers' demands being met to the letter. Namely, that fifteen million US dollars be delivered and once the money had been received and verified, the location of the hostages would be provided. If the Somali security forces were informed, the hostages would be killed. If the UN were informed, the hostages would be killed. If there was any deviation from the plan at all, the hostages would be killed.

The silence was broken by the sound of Hopkins's phone ringing. Jack sat back and took a long drag of his cigarette as Hopkins picked up and answered.

'Hello?' He waited to hear the codeword that had been agreed. 'Okay. Proceed . . .'

Hopkins began to scribble details onto a piece of paper, while Jack added his latest cigarette to the pile. Under his shirt, he was wearing low profile Englands' body armour. He had a Steyr A2 MF pistol magazine loaded with seventeen rounds, stashed in the waistband of his trousers and four M84 stun grenades – Jack's particular favourite for creating maximum effect in a controlled urban environment – in a backpack. He also had three duffle bags containing a small fortune at his feet.

'Bollocks,' Hopkins said with a sigh. 'Bakara Market.'

'Fuck it. We'll make it work. Let's just get it done,' Jack said, already getting to his feet. 'Mace, acknowledge?'

'Roger that, mate,' Mason replied in Jack's earpiece. 'Right behind you all the way.'

They crossed town in their SUV, the duffle bags tucked securely behind the driver's seat. The vehicle weaved through the traffic. It would have been better to be in something less visible than an SUV but there hadn't been time to organise an alternative, besides the SUV meant extra security in the event that the kidnappers were planning a double-cross. Hopkins had programmed the coordinates into the satnav to take them via a less direct route just in case their location had already been compromised.

The SUV's engine screamed as they sped along the port road and past the pristine sands of Liido Beach where fishermen were busy hauling in their catch on the water. They continued north, past the walled low rise compounds with their corrugated iron roofs. The streets of Kismayo were busy, women wrapped head to toe in jilbaabs, men openly carrying rifles over their shoulders. They slowed as they reached the market and pulled over, parking the SUV two blocks to the west, sheltering underneath the cover of an old bank, pockmarked with bullet holes.

They had run the plan several times already, just as they would have done back in the days when they were still in the Regiment. Old habits were what they were getting paid for. The cash remained in the SUV, Jack held the key while Hopkins dealt with the hostages. Mason would peel off and shadow from a distance, unseen by the enemy, ready to cover at a moment's notice. The key didn't get handed over until Hopkins had confirmed proof of life, upon which he would signal Jack to make the handover.

The location was inside the fish section of the old market, a hundred-metre-long single-storey building where the city's fishermen brought their catch and market traders lined it up for sale. It was the last place Mason would have agreed to do a handover, too many people, but they'd not had much choice. James had made the arrangements and there was no going back on them. Hundreds of men and women were packed into the vast white-tiled room, vying for places to get close to the freshest fish. Everywhere traders roared out prices over the din of the crowd and when the orders came, their assistants gutted the fish;

marlins, swordfish, snapper, and tuna, blood and guts sloshing over the tiles into open drains. Hopkins scanned the faces in the crowd, while Jack held his nose at the stink and surveyed the roofs of the surrounding buildings. Both men were in no doubt that they were being watched. And not only by Matt Mason.

Matt Mason was there, but nobody paid him any attention. He was dressed the same as many of the older Somali men – sarong and linen tunic, a white koofiyad on his head. With his beard grown out and his deep tan, he easily passed for one of the many Arabs who were commonly seen in the city. As he pretended to browse the fish, he felt his phone vibrating in his pocket. He could see through the crowd that it wasn't Hopkins or Jack calling, which meant whoever it was would have to wait. He looked around again and checked for anyone who might be following them. Seeing nobody suspicious, he pretended to return his attention to the fish.

Seconds later, Hopkins's phone began ringing. He glanced at the screen before he answered it. The voice on the other end of the line said only one word, 'Wait!' A moment later, he heard another voice.

'Hello?' Hopkins assumed it was Captain Ben Warmington from the accent. He sounded weak but alive. 'Please help us.'

The first voice returned on the line. 'Okay, you hear he alive, yes?'

'I need to see them and I need to see them all,' Hopkins said firmly.

'Okay. You. Alone. The other one stays.'

Hopkins looked to Jack for confirmation. The big man nodded. Neither was surprised that they'd been followed, but both were relieved to hear that Mason's presence had gone undetected. That was exactly how they'd hoped it would go down.

'Once I see the hostages,' Hopkins said, 'the cash is yours.'

After a pause, the caller spoke again, 'Very well. Come outside the market. There you will see a building. It is blue. Second floor. Room six. Here are your friends.'

'Blue building. Across the street, room six,' he repeated for Mason's benefit. 'I'm on my way.'

Hopkins walked fast, out of the fish market, along the narrow path between the stalls, firmly pushing his way through the crowds until he was back on the street. He looked up and down and spotted a blue four-storey building at the end of the block. A minute later, he was inside, climbing the staircase, pistol drawn, a bullet already in the chamber.

The quiet of the building compared to the bustle outside made him aware that he was alone. He suddenly felt the fear. He could be walking into a trap. The adrenaline was coursing through him and he was blowing harder than he would ordinarily have after climbing two flights of stairs, but he steadied himself and took stock of the situation. There was no way back now.

At the top of the stairs, a single corridor ran east/west. The floor was clean. White polished floor tiles. There were white apartment doors on either side. Number one on the left, two on the right. He edged his way along until he reached the third door on the right. Number six. By now he knew that the kidnappers would have closed in on

Jack, who would wait for Hopkins to give him the all-clear before he handed over the cash. This was the most dangerous moment of a hostage handover. If something was going to fuck up, then it was now. He let out a breath as he knocked on the door.

There was no answer. Staying to one side, he turned the handle and pushed it open. He peeked around the corner looking inside, where he caught a glimpse of Ben Warmington and Paul Woods lying on the floor, tied with their hands behind their backs. But before he could do anything else, the windows of the room came crashing in towards them.

Hopkins felt the force of the explosion long before he ever heard it. The glass from the windows showered the room and a rush of hot air followed closely behind with a force that threw him back against the wall of the corridor. Then came the sound. An ear-splitting crash filled the whole space and the building shook with its strength. He heard car alarms, several screaming in unison and somewhere beyond that, the sound of human screaming. He slumped down onto the tiled floor, the air knocked out of his lungs by the blast. His mouth was dry and his eyes were stinging from the dust. He briefly checked his body for injuries, relieved not to see any sign of damage. He had no idea what had just happened, but still he crawled forward on his belly, dragging himself into apartment six.

THIRTY-FIVE

Kismayo, Somalia

The explosion outside of the market had put Jack on his arse. He picked himself up off the floor, cursing that his clothes were now covered in fish guts. All around him, people were panicking, running in every direction. Mothers were screaming for their children, men were shouting at each other to get out of the way, get help, get themselves together. Judging from the blast, Jack's best guess was that it had been a car bomb. A big one. Not too far away. Somewhere near the edge of the market. It had done its job too because the people running his way were covered in blood.

He reached for his phone, figuring that Hopkins should be with the hostages by now, should have called to give the okay for him to hand over the money. But his phone had no signal. Looking around, he could see other people struggling with their phones. The explosion must have taken out the local masts and what bandwidth was left was probably jammed up by people calling for help. He grabbed for his weapon and staggered to his feet, suddenly realising that he'd injured his knee in the fall.

As he reached the exit to the fish market, two men stepped out of the bright sunlight, directly into his path. Both were skinny, bearded, wearing long white thawbs and carrying Norinco QBZ-191 carbine assault rifles. *Nice kit*, Jack thought. Chinese made, with a much shorter barrel than the AK which meant it was much better in a tight spot like this. But it was still relatively new to the market. In fact, Jack hadn't seen one in the field before.

The shorter one glanced down at Jack's gun and held out his hand, while the taller one pointed the Chinese rifle directly at him. Jack stopped dead and looked again at his phone. Still nothing. The plan was to only hand over the cash once he'd had a call from Hopkins. He stood bolt still and shook his head.

'Sorry fellas. No call, no money.'

The taller man smiled and lifted the rifle higher, pointing it at Jack's head.

'Easy fella,' Jack said in a calm voice.

The three men were the only people standing still in an otherwise chaotic scene of panic and carnage. The tall guy eased his finger over the trigger. Jack lifted his head and jutted out his chin, staring defiantly down the barrel at the man who was preparing to kill him. As they locked eyes, a bullet exploded out of the back of the tall guy's head, taking most of his brain with it. Man and rifle dropped, while Jack, without missing a beat, swung his pistol up and tapped two rounds into the other guy's chest, propelling him to the floor. A second later, Mason appeared, administering another two rounds to the head, just in case the fucker was thinking of getting up again.

Mason looked down at Jack's knee, which was now bleeding heavily. 'Can you walk on that?'

Jack growled back, 'I'll hop on the other one if not.'

Mason swung Jack's arm over his shoulder and the two men hobbled into the stampede of people, now piling out of the market onto the street. Mason stopped momentarily at a clothing stall, blown to pieces by the bomb. He tore a thawb from one of the racks, ripped off a length of material and tied it tightly around Jack's wound. It would stop the bleeding for a while.

As they reached the street, they pulled away from the crowd again and moved as fast as Jack's leg would allow until they reached the blue building. As Mason set Jack down on the steps, he saw the man he recognised as Ben Warmington stumbling out of the door. A moment later Hopkins appeared, helping Paul Woods who was bleeding heavily from a wound in his back. Mason ran to help them, wrapping an arm around the other side of Woods, sharing the load as they lifted him down the stairs.

'Where's Joanna?' he asked.

Hopkins shook his head. He'd searched the whole apartment, checked everywhere, called out in the corridor for her several times. But she wasn't there.

Mason shook his head in disbelief. 'Nah, fuck that,' he said, running back into the building.

'Mace!' Hopkins cried after him but he knew there was no stopping him. Mason had to see for himself.

Mason was already running up the stairs, two at a time. He sprinted along the corridor, now filling up with stunned people piling out of their apartments. He bolted through the open door to apartment six and searched every room for his daughter. But just as Hopkins had said, Joanna Mason was not there.

Mason was crushed. His head fell and he closed his eyes. The pain in his heart was unbearable. His breathing was short and he felt a tightness grip his chest. He kicked the front door, kicked it again and again until it came clean off its hinges, the anger rising inside of him like a volcano ready to erupt.

He slumped forwards and laid his hands on his knees, blowing out one long exhale to get control of his breathing. He had to pull himself together. Joanna was out there somewhere, still alive. He wasn't giving up. He was going to find his daughter and then he was going to kill every last one of the people who had taken her, but first, he had to save himself and the others. He had to deal with the task at hand. Then move on to the next. Just as he'd been trained to do. He retreated from the apartment and hurried back down the stairs.

Outside, Mason and Hopkins helped the others down the street towards where they'd parked the SUV. The scene wasn't pretty. There were bodies and parts of bodies strewn everywhere, blown apart by a massive car bomb. A specialty of Al-Shabaab. Mason could see the death toll was going to be heavy.

What had happened was starting to make sense. The kidnappers had double-crossed them and only brought two hostages. The car bomb was designed to ensure that comms went down for long enough to create confusion and give them time to get away with the cash. You had to be a particularly evil bastard to detonate a car bomb in a crowded market just to create a diversion.

Mason saw Hopkins checking his phone. 'Don't bother. Useless.'

There was no way they were going to get through to anyone for help. Their only option was to get back to the vehicle and get Jack, Ben, and Woods to safety.

'Come on,' Mason said, lifting Woods over his shoulder in a fireman's lift. 'Let's get the fuck out of here before this one bleeds out.'

THIRTY-SIX

Mombasa, Kenya

Razir Al-Haq checked his phone again as he stepped onto the dock from his Baja 36 Outlaw. The speedboat, which his men had taken from a group of tourists several years ago, was a beast. It was capable of doing over seventy knots, which made it by far the fastest and most comfortable way of getting from Somalia to Kenya. It also meant it was easily fast enough to outrun the Kenyan coastguard should they ever object. Not that they ever did. The minute they saw the distinctive green flash along the Outlaw's hull, they knew who it belonged to and they knew to leave it alone.

The journey from Kismayo had taken just over four hours and Al-Haq felt in need of some mint tea and a cigarette. But first, he wanted to hear from his cousin, Raghe. It was nearly 5 pm, so the handover in Kismayo should already have taken place. He was still tense about how little time the Iranian's request, more like demand, had given him to change his plans. He didn't like last-minute changes, they usually led to problems.

Before he left Somalia, he'd personally gone over the changes with his men. The two hostages that the Iranians

247

had asked for would no longer be part of the handover. But if his men followed his new instructions, they could still claim all of the ransom because the British wouldn't realise what was going on until it was too late. The car bomb outside the market would knock out the cell phone masts and create a distraction so that they could separate the British from the ransom money before they realised what was happening. He checked his phone again and cursed. There were still no messages.

A black SUV was waiting with two armed men standing by. He stepped into the back of the vehicle and told the driver to turn on the radio. The main news item concerned an explosion in Kismayo. Thirty-three people were dead. Al-Haq relaxed a little, satisfied that his plan had been followed. He informed the driver to drive directly to the madrassa and dialled Raghe's number again. After a couple of rings, he heard his cousin answer.

'Why have you not called me?' Al-Haq demanded.

'Cousin,' Raghe sounded shaky. 'We have a problem.'

'What problem?'

'The package was not delivered.'

Al-Haq felt his pulse rising. 'Where are the assets?'

'They have been lost.'

'Very well,' Al-Haq said and hung up.

He began breathing deeply. His grip on the phone grew tighter and tighter until, finally, he snapped. He smashed the phone against the central dashboard, over and over, cursing at the top of his voice, until the handset came apart, showering fragments of glass and plastic all over the inside of the vehicle.

He had wanted a simple confirmation that everything had gone smoothly and that the money was secured. Instead, he had lost two hostages to the Iranians, lost another two to the British, and had nothing to show for either. Fifteen million dollars. He cursed the Iranians for compromising his whole plan. And yet, to make matters worse, they were still demanding he personally oversee the delivery of the two remaining hostages to them. He cursed his bad luck and resolved to write the whole sorry endeavour off. He would finish the job tonight and think about it no more. Tomorrow he would put the whole sorry business behind him. The relationship with Tehran and their continued funding of Al-Shabaab's operations in Somalia was the most important thing. The ransom money was small change in comparison, so now he had to just keep the Iranians happy and, in time, the rewards for that would far outweigh what he had lost today.

THIRTY-SEVEN

Mogadishu, Somalia

James Beeby was in a bit of a pickle, if indeed that is the best way to describe waking up with the barrel of a pistol in your mouth. While the initial shock was still taking a hold of his body, his eyes, blurry from less than an hour's sleep, struggled to focus on who the holder of the gun might be. Eventually, they settled on the angry face of Matt Mason.

'Oooffgh,' James tried to say.

'Don't say a fucking word,' Mason replied, pushing the barrel so far into James's mouth that he wretched.

'We know, James,' he recognised the second voice as that of Agent Redford, but the presence of the Browning 9mm in his mouth prevented him from turning his head to face her.

He ran through the implications of what Redford had just said. He'd sensed that she'd been a little off with him the previous day, but he'd dismissed it as her concern for the team's wellbeing. The handover had been a total shitshow, and when they returned with two men seriously wounded everyone had scrambled to get them to the international hospital. Jack had been taken in for immediate surgery. Only once they'd been satisfied that both men were in a stable condition, had they returned to the Sahafi for a debrief. When Redford and Mason had requested that they be left to talk privately, he'd decided to take himself off to bed.

Meanwhile, Redford had updated Mason on what she and Langley had uncovered about James Beeby. As well as showing Mason proof that James had made the call to Al-Haq before the *Falcon*'s interception, she now had phone records detailing several more calls from James to Al-Haq over the previous three weeks. The conclusion that they'd drawn was that the De Grasse chief executive had been directly involved in the plan to kidnap Chow and his crew. It was fair to say that Mason hadn't taken it well.

'You speak only to answer the questions that we ask. I don't want to hear any other bullshit. Do you under-stand?' Mason's finger was way too close to the trigger for James's comfort. He nodded as much as he could manage to acknowledge that he got it. Mason eased the pistol out of his mouth.

'I can explain—'

'Did you hear what I just said?' Mason was pushing the gun against James's lips again. James stopped talking.

'When did you first make contact with Razir Al-Haq?' Redford asked.

'This has gotten so out of hand,' James sighed.

Mason jabbed James with his spare hand, breaking his nose. 'That's not what she asked.'

'Aaaaargh' James cried and threw up his hands to his face. Mason pushed him back and again pointed the gun at him. 'He's Al-Shabaab.'

'We know that,' Redford replied.

'We've worked with him six or seven times in the past,' James said, his nose was bleeding and he looked like he was going to cry. 'The last time was the *Greensilver*?'

Redford nodded. She remembered the story. The *Greensilver* was a Panamanian-flagged container ship, Israeli owned, taken off the Somali coast by pirates in 2018. Everyone had made it out alive and the ship was returned for an undisclosed ransom believed to be in the millions of dollars. De Grasse had handled the negotiations. She handed him a towel for the blood.

'But he's never pulled anything like this before. It's always been bish, bash, bosh. Hand over the ransom, hand over the hostages, no fuss, no nonsense. It's how this business works. Or at least it was.'

'But *you* called *him*,' Mason said.

James squirmed again in his bed. He looked like he'd been caught cheating on his wife, which would have been infinitely preferable to what they'd actually discovered.

'Look,' he said, 'I called Al-Haq when I heard Chow wanted to take the *Falcon* to the Zubair Group. But it was meant to be a simple, run of the mill handover for ransom. Al-Haq was supposed to organise things at his end and then I would just . . . swoop in and save the day.'

'And get a slice of the ransom,' Redford said with utter disdain.

'Fifty–fifty was the deal.'

'Seven and a half million dollars to kidnap your own client? And my daughter.' Mason wanted to shoot him on the spot.

'Things have been really tough,' James whined 'Hostage release is our bread and butter but we haven't done any for over three years.'

'You fucking entitled piece of shit!' Mason was growing impatient. 'Not enough piracy out there for you any more?'

'De Grasse is on the skids,' James's eyes darted back and forth from Redford to Mason, looking for sympathy. He didn't find any. 'We're weeks from bankruptcy.'

'And this was your plan to get out of it?' Redford couldn't believe what they were hearing.

'Chow was too good an opportunity,' James replied. 'Al-Haq got it right way. He had all the contacts to control the chain of custody and I was in the right place to ensure the pay-out. It should have just gone smoothly.'

'So why hasn't it?' Redford asked.

'It's not my fault,' James protested. 'You have to believe me. I did't know anything about this Iran thing until yesterday.'

'Iran?' Redford repeated incredulously.

'I don't believe a fucking word,' Mason growled and tightened his finger over the trigger.

'Wait, Mace,' Redford held up a hand. 'What do Iran have to do with any of this, James?'

'I swear on my daughter's life. Al-Haq said the Iranians forced him to hand over Chow and Joanna to them. That's why they weren't in Kismayo with the others.'

Redford looked to Mason to see whether he now believed what James was saying, but Mason looked like he wasn't sure.

'Who is Al-Haq's contact in Massawa?' Redford asked.

'Oh fuck,' James said, squirming again. They knew every-thing. He was well and truly fucked. He was either going to be beaten to death by Mason or thrown in prison for the rest of his life for terrorism and piracy.

'I don't know his name. He's a nobody, just a guy who passes on information for Al-Haq to people in the Eritrean Navy. He's the same person Al-Haq uses for all his smug-gling operations.'

'Drugs?' Mason asked.

'If only,' James sighed. 'They've been running Chinese-made weapons through Iran to terrorist organisations in Africa – TPLF in Tigray, Al-Qaeda in Sudan, Al-Shabaab in Mozambique.'

'Mozambique?'

'Anyone who can destabilise things. They've totally derailed the French gas project down there. And guess who benefits from that?'

'Iran,' Redford answered. The Iranians were the number one gas supplier to Africa, but the Mozambique project would have challenged that.

'Of course,' James said.

Mason rubbed his eyes with a heavy sigh before he looked back at James with a stare that almost tore him in two. 'What the fuck do Iran and China want with my daughter? Last chance, cos I'm running out of patience for this shit.'

'I don't know. Really, I don't. Maybe the Iranians are handing Chow over to keep the Chinese happy?'

Redford looked to Mason again. It was possible that what James was saying was correct. He'd schemed to make some quick money out of Chow, an opportunistic act of betrayal to get himself out of a financial hole, but then things had gone sour when Tehran discovered what was going down and took advantage of the situation to do a favour for China. If Iran really was supplying Al-Shabaab with weapons then Al-Haq knew he stood to gain a lot more from playing ball with them than he did with James Beeby.

'Look, I'm sorry about your daughter,' James said, spreading his arms in plaintive innocence. 'If I'd known she was on that boat, then I'd have made sure they left her there. Honestly.'

Matt Mason looked at James Beeby in incredulous disbelief. Then he punched him hard in the face, again, this time knocking him out cold.

'What now?' he asked Redford.

Redford didn't have an answer. She looked worried. If the Iranians were handing Chow over to China as some sort of quid pro quo, then that was seriously bad news. And, somehow, Joanna Mason had got mixed up in it all, which was even worse.

'We gotta find Al-Haq,' she said. 'Before he sends your daughter and Chow to Iran.'

THIRTY-EIGHT

Mombasa, Kenya

Wang Li Lan felt a spot of rain fall on her skin. The rainy season was not due for another month, but recently the seasons hadn't followed their usual predictable pattern. These days, storms came during months that had once been dry, while rainy months passed by without so much as a single drop. Either way, Li Lan hated getting wet. She put up her umbrella and looked anxiously down the Shimanzi Road.

She had sent Kassim to meet Al-Haq the one-eyed Somalian at his madrassa over two hours ago. Kassim's instructions were to collect the girls and deliver them directly to the WellBox premises. Li Lan had made the necessary adjustments to accommodate Al-Haq's latest request so that now the girls could be loaded into the false compartment that Aku had built. The seal would be invisible to the naked eye and nobody would notice anything out of the ordinary when it was loaded onto the *Neptune* the following morning.

Li Lan had thought of everything. By mid-afternoon, the cargo would be en route and she had already greased the necessary wheels to ensure that it avoided customs. Meanwhile, she had reloaded the elephant tusks from Mozambique onto another container bound for Hong Kong. By next week, she would have completed the delivery of both shipments and been paid handsomely for it.

Despite the rain, Li Lan felt a giddy excitement rising in her stomach. She was close to pulling off an audacious plan and, with it, opening up what could prove to be a whole new income stream for her family's company. Until now, ivory had been the most profitable source of revenue for the Wang Trading Company, but it was small change compared to the potential that this new relationship could deliver.

She felt her phone buzz and she frowned at the screen before she answered, 'Yes, brother?'

'Why have you not followed my instructions?' It was Oo, and he sounded angry.

Li Lan had anticipated her brother's mood and she silently reminded herself to remain calm. Her brother needed to feel like he was in control. He had always been fragile that way. Even when they had played together as children, whether racing their old bone-shaker bicycles along the flat white sands or playing draughts under the shade of the palm trees, Oo would cry every time he lost. Li Lan's mother would scold Li Lan for upsetting her brother until, finally, Li Lan learned that winning wasn't worth the hassle, the juice not worth the squeeze. Even in Zanzibar, the son in a Chinese family came first and the daughter was a poor second.

'Sorry, brother,' she said with as much deference as she could muster. 'We had a few problems with Kenyan customs.'

'What sort of problems?' Oo replied curtly.

'Nothing that I couldn't handle,' Li Lan replied. 'But the cargo will be delayed by a few days.'

'A few days?!' Oo sounded like he was going to explode. 'The customer will be angry, sister. I will lose my face.'

Li Lan understood. Losing face was the worst thing that a Chinese man could ever suffer. Even more so in front of a client. She smirked as she imagined how Oo would have to apologise and take the criticism in order to maintain the relationship. The thought of it amused her, but she didn't let it show.

'I am so sorry, brother,' she said as seriously as she could. 'I suggest you tell the client that next time; you will come to Africa to oversee the shipment personally.'

'Come to Africa?!' Oo repeated.

Li Lan was fighting the urge to laugh. She knew how much her brother hated Africa. He was so comfortable in his new life in Hong Kong, that he could hardly bear coming home for Chinese New Year, let alone return for work.

'Just make sure there are no more delays,' he barked.

Li Lan saw the glare of headlights in the distance. It was Kassim returning, which meant that it was time to get back to work. Real work, making real money, not this pathetic nonsense that her sibling did to feed his flimsy ego.

'I have to go now, brother,' she said before ending the call abruptly.

The headlights came closer and Li Lan opened the WellBox gates, locking them again once the truck was safely inside. She walked around to the front of the vehicle and was surprised to see Al-Haq step down from the passenger side. She had expected Kassim to return with the girls alone.

'You are ready?' he asked.

'Of course,' she replied.

'You will make one more slight alteration,' he said.

Li Lan remained unmoved, her face giving nothing away. She watched Kassim get out of the truck, trying to read his expression. He was shaking his head with a look of concern.

'Two extra people,' he said.

Li Lan considered this. She and Aku had made their calculations very carefully. That was what she did. She planned and delivered. There wasn't any margin for error. The space inside the container was just enough to keep ten people alive for ten days. Another two people would compromise the survival of the others. But usually, where there was a problem, there was an extra buck to be made. She looked to Al-Haq and nodded confidently.

'I'm sure we can accommodate whatever it is,' she said. She pointed to the rear of the truck. 'Can I …?'

Al-Haq motioned for Kassim to open the back of his truck so that Li Lan could see what she was dealing with. The door rolled up and she saw what was inside. Whatever she'd been anticipating, this wasn't it.

Al-Haq seemed to enjoy the look of surprise on Li Lan's face. He would admit that the Chinese woman had dealt with everything very professionally up until this point, but surely now he'd managed to challenge her. Li Lan simply looked back at him, non-plussed.

'Okay. But more money,' she said, calmly.

'Okay?' he said, mimicking her accent.

'Yes,' she repeated. Li Lan was not laughing. 'Double money. Okay?'

The smile fell from Al-Haq's face. He was starting to resent this woman. She cared about money more than anyone he'd ever met. Money and nothing else. He wished he'd never involved himself in this whole sorry enterprise.

'Sure,' he said. 'Double money.'

Li Lan nodded and looked back inside the truck. This was a surprise. It was a big surprise. But it was nothing she couldn't deal with. Every problem had a solution. Every solution had a price. This was what she lived for. She would turn this problem into an opportunity and the client would be happy. They would see that Wang Trading Company was a company they could trust to get the job done.

THIRTY-NINE

Mogadishu, Somalia

Matt Mason returned to the meeting room in the Sahafi and slumped down into a chair, tossing his mobile phone onto the desk. He filled his cheeks and let out a long sigh, raising his eyebrows in the direction of Redford. The American CIA agent knew that the call he'd just made wouldn't have been easy, so she said nothing. Better to let him speak when he was ready. It didn't take long.

'Well that was shit,' Mason said.

'Wanna talk about it?' she asked.

'We haven't spoken in months.' Mason rubbed his eyes. He looked exhausted. 'She'd been trying to call me for days and then when she finally gets through, I already know. So now, she's doubly fucked off with me.'

'Sounds rough,' Redford said.

'And of course, it's all my fault.'

Redford had never met Kerry Mason, but even from what little Mason had told her, she knew that the woman back in England was a devoted mother. The news that Mason had just shared with her would have turned her world upside down and it wasn't surprising to hear that she had lashed out at the only other person who could understand her pain – Mason himself.

'She doesn't mean that,' Redford said, trying to sound supportive.

'Yes she does,' Mason replied. 'She said unless I find Jo and bring her home, it'll stay my fault too.'

Redford didn't argue. Matt Mason was a man of action. In Yemen, she'd seen with her own eyes what he was capable of when his mind was focused. Right now, it suited her for him to blame himself. Mason wanted his daughter back even more than she wanted Chow, and he was going to do everything necessary to make that happen. There was no better tool to get the job done than Matt Mason.

'You'd better listen to this,' she said, handing Mason a set of headphones.

She booted up a recording that had come through from Langley that morning. Since they'd got a positive ID on Al-Haq, Langley had upped the surveillance on him. With access to his phone numbers, they'd been able to engage Pegasus, the Israeli-designed spyware that enabled them to activate his devices without the need for him to even switch them on. With Pegasus in play, they'd been able to listen in on Al-Haq for the last twelve hours. The analysts in Virginia had distilled the key contents into a single audio file and sent it through to her in Mogadishu.

She scrubbed through the audio file, looking for a conversation that she'd heard moments before.

'Here,' she said, 'this is it.'

Mason squeezed the headphones tighter to his ears. The sound quality was bad, muffled and covered with interference. Al-Haq's phone was bouncing around in his pocket and there was a deep mechanical hum that sounded to Mason like a diesel engine. Suddenly, the vehicle stopped and Mason heard the sound of a door slamming. It sounded heavier than a car. Possibly a truck.

The conversation that followed was a little clearer. Al-Haq seemed to be delivering something.

'Sounds like the port,' Mason said. Redford nodded in agreement.

They listened together to the discussion that followed. Al-Haq had delivered extra cargo and was prepared to double his fee if the courier would take it. After that, the recording became muffled, but they could intermittently make out the courier giving instructions and the sound of people moving around. Finally, the truck engine started up again and drove away again with Al-Haq inside.

'It's got to be them,' Mason said. 'Do you have a location?'

'Working on that,' Redford said, typing furiously on her keyboard as Mason rewound the file to the start of the conversation again and hit play.

'Listen to this again,' he said. 'Why's he taking the piss out of her?'

Redford listened again to Al-Haq mimicking the woman. They were speaking in English. Both were heavily accented, but while Al-Haq had a strong Middle Eastern twang, the woman sounded distinctly different.

'Is she Asian?' Redford said, thinking out loud.

As Mason listened again, Redford's attention returned to her screen. She'd received a new message from Langley.

'We got a location. Mombasa. Here ...' She turned the screen so that Mason could see. 'A container repair workshop at the docks. The property is registered to a company out of Nairobi called WellBox.'

'Eh?' Mason sounded incredulous.

He looked at the screen and thought again about what Redford had just said. Al-Haq was meeting a woman, an Asian woman, at the WellBox workshops in Mombasa. The same place that he'd been to three days ago.

'I know who she is,' he said.

Redford looked baffled. 'How could you possibly—'

'Look up Wang Trading Company, Pemba,' he said, pushing the laptop back to Redford.

She looked baffled, but she did as he said, tapping on the keyboard again as Mason explained.

'They're officially a seafood company, but they're smuggling ivory out of Mozambique. I followed them as far as Mombasa. There was an Indian bloke getting boxes on and off ships for a Chinese bird running it. I was waiting for them to load up again so I could follow it, but then ... this happened.'

'Not only smuggling ivory by the sounds of it,' Redford said, still typing furiously. She instantly regretted it.

'He said people,' Mason said, rubbing his eyes with the back his hand. 'He means Joanna, doesn't he?'

For once, Redford didn't know how to respond. There was a growing underground trade in human trafficking from the region, specifically the selling of young women from Africa to the Gulf States to work in big houses as domestic slaves. She could see Mason's mind running through the angles, wondering if Al-Haq had seen a way to make some extra cash by throwing Joanna in with his latest shipment. He stood up sharply and began pacing around the room. If she didn't know him better, Redford would have said he actually looked frightened.

She returned her attention to the screen and found what she was looking for. 'The company is listed out of Tanzania,' she said. 'It's a family business with a head office in Pemba just like you said, and another in Hong Kong. The African side of the business is run by Wang Li Lan. This is the most recent picture we have.'

She turned the screen to show Mason and he instantly recognised the woman in the picture as the same woman he had seen with Aku. If she and Aku had been preparing the container in the workshop to smuggle girls out of Mombasa for Al-Haq, then it made perfect sense for them to add Chow to the shipment, and smuggle him along with the girls to the Middle East. The Iranians could send him on to China from there.

'We have to get to Mombasa,' Mason said, already gathering his things.

'We need a little more to go on than this, Mace,' Redford replied. 'If they're running contraband out of Mombasa, then there's a million ways they can do it. A million containers they could use. We're still looking for a needle in a haystack.'

Mason opened his phone and drew up an image of the container that he'd seen in the WellBox workshop. He showed it to Redford. 'We've got the serial number of the needle.'

Redford shook her head in disbelief. Matt Mason was an endless source of wonder. There'd be time for questions later, about just how he'd come to know the exact container number for the one box out of the hundreds of thousands that were currently in Mombasa port. But all that could wait. She was already on the phone, calling for the chopper to get ready. In less than an hour, they would be airborne and an hour after that, they'd be in Mombasa. Until then, she prayed that Joanna Mason and Wei Lun Chow were still there.

PART FIVE

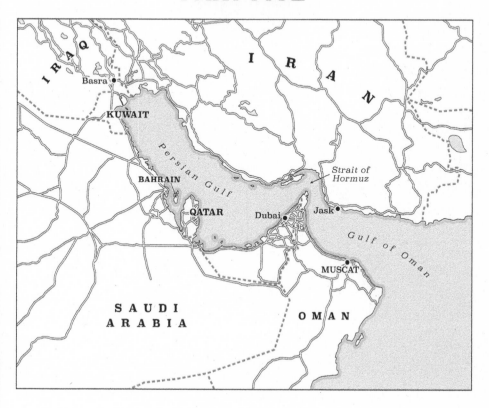

FORTY

Mombasa, Kenya

There are no tourists in the Mwangeka bar. Ever. Sailors? Always. Prostitutes? Usually. Drug dealers? Sometimes. But never tourists. Its corrugated iron roof has been fixed up so many times that the place looks like it might fall down any second. The temperature inside the bar rarely drops below forty degrees and every afternoon, the bar's owner, Jeffery, a wiry, old third-generation Kenyan-Indian, has to slop out the dead cockroaches and rat droppings onto the street. The music inside the Mwangeka is hardly inviting either. Jeffery's playlist consists of a booming cacophony of Kalpop and Swahilian soukous, turned up to a volume that would make even the hardest German techno aficionados blanch. No. No tourist would ever dare walk through the door of the Mwangeka, which is exactly why Dahir Jama, the huge seaman from Somaliland liked it. At Jeffery's bar, he was left in peace to drink rum until it was time to go back to sea.

Dahir had been in port now for three days and had lost count of how many bottles he'd put away. Fortunately, Jeffery's prices were the cheapest in town. All his liquor was smuggled contraband, which meant that Dahir's pay packet went a long way. As Jeffery refreshed his glass, Dahir caught a look of total surprise on the barman's face. This was unusual. Jeffery was not a man who was easily surprised. But as Dahir turned to see what Jeffery was looking at, he was just as shocked.

'You're not an easy man to find,' Matt Mason shouted over the music as he strode to the bar, flanked by a tall good-looking woman with long red hair. Mason threw a one-hundred-dollar bill onto the bar. 'Does that cover him?'

Jeffery slid the hundred dollars into his pocket. His eyes remained fixed on the two strangers as he laid fresh shot glasses down on the bar for them.

'You're alright,' Mason said. 'We're not staying.'

After they'd landed in Mombasa, Mason and Redford had gone straight to the WellBox offices and demanded they be given access to the workshop where Mason had seen the Wang container. They found nothing. The container was gone and according to the WellBox administrator, the container had never been there in the first place. The guy swore blind that he'd never heard of the Wang Trading Company or an Indian seaman called Aku. Mason had immediately started looking for Dahir.

'Matt Mason,' Dahir said, slightly slurring. 'What brings you to this wonderful establishment? You missed me?'

'I need your help, mate.'

'Why so serious, Mace? You look like you could use a drink.' Dahir waved for Jeffery to pour, despite Mason's protestations. He almost fell off his stool from the effort.

'My daughter's missing,' Mason said, steadying the Somali-lander with his arm. 'I think you might know where she is. Where's Aku? Has he been reposted?'

Dahir blinked and shook his head, trying to take in what Mason had just said through the rum-induced haze. Mason had talked about his daughter back on board the *Sirrah*. *Now she was missing?* He shook his head and desperately tried to sober up. He had to think. *Where was Aku?* The question took a second to settle in his brain before he could process it. Finally, he had it. *Aku. Where was Aku?*

Dahir and Aku were part of a rota of seamen that some-times worked together, sometimes not. It depended on what each ship needed. While it wasn't unusual to work with the same people on a couple of jobs in a row, it was just as common to not see someone you'd worked with for another year or two. So while Dahir had been rota-ed onto a ship to Europe the following day, he wasn't surprised that Aku's name wasn't on the manifest.

'He's not on my next ship,' Dahir said.

'That's not what he asked,' Redford said, her tone was curt. 'What ship *is* he on?'

Dahir bristled a little. 'Okay, ma'am,' he said in his deep voice. He tapped his forehead twice with his finger to help himself to focus again. 'There was another ship left two days ago,' he said, banging his hand on the bar, fighting the effects of the rum, forcing his brain to remember. 'The *Neptune*!' he said triumphantly and punched himself in the chest. *Thank God. That was it. The* Neptune. *Where was the* Neptune *going?*

Dahir delved again into his memory. It felt like swim-ming through honey, looking for something buried in the bottom of the pot but, again, he found what he was looking for. 'For Dubai. Dubai. Dubai. Yes, Dubai,' he said, swaying again in his stool. 'If Aku isn't in Mombasa, my friend, then he's on the *Neptune* for Dubai.'

Mason put a hand on Dahir's shoulder. He knew what it was like to be that shit-faced and so he passed no judgement. Like so many lads who'd been to war, Dahir had found his own way of getting through life. He'd fought for his country and he deserved respect, whatever troubles he had now.

'I'm sorry for your daughter, Mace. I hope you can find her,' Dahir said and Mason knew that he meant it.

Some people might think it takes a lifetime to build the kind of friendship where you trust someone with your life. But soldiers like Dahir and Mason knew different. On the battlefield, you put your life in the hands of a man you'd only met months or even weeks before. To put your life in the hands of a man you hardly knew in the name of a common cause, that was how men made bonds that lasted a lifetime. The connection that Mason and Dahir had made in the short time they'd known each other felt more valuable to Mason than some of the relationships he'd had with people he'd known his whole life.

Mason put his hand on Dahir's shoulder again and searched in his eyes until he found a connection there. Dahir was struggling to focus, still swaying a little, but Mason could see that he knew what Mason was feeling. The big man had helped him more than once and one day he hoped that he could repay that debt. A man who helps someone in need is a man who can hold his head high and Mason would forever respect the big guy from Somaliland.

'Let's go,' Redford said.

Mason put another hundred on the bar and locked eyes with Jeffery. 'Make sure he gets home,' he said.

He gave Dahir a final deferent bow before he followed Redford out of the Mwangeka. As they sprinted down the road to their vehicle, Redford was already on the phone, calling Langley to prepare the chopper and divert the team to start searching for the whereabouts of a ship called the *Neptune*.

FORTY-ONE

Gulf of Oman

Aku enjoyed standing on the bridge during the hours before dawn. He liked the way the super-container ate up the dark ocean below at over twenty-five knots. The *Neptune* was one of the fastest of the new breed of neo-Panamax ships, so-called because they were too big to fit through the Panama Canal's old locks. With a beam of forty-three metres and a length of over three hundred, the *Neptune* could transport over twelve thousand boxes to the other side of the world. The ship was equipped with the latest AI-driven navigation system which far exceeded the limitations of older ships like the *Sirrah*. Even navigating in crowded waterways or operating in low-visibility conditions, the ship could maintain top speeds with zero risk of collision. In short, the *Neptune* was superior to the *Sirrah* in every possible way.

Off the port bow, Aku saw the lights of Muscat. The Omani capital's high-rises, mosques, and minarets stretched up into the desert sky, lighting up the peninsula like a fun park. It was for moments just like this that he preferred working the night shift. He volunteered for it whenever it was available and his peers were usually happy to oblige him. Most of them favoured working office hours. Especially the officers. Another perk of working the graveyard shift was that, unless there was an emergency, you had the bridge all to yourself.

The diminutive Indian took off his glasses and rubbed his eyes wearily. He was heavy with fatigue. The last-minute change of plans had meant that he'd worked non-stop for the last couple of days to ensure that the Chinese woman's cargo was loaded on board but wasn't logged onto the system. The Chinese woman was a hard taskmaster and she expected the best. All the time. The one saving grace was that she paid well, much better than the shipping company ever did anyhow. This latest job would net him more than three months' salary. He put his glasses back on and imagined himself sleeping in a big, soft bed in a fine hotel when this was all over.

The screen on the bridge showed the *Neptune*'s current location. The green dot was tracing the route that had been planned out by the ship's captain before he retired for the night. The automatic navigation system was now guiding them towards Dubai just as it had been programmed to do. They would shortly enter the Hormuz Strait, the narrowest part of the Gulf, where the distance from UAE to Iran was only forty miles, and from there, the port in Dubai was less than three hours away.

But the position of the green dot on the screen was not showing the actual location of the *Neptune* at all. The true location was nearly twenty kilometres away from where the navigation system said it was, and Aku was the only person on board the *Neptune* who knew it.

The reason for the discrepancy was that thirty minutes earlier, the *Neptune's* state of the art navigation system had received a series of counterfeit satellite automatic identification signals containing bogus GPS data. The signals had effectively spoofed the *Neptune's* computers into believing that the ship's coordinates were somewhere that the ship was not.

This communications failure had been meticulously planned. The counterfeit signals had been originated from the Islamic Revolutionary Guard Corps Navy's control room in Jask. While Aku stood silently watching the screen on the deck of the *Neptune*, General Haddadi, back on the shore, was watching another screen in the Jask control room. Only Haddadi's screen showed the actual location of the *Neptune*. It showed that the ship had veered from its intended course and was bound not for Dubai, but rather for Iran. In less than twenty minutes, the *Neptune* would enter Iranian sovereign territory.

There is no single legal definition of what constitutes 'international waters'. The term has come to be understood as a result of various conventions agreed upon between countries over time. The most fundamental protocol, the United Nations Convention on the Law of the Sea, holds that a country has a sovereign right to waters within two hundred nautical miles of its coast. However, in parts of the world, such as the Persian Gulf, where the sea is much narrower, the eight countries around its coast have had to fight over who controls what. It has taken many centuries and dozens of agreements over the years to finally settle the boundaries so that now an elaborate mesh of treaties defines every last drop of the body of water at the heart of the world's most incendiary region. Woe betide anyone who even 'accidentally' strays where they are not supposed to go.

He checked the screen again. According to the ship's navigation system, they should now be one hundred kilometres from the Oman coast, comfortably within the internationally agreed shipping lanes, but Aku could see from the lights off the port bow that Oman was more like one hundred and twenty kilometres away. The *Neptune* was edging steadily towards Iran so that by the time the sun came up, and the morning shift took over the bridge, it would be too late to stop the container ship from breaking the treaty between Oman and Iran. Iran would be well within its rights to launch a full military engagement.

Aku had no idea who it was in Iran that was now covertly controlling the ship from the other side of the Strait. He didn't care. His job was simply to ensure that the alarm wasn't raised. When the time came, he would then reveal the location of the Chinese woman's container to whoever came to collect its cargo.

Aku realised that he had never met an Iranian. He had grown up far away from Iran, two thousand miles away, across the Arabian Sea. He had never given the country much thought. He wondered for a moment what Iranian women might be like, but thought, on balance, they wouldn't be for him. In any case, his brothers would kill him before they let him marry a Muslim. Things were like that back in Mangalore. People weren't so open-minded as they were in other countries.

Three blue dots appeared on the screen just off the coast of Iran. Then four more. Pretty soon there were twelve blue dots. Aku checked their speed and bearing against those of the *Neptune*. They were heading towards each other at a combined speed of nearly eighty knots. At their current bearing, they would reach the ship in just under an hour, exactly when his shift was due to end. He let out a grunt of satisfaction. The Chinese woman would be pleased. Everything was going exactly to plan.

FORTY-TWO

Gulf of Oman

Joanna Mason felt her stomach turn over on itself again, but again she fought the urge to vomit. She had to hang onto every last drop of moisture in her body because the water was already running low and she had no idea how much longer they would be locked up. Her best guess was that they had been rocking back and forth in the dark for two days, but she could easily have been out by a day or two. What she *was* sure about was that not everyone inside was going to survive the time they had left.

Several of the captives inside the secret compartment of the forty-foot container weren't coping with seasickness as well as Joanna. Frequently, someone scrambled without warning, groping for the bucket in the darkness. Joanna listened to them puking uncontrollably, empty stomachs retching over and over, adding to the dehydration, piling on more stress to already tired and malnourished bodies.

The smell inside the space was sharp with the ammonia-laced odours of all forms of human waste. They had agreed between themselves to save the capacity inside the buckets for vomit and stools, and to urinate directly onto the floor.

There were enough cracks in the steel to let the puddles seep away slowly, but sometimes, if a few people went at the same time, the piss built up and soaked their clothes.

Joanna tried to block out the near-constant sobs and groans and prayers of the others by focusing on the white noise of the ship's diesel engines, rolling over and over, carrying the ship across the ocean to where she knew not. She knew that container ships did twenty-five knots, so by her reasoning, depending on their bearing, they were either approaching the Suez Canal or were halfway to the Middle East. She figured the latter was more likely.

The girl who occupied the space next to her was Maria, a sixteen-year-old girl with soft hands and an even softer voice who spoke just enough English to explain to Joanna how she had been kidnapped by the jihadists from her village in the coastal region of northern Mozambique. Maria described the terror that had forced her to flee from the men who had come at night. She had seen murder and rape along the way and she worried about the impending war that would soon follow. Joanna had tried to get a sense from her of whether the jihadists had operated as far north as where her father was working, but Maria didn't know. Joanna could only pray that her dad was either far enough from the fighting to be safe or, if not, that he had managed to escape in time.

They had no space and resources were minimal, but Joanna tried to impress upon everyone that if they worked together, then their chances of survival would be far greater. She knew that it was vital to build a sense of camaraderie between themselves, to make everyone see that the only hope of getting out alive was to work together, to share what little they had and protect the most vulnerable among them. But she had met with some resistance. Not everyone inside the tight, dark space agreed with her strategy. A hierarchy had already developed, and some had begun bickering and fighting in their own languages.

The longer they remained in the darkness, the greater the fear and confusion they felt. The heat didn't help to calm them any. The temperature outside was over forty degrees in the day. Inside, it was compounded by the heat from the engines and the lack of air. Other than the gaps in the corroded metal, the only ventilation came from two small air holes which Aku had drilled into the roof. He'd erred on the side of caution, not wanting to draw attention, and the result was that they simply weren't large enough for purpose.

Sleep was hard to come by. As she had done several times before, Joanna felt herself jolt upright and realised that she must have dropped off but for how long was anyone's guess. There was no judging time when you were locked in the dark without room to move or air to breathe. She reached out instinctively for Maria's hand. The younger Mozambique girl had inadvertently become Joanna's comfort and support. The touch of a friend was enough to keep the darkest thoughts of what their future held at bay. For a while at least.

Joanna instantly felt that something was not right. She fumbled in the dark until she could feel Maria's hand, but the flesh was still and lifeless. When she pressed her own hand into Maria's fingers, they offered nothing in return.

For a moment, she wondered if she were merely sleeping, but her gut told her that it was something else. Still, she shook her gently and called out her name.

'Maria,' she said gently. 'Maria.'

'She dead,' a voice said in the darkness.

'No,' Joanna said, shaking Maria more now. 'No she's not. Maria. Maria.'

Joanna cradled Maria's head in her lap and slapped her gently on the cheek, repeating her name as she fumbled for a cup of water and forced the warm liquid between Maria's chapped, dry lips. At once, she felt Maria move. Only slightly but unmistakably moving her head.

'Yes, drink. Drink it slowly,' Joanna said, steadying the cup. Feeling the whole while with her own fingers to ensure that the water was directed into Maria's mouth.

Joanna let out a deep sigh of relief. Maria was alive. Just. For now. She didn't know for how much longer. She put down the cup and clenched her fists tightly, allowing herself to scream out in frustration. She'd had enough, she didn't know how much longer she could face it, face being incarcerated, not knowing her future, watching people die around her. This was not supposed to happen to people like her and she wanted it to stop.

'Thank you,' Maria's voice sounded weak, barely more than a whisper.

Joanna again reached for the young woman's hand. This time she felt Maria's fingers squeeze around her own. Her grip was weak as a baby, but Joanna held onto it for dear life. The two women from opposite lives, brought together by cruel destiny, held onto each other in the dark, knowing that, for now, all they had was the little strength that remained within them until this living hell came to an end one way or another. Until that moment came, they would do everything they could to survive because, in the end, that was all they could do.

FORTY-THREE

Gulf of Oman

The air rushed hard and fast around Matt Mason's ears so that he could hear nothing else. It felt good to block everything out for a few moments. The pilot was keeping the helicopter low, skimming over the dark waves at one hundred and thirty knots, careful to remain below the scope of any radar that might spot them. As they weaved in and out of the shipping lanes, Mason saw the lights from the decks of container ships and tankers hauling cargo back and forth from east to west. Somewhere down there, his daughter was locked inside a shipping container and he didn't want her to have to be there for a second longer than she had to be.

No matter how hard he tried to keep it out, the conversation he'd had with his ex-wife, kept replaying in his head. Kerry had been angry, taken it out on him, blamed him for everything that had happened. She'd made him promise that he'd come home with their daughter, whatever the cost. He knew he owed her that. He hadn't been able to keep the last promise he'd made to her, the one at the altar eighteen years ago, but he was going to keep this one.

Next to him, Agent Redford sat silently, buckled into her seat, eyes focused intently on the pilot's console. Using live Marine Traffic software, one of the screens lit up the inside of the chopper, mapping the location of every vessel on the sea below. Tankers were marked by red dots, cargo vessels were green, fishing boats orange, while special craft like naval vessels were blue. Each one appeared to be following along behind the other in lines of clear traffic like a Californian freeway in the rush hour. As the lane from Africa to the Middle East crossed the lane from Asia to the Red Sea, the traffic crossed, like a busy intersection where the lights were out. To the layman it looked like chaos, but every captain on board those ships knew exactly how to pass safely without a collision.

The helicopter pilot, Frankie Ford, a twenty-eight-year-old Nebraskan with a heart of gold and a chin as broad as a coal shovel, pulled back on the controls, edging them a little higher to avoid the melee. On the other side of the crossing, Frankie dropped in low again, banking left a little, overtaking the traffic skirting around the Omani coast. A couple of minutes later, he turned north into the Gulf of Oman and Redford blew out a breath in exasperation. The volume of ships had suddenly increased exponentially and there were now hundreds of vessels packed into the shipping lane that bisected the Gulf. The screen was filled with blue, red, and green dots. One of them was the *Neptune*.

'You good?' Redford called out into her comms.

Mason pulled himself back inside and nodded. Redford had commandeered the Air Branch chopper to fly down from Lemonnier. The Air Branch is the aviation wing of the CIA's Special Activities Division and their role is to fly missions in support of CIA operations. Air Branch pilots, like Frankie, were some of the best in the world and the craft that he'd brought to Mombasa wasn't bad either – a Mil Mi-17, Russian-made military helicopter, kitted out to look like a civilian transporter.

The CIA avoided using anything that might be associated with the US military. The Mil Mi-17 was perfect for covert operations as nobody would suspect them of flying a Russian aircraft. But as soon as Mason jumped on board, he'd been in no doubt that he was on an American, not a Russian, chopper. You could tell from the range of kit it was carrying. The Yanks could always be relied upon to turn up with all the latest toys. As well as a suppressed HK 416 assault rifle with an Aimpoint red-dot sight and weapon light, he'd holstered a 9mm Glock pistol.

'Agent, we have a problem,' Frankie was saying from the front.

Redford and Mason looked up to see what he was talking about. The pilot's finger was pointing to a large green dot on the screen.

'See that?' Frankie said before he looked up across the water. 'That green dot there? That is supposed to be the *Neptune*.'

'Supposed to be?' Redford replied.

'Yeah, because it ain't there.'

Frankie was staring into an empty stretch of sea that lay between two tankers. The screen showed the two tankers, two red dots, but between them, a green dot depicted what was supposed to be the *Neptune*. But either the *Neptune* was invisible or the GPS was wrong.

'What do you mean it's not there?' Mason barked. 'Where the fuck is it?'

The pilot's eyes darted around the screen until he saw something even more unusual. 'Okay, you see those?'

His finger fell on a group of a dozen blue dots, moving fast across the Gulf.

'What are they?' Mason asked.

'They launched from Jask, Iran, forty-four minutes ago,' Frankie replied. 'And from the speed, I'd guess they're military.'

Redford looked at Mason. They were both thinking the same thing. The *Neptune* disappearing at the same time as Iran launched a fleet of naval vessels into the Gulf was too much of a coincidence.

'Fly at them,' Redford ordered.

'What?!' Frankie was shaking his head. 'They are still easily within Iranian waters, Agent.'

'Just do what she told you,' Mason said in a tone of voice that didn't leave room for disagreement.

Mason felt something change within himself. He'd found a kind of peace at the Niassa reserve, a sense of connection to the place and the animals. That feeling was genuine. He hadn't made it up. But what he was feeling now was something else. It was older, more instinctive, sensations that had been buried were coming back to the surface. He'd been a soldier for all of his life and he couldn't deny that. His body was telling him that he wasn't done yet. He'd been trained for moments like this.

It was what he lived for, what made him feel himself, where he truly found peace.

'What's that?' Redford was leaning forward and pointing out of the window to the light from a ship on the horizon.

The pilot looked down at the screen and back again to where Redford was pointing. His face was contorted in confusion and bewilderment as though he were seeing a ghost. He did another double-take.

'I don't know,' he said. 'I mean it's there but it's not there.'

'It's the *Neptune*,' Redford replied. 'The Iranians must be spoofing it.'

Mason nodded his agreement. He'd heard of this before but never seen it with his own eyes. He'd always assumed that the systems in place were too good to be fooled, but right in front of him was one hundred and fifty thousand tonnes of hard evidence to the contrary. That was a container ship and there was no point denying it.

'Those military go-fast boats are twelve minutes out,' Frankie said as he traced his finger across the line of a dozen blue dots racing towards the true location of the *Neptune*.

'What's our ETA?' Mason asked.

'Two minutes, a bit less.'

'That gives you ten minutes, Mace,' Redford said, setting her watch.

'Plenty of time,' Mason replied.

He looked down, out of the helicopter. They were less than five hundred metres from the *Neptune*. He had to think fast.

'Come around the port side, Frankie. And stay low,' he said. 'I'll fast rope, low-level drop, blindside of the threat.'

Frankie gave a thumbs-up as Redford leapt to her feet to prepare the fast rope.

'You create a diversion with the heli. Mayday with smokescreen.' He passed Redford two AN–M8 HC smoke grenades from the kit-box. 'Smoke grenades. 12 o'clock of the enemy.'

Redford took the grenades from him. 'Copy that,' she said.

Frankie brought the chopper in around the *Neptune's* stern, careful to keep the ship between them and the go-fast boats. As he flanked the port side, he raised the nose again until they were hovering twenty-five metres above the deck. Mason gave him a thumbs up.

'When you see I'm on, get out there,' Mason pointed forward before looking back and forth between Redford and the pilot. 'As low as you can. Use whatever you need. Like you're in distress. Understood?'

Redford nodded. She knew what he was asking her to do. Mimicking a mayday distress was a technique that she'd learned during her training at the Farm. A chopper in trouble could be a good distraction.

'It might buy us a couple of minutes,' Mason said.

The pilot gave a thumbs up before Mason turned back to Redford. 'Just try not to fall out this time.'

Redford managed a wry smile. She'd never forget how Mason had saved her life, stopped her from falling out of a chopper in Yemen, but she still marvelled at how he always seemed to have a smart-aleck remark to make at the most inappropriate times. It was a very Matt Mason trait.

'I think, I'll be fine,' she said, witheringly.

'Right,' Mason held up the radio before he secured it. 'I'll radio for SPIE rope water extraction from blindside. Ten to Twelve mins. Engage if necessary. Questions?'

Redford shook her head. It was a bold plan, but in the circumstances, she agreed with every part of what he'd said.

'Right then, let's do this,' Mason said, before he threw himself out of the helicopter.

Redford peered over the side and watched Mason slide faster than she'd ever seen a man fast-rope before, landing onto the *Neptune*'s deck like a cat. As soon as Mason's feet made contact, he released the rope and she signalled for the pilot to pull out.

'Get us out of here, Frankie,' she shouted into her comms. 'Let's see if we can't slow those boats a little.'

FORTY-FOUR

Jask, Iran

Militarised speed boats have been at the core of the Iranian naval strategy for the last fifteen years. General Haddadi was personally responsible for putting in place a chain of secretive deals that brought one British-designed BladeRunner 51 speedboat, the fastest boat in the world, to Iran via a South African intermediary. Thanks to some very clever reverse engineering by IRGCN's top people, Iran began producing a near clone, the Seraj-1, a boat capable of doing over eighty knots while carrying a 12-tube, 107mm Chinese-made rocket launcher and a Russian DShK heavy machine gun. Haddadi's cunning plan had created a rapid response fleet capable of countering the USA's massive warships at a fraction of the cost.

Haddadi's strategy was to strategically launch spontaneous attacks with large numbers of the fast-boats against coalition military or commercial vessels as needed. Launching from the shore like a swarm of wasps attacking a larger foe, the fast-boats could swiftly outmanoeuvre larger military ships and overwhelm their defensive targeting systems. Iran's fast-boat fleet, combined with the new offshore-based missile capabilities Haddadi was constructing at Jask, meant that soon they would have effective control over the Hormuz Strait.

This morning, Haddadi had sent a message to his Chinese counterpart reassuring him that the request he had made at their meeting last week would soon be honoured. The Chinese minister had been very complimentary about the general's efficiency, which Haddadi had lapped up with pride. He had reminded Secretary Xi, that Iran was not only a friend to China but a friend that could be relied upon to deliver when needed. It boded well for their ongoing relationship together as they expanded the Iranian naval base with Chinese money and weapons.

Standing in the base's new control room, the general looked at the screen on the wall, watching a dozen blue dots, one for each fast-boat, racing across the sea. They would intercept the *Neptune* in less than eight minutes, whereupon they would collect the valuable cargo and return it to port. However, as the general watched their progress, he was troubled by something else he saw on the screen. It was an airborne vessel, a helicopter, that was moving even faster than the go-fast boats and heading in their direction.

On board the chopper, Frankie was pushing the Mil Mi-17's capabilities to their absolute limit. Helicopters are designed to fly at steady altitudes, rising and falling gradually with subtle alterations to their controls, but, right now, the Nebraskan CIA-trained pilot was flipping the control stick around like it was a timber rattlesnake. The chopper climbed and dropped, heading at the approaching fast-boats, as though it was completely out of control, which was exactly the effect that Frankie was going for.

In the back, Redford was being thrown around like a rag-doll. She managed to grab a hold of the back of Frankie's seat with one hand while she looped a pair of smoke grenades firmly around one of the passenger harnesses. She discharged them both and tossed them out of the cabin door. The grenades began to pump out thick white smoke, which caught in the draft of Frankie's erratic flight path and engulfed the whole craft in a white fog. The combination of smoke and loss of altitude made the Mil Mi-17 look like a Russian transporter that was in the midst of a catastrophic emergency.

Upfront, Frankie locked eyes on the lead fast-boat. At their combined speeds, the space between them was getting swallowed up at nearly two hundred and fifty miles per hour and every time that Frankie nudged the controls forward another inch, the Mil Mi-17's altitude dropped lower and lower so that its trajectory put them on an imminent collision course.

Redford crawled her way forward and dragged herself up behind Frankie's shoulder. The distance between the chopper and the lead fast-boat had dropped to less than a hundred feet, and the G-force of the dive was beginning to make her head shudder like a washer in a spin cycle. She couldn't keep her eyes open from the vibrations, so she held her breath and squeezed tight on the pilot's shoulder, her body instinctively bracing itself for catastrophic impact. This was madness.

'Pull up!' she screamed.

'One more second,' Frankie shouted over the whistle of the engines, maxed out to capacity.

He blew out his cheeks as he continued to dive, racing headlong into a life or death game of chicken with the IRG naval vessel. Through the smoke, he tried to make out the face of the guy driving the boat, but the fog now was too thick. Frankie closed his eyes and said a prayer. He could hear Redford still screaming to pull up again, but he knew it was too late now. He had no idea if what they were doing was going to work or not, but he knew that if that guy down there in the boat didn't pull out in the next four seconds, then there was going to be parts of helicopter and speedboat scattered all over the Persian Gulf.

A second later he opened his eyes again and pulled back hard on the controls. The lead fast-boat had already lurched to starboard, turning back on itself in a wide circle. The rest of the boats following behind did the same, like a flock of birds trailing their leader. The whole fleet, a dozen boats, span around as Frankie brought the Mil Mi-17 back onto the level and then climbed to a safe altitude.

'You crazy bastard,' Redford said. She was laughing nervously, almost hysterically, from the rush of relief that she was feeling.

'It worked, didn't it?' Frankie said.

He pulled the chopper up and banked left. They both looked down, out of the starboard window of the cockpit, to where the fast-boats were completing their wide turn. The smoke that the grenades had thrown out across the sea was beginning to clear and Redford could see that the game was up. The guys on the boats down there would have worked out by now that their mayday distress swan dive was nothing more than a ruse.

Indeed, a most irate general back in the control room at Jask was already radioing to the senior IRGCN officer on board the boats to order him to turn back for the *Neptune* at once, stating very clearly what the consequences would be for the officer concerned if he didn't return to his original course immediately.

Redford watched the fleet of fast-boats regroup and ramp up again to full speed. At most, they had bought Mason an extra four or five minutes on the *Neptune*. As Frankie turned the chopper around and headed back to the ship, she could only hope that was long enough.

FORTY-FIVE

Gulf of Oman

The second that Matt Mason's boots landed on the upper deck of the *Neptune*, the hairs on the back of his neck stood up on end. He knew that feeling well. He was adrenalised and it felt pretty damn good. Good to be back on task, good to be in the heat of the action, even better to know that soon he'd have his precious daughter back in his arms. Once that part of the job was done, and he'd got Jo to safety, then he'd start work on the next part; killing the people who'd been responsible for taking her in the first place.

First, he had to find Joanna. If things on board the chopper had gone to plan then Redford and Frankie might have bought him an extra few minutes. Either way, he still didn't have long before the go-fast boats caught up with the *Neptune* and made life very uncomfortable for those who were aboard. Mason didn't intend to be one of them.

Looking around, he saw the biggest ship he'd ever set foot on. The upper deck was bigger than a Premier League football pitch and was carrying over a thousand containers. He figured that the holds below deck would have room for another three and a half thousand more. He didn't have time to work his way through four and a half thousand boxes. He needed to whittle things down.

The position of every container on a ship is considered very carefully before being loaded. Each box is stacked in a way that doesn't compromise either the ship's schedule or stability. If a ship is due to call at three ports, then a container to be unloaded at the first port wouldn't be stowed under a container to be unloaded at the last. But at the same time, the loader has to consider the weight of every container so that heavy boxes aren't stowed above the lighter ones. To do that would raise the centre of gravity of the vessel and reduce the ship's overall balance. This complex problem is solved by a computer program and Mason knew that even if Aku had overseen the loading of the Wang box onto the *Neptune*, he'd still have had to comply with the rules of the algorithm.

That allowed him to make two assumptions. First, Aku intended to use the trapdoor to sneak out the stowaways and hand them over to the Iranians. In which case, he would rather keep it below deck, away from anyone watching from the bridge. Second, the additional weight of a dozen people on top of the rest of the cargo in that container, around a thousand extra kilograms, meant that the algorithm would assign the container to the bottom of a stack. Put together, that suggested that the container he was looking for was at the bottom of a stack and in one of the holds.

Fifty feet along the port side, he found a metal hatch and unscrewed the lid. He threw himself in feet first and descended the ladder inside, dropping down into the bowels of the ship, two steps at a time, his rifle slung over his shoulder until he reached the bottom. The inside of the hold was dark except for the dim glow from the overhead strip-lights, but he could see that he was standing at a junction of two corridors, one running along the port side of the ship and another at right angles across the beam. The deep hum of the ship's long-bore diesel engines drowned out everything else in the space.

Mason took the corridor towards the bow, moving along the narrow walkway, through a series of hatches. A metal staircase took him down another floor to the bottom deck where the corridors were even darker and narrower. He moved fast, weaving his way between the ventilation shafts that ascended towards the top deck. All around him were walls of containers, like a huge steel three-dimensional maze made from boxes. Despite the claustrophobia, he tried to get a sense of how vast the space was. The containers were piled up, twenty rows end to end from bow to stern, twelve across the beam, six high on the middle deck, another six on the deck below. Over one thousand two hundred boxes in total. The corridors that criss-crossed the ship were bolted to the steel carcass that stopped the containers from moving around in transit, effectively sectioning them off into cells, sixty or so to a cell.

Mason was in a stronger position than he had been when he was looking for the container on the *Sirrah*. This time, he at least knew what the box he was searching for looked like. He'd seen it with his own eyes in the WellBox workshop. It was white, with the distinctive Wang Trading Company logo emblazoned in large red letters across its side. If his logic was right, then one of the cells contained a red and white box at the bottom of a stack. That at least reduced the odds in his favour. It meant that Joanna was in one of just two hundred containers. A bit more manageable.

He started at the bow, descending a series of staircases and ladders until he could go no further. He was at the very bottom of the ship. The containers on either side of him now were the bottom of the stacks above them. He worked his way along each row, scanning the boxes, working his way methodically, moving along, looking for the white box with the red Wang logo.

As he reached the last box in the first cell, he ducked through another hatch into the second cell and repeated the process. As he got closer to the stern, the roar of engines became almost deafening.

The noise was so loud that Mason didn't hear the sound of the dog. But he saw it. He turned the corner at the end of the row just as fifty kilograms of pure Doberman Pinscher launched itself towards him. As he fell backwards, Mason thought he caught sight of a guard running desperately towards him, but Mason's focus was firmly on the animal.

The dog climbed up onto Mason's chest, growling and snapping at his face, nearly taking a chuck out of his chin. Mason flipped himself onto his side, knocking the dog off balance for an instant, giving him a chance to bring his knees up hard under its snout. The dog flew back against the steel wall with a yelp, but moments later it was back on its feet ready to launch another attack.

Dog and man came together with full force, Mason letting out an almighty kick just as the dog snapped down onto his ankle, getting a firmer grip. Mason screamed out in pain, kicking at the hound again and again with his other foot. But the dog knew it had its man and nothing short of its owner's command would convince it to release. Or at least that and a 9mm round.

Mason let off two rounds right between the Doberman's ears, killing it dead. By now the guard, a chubby woman in black fatigues, hair tied back with a greasy ponytail, had caught up with them and fell to her knees in horror. Her precious dog was dead. Mason retargeted the gun onto her, but before he could act, he heard the sound of a bullet ricocheting off the steel roof, inches above his head.

'Back off!' he roared at the security guard, fixing the Glock on her. She took two steps back, her hands aloft as another round echoed off the containers.

Mason and the guard both hit the deck. The guard froze solid while Mason slithered on his belly through the nearest hatch for cover. His leg was now bleeding freely from the dog bite, but he put the pain out of his mind. Rounds continued to ping off the containers around him and he could just make out the muffled register of a pistol coming from back along the corridor. Someone was shooting at him, moving along the walkway to the port side of the ship, taking pot-shots.

He pulled himself back to the edge of the hatch and unlocked the safety on his rifle, peering in the direction the bullets had come from. There was no sign of anyone there. The end of the corridor was ten metres away and he calculated that the shooter must have taken cover around the corner towards the bow. He didn't have time to wait for another assault. The clock was ticking and any minute twelve go-fast boats full of IRGCN operators were coming aboard.

Mason stood up, wincing from the pain that the Doberman had inflicted on him, and hobbled as fast as he could towards the position from where the shooter had fired. He fired into the likely cover to keep the gunman's head down, rapid, aimed, single shots, one round every three seconds, making sure that whoever was around that corner had no chance to get another shot at him. When he reached the corner, he pivoted around it, unleashing a fresh volley of bullets. The first three rounds struck Aku square in the chest as he fumbled with his pistol. The Indian seaman went flying and landed heavily on his back.

Mason kicked away the gun. He wished that he had more time. More time to make Aku suffer. More time to find out what else he knew. But there wasn't time. In any case, the fact that Aku was there told Mason that he must be close. The only thing there was time for now was to administer a final shot to the centre of Aku's forehead.

He slung the rifle over his shoulder again and sprinted back along the corridor, calling out Joanna's name, screaming over the engines to be heard. He found the guard, huddled over, crying into the still-warm body of her precious pet. Mason grabbed her by the collar and yanked her to her feet.

'Where is it? Wang Trading Company,' he said.

The guard hesitated for a moment, but Mason's face convinced her otherwise. She lifted her hand and pointed towards the final cell at the end of the hull.

Mason shoved her in front and they moved together into the cell containing the last stacks of containers. He saw it immediately. The white and red box was on the second row, the door facing out, locked and sealed. Mason ran around to the other side and began feeling for the edge of the trapdoor that he'd seen in the workshop. He smashed it open with his rifle butt, sending the rectangle of metal flying.

'Joanna, Joanna,' Mason cried out as he shoved the guard into the box ahead of him.

The container was pitch black and there was a foul smell of human waste. As his eyes adjusted to the darkness, he saw a figure cowering on the floor. He strode forward and reached out, but when he saw the face looking back at him, he stopped.

'Where the fuck is my daughter?'

'I don't know. They put her in a different container,' Wei Lun Chow replied. 'Don't shoot.'

The Chinese billionaire had his hands raised above his head and was trembling with fear because Matt Mason's rifle was pointing directly at his head.

'Where?' Mason said without lowering the rifle. 'Is it on this ship?'

Chow shook his head. 'No.'

'Are you sure?'

Chow kept his hands raised and nodded slowly.

Mason screamed out at the top of his lungs, 'Fuck!'

He kicked over the bucket of shit and piss that Chow had been using for the last two days and grabbed a hold of him by his shirt. 'Go!'

Mason pushed Chow out of the container and locked the guard inside. Chow's feet barely touched the ground as Mason dragged him back along the narrow corridors, back up the metal staircases and shoved him into the hatch that led to the top deck. Mason followed him up the ladder, checking his watch as they climbed. It had been thirteen minutes since he'd landed on the deck of the *Neptune*. He didn't know what he was going to find up there. He'd taken more time than he'd wanted. Now, he had to be ready for anything.

Chow pushed open the hatch's lid and the first rays of morning sunlight poured in. The sky was petrol blue and the day was already reaching thirty degrees centigrade.

'Sssh!' Mason held his finger to his lips. He was listening for the sound of approaching craft. 'Shit,' he said.

There was the unmistakable sound of go-fast boats. 'They're close. Go! Go!'

He shoved the Chinese billionaire by the seat of his pants out onto the deck and pointed to the port edge of the ship, 'Wait there!' he ordered.

Chow did as he was told as Mason span three hundred and sixty with his rifle to check for any other attackers. Satisfied that there was no immediate threat on the ship, he ran in the opposite direction to Chow to get a look off the starboard side. Mason saw exactly what he'd heard. The Iranian go-fast boats had regrouped and were now less than a minute from the *Neptune*. Once they arrived, he knew they would circle the ship. But before that happened, the *Neptune* offered them a brief window of cover.

Mason turned back and ran as fast as he could to where Chow was waiting. 'Can you swim?' he called out.

Chow looked confused for a moment before he realised what Mason was asking. He looked over the edge of the ship, down to the water, thirty feet below.

'NO!' Chow cried, his eyes wide with fear.

'Well you better hang on then,' Mason said as he grabbed a hold of Chow and flung them both off the deck into mid-air.

They fell thirty feet and plunged together deep into the warm water of the Persian Gulf. When they surfaced again, the *Neptune* was another hundred metres away and now flanked by the go-fast boats on both sides. Iranian sailors were throwing grapple hooks up onto the ship so that they could climb on board. Mason knew that meant that they hadn't seen them jump. The bulk of the ship must have covered their fall from view and the *Neptune* would be miles away before the Iranians discovered Chow was gone.

While Chow panted and coughed up a lungful of sea-water, Mason activated the PTT on his radio and called Redford.

'You still out there?'

'Coming back for you now, Mace. You got Chow? You got your girl?'

Mason's heart broke again in that moment. It wasn't Chow's fault, but right then he'd have happily sacrificed him in exchange for his daughter. Mason would have given anything for Joanna to be the one floating with him in the Persian Gulf while the chopper came back around for them.

'That's a negative,' he said into his radio. 'Prepare for double extraction, but Joanna wasn't on board.'

There was a pause before he heard Redford's voice again, 'Sorry, Mace.'

He heard the chopper circle again overhead before he saw it banking back towards them. With the *Neptune* already almost out of sight, he released a marker buoy so that Frankie could get an accurate location. Two minutes later he caught the SPIE rope that Redford threw down to him and the chopper winched them out of the water, turning back away from the Iranian coast, returning to the safety of international waters.

FORTY-SIX

Jask, Iran

The *Coral Queen* sailed slowly into the shipping port of Bandar Bushehr as it had done hundreds of times before. As the pilot guided its ten thousand tonnes of cargo into a freshly vacated loading bay, he radioed to his colleague in Iranian customs to come aboard and begin his usual checks. Meanwhile, he and the captain exchanged the gossip they'd heard since they'd last seen each other. The two men caught up on the latest comings and goings in the shipping company, proposed changes to protocols, political appointments, the usual chat that accompanied the arrival of every ship into port. That is to say that everything that was happening on board the *Coral Queen* was entirely ordinary. Nobody would ever have suspected that there was one container on the *Coral Queen's* top deck that contained eleven tired and hungry women who were being smuggled into Iran from Mombasa.

Three hours later, the gantry crane offloaded the container onto the back of a flatbed eighteen-wheeler truck. The truck's driver was under strict instructions to drive directly to an address outside of Ahvaz, the capital of

Khuzestan Province. The whole way, he listened to IRIB Radio Quran, the national radio station whose only content is verses from the Holy Book, recited 24/7. The five-hour journey passed without incident and when he reached his destination, a canned fish plant on the edge of an industrial estate, the driver waited while the container was offloaded. Soon after, he left again without having spoken to anyone other than the man who signed his paperwork, a young Arab who looked to the driver like most of the other people who came from the northern province that bordered Iraq.

As soon as the truck passed back out through the factory gates, the young Arab, whose name was Massoud Najafi, told the factory foreman to give his workers an early lunch. Once the place was deserted, Najafi made a phone call and lit a cigarette. By the time he flicked the butt into the dirt, two more vehicles had arrived at the gates. The first was an old Mercedes van he knew well, but the following vehicle, a brand new Toyota Land Cruiser, was not one he had seen before. Najafi's eyes remained locked on the Toyota as it pulled up next to him. When the rear door opened, Najafi's eyes almost popped out of his head, because stepping out of it was one of the most powerful men in Iran – General Haddadi.

Haddadi barely acknowledged Najafi as the young man stood upright and saluted. Instead, the general walked directly to the container and pointed to its doors. Najafi ran back inside the factory, reappearing with a set of bolt-cutters and a blowtorch. He cut the container's seal and threw open the steel doors, immediately recoiling and cursing at the foul stench that oozed out. The general was unmoved and shot him a look that shut him up immediately.

Haddadi stepped into the container and examined the contents. It contained sacks filled with worthless scrap metal, ballast to ensure sufficient weight not to arouse suspicion. But he walked directly past the sacks to the end of the box. He had already been informed about the false wall. He called Najafi to his side and pointed at the wall.

'Open it,' he said.

The temperature inside the metal box was hotter than an oven and the smell of excrement and death filled Najafi's lungs, burning his airways like acid. But he knew better than to disobey a man as powerful as Haddadi. He ran his fingers along the wall and quickly found the thin layer of solder where the false wall had been fixed to the frame. He was working efficiently, as he had many times before, using the blowtorch to soften the solder, working the metal away from the edge. When he was done, he kicked it hard with the sole of his boot, first once, then again and again until it buckled and one side became completely detached. Najafi wrapped his fingers around the edge and pulled with all his strength until the wall came away entirely, landing in front of him with a thunderous crash. When he looked up again, the general's eyes were fixed on what was on the other side.

Eleven women, crammed tightly together, stared blankly back at them. Two of the women were already dead. Another would die soon. Two excrement buckets next to them were full to the brim as well as a fifty-gallon water butt long since emptied of the water it once contained. None of the women moved except to gasp for the first whisps of fresh air that they had breathed in nearly four days.

Najafi snuck a look at the general, wondering what reaction to expect. The young Arab had been in the people-smuggling business for nearly five years, working through Razir Al-Haq and his team of intermediaries in Somalia, trafficking young African girls via Iran to work as domestics for wealthy Arabs over the border in Kuwait. He found his customers online through social media sites and there was no end to the demand. Business was booming in Kuwait and a good strong girl who spoke a little Arabic could fetch as much as three thousand US dollars.

But the presence of an Islamic Revolutionary Guards general was unexpected. Najafi already paid several bribes to various authorities to ensure that his cargoes were not investigated. But he never expected the IRGC to be on the list. *Surely this was below their area of interest?*

'This one is mine,' Haddadi said, striding forwards.

Najafi realised what he was talking about. He had to double-take to make sure he hadn't imagined it, but it was real. Sitting in the middle of the women, cradling the head of another girl who looked close to death, was a blonde-haired white woman. The general reached down to pull her to her feet.

'No,' Joanna Mason shrugged him away. 'This woman needs water.'

Joanna's mouth was so dry that she could barely say the words, but Maria, whose head she held in her arms, was going to die soon without fluids. She shook her head at the general as he considered her. After a moment, he smiled.

'Bring water,' he said.

Najafi ran from the container, returning at once with a bottle. He went to hand it to Haddadi.

'To her, you fool,' Haddadi snapped.

Najafi took a second to realise what he was being told, but then he bent down and passed the water to Joanna, who held it to Maria's lips and poured a little inside.

'Not too much,' the general said. His voice was low and even. 'Or she will be sick.'

Joanna nodded that she understood. Maria licked her lips and Joanna passed the bottle to another woman by her side.

'Bring more water,' Haddadi said to Najafi. 'Give all these women food and water.'

'General, I—' Najafi spluttered.

'Nothing more,' Haddadi said, raising his hand to show it was not a conversation.

Najafi ran off again to fetch water, and again Haddadi reached out for Joanna Mason's hand. Only this time, he was asking her to come with him rather than demanding it. He respected people who showed compassion for those weaker than themselves.

Joanna saw that she had no choice. She stood up, wobbly at first on legs that had been bent double for days, and slowly followed the general from the container into the bright sunlight, shielding her eyes from the glare. Najafi passed her, carrying a bucketful of water for the others she was leaving behind.

When they reached the car, Haddadi called one of his men to bring water for Joanna. She accepted, sipping from the bottle as her eyes darted around, trying to make sense of it all. *Where was she? Who was this man?* None of it made sense.

'Welcome to Iran, Miss Mason,' Haddadi said, opening the passenger door and gesticulating for her to get inside. 'Now please, we do not have much time.'

Joanna got into the Land Cruiser and it roared back out of the factory gates. Haddadi sat silently by her side, considering his position. It was a shame that they had lost Chow, but the Chinese would get over it. He would make them see that Iran had tried its best and understand why, with more resources, they could have achieved a better result. He would use the loss of Chow to his advantage, and in any case, he wondered if Chow's talents might have allowed China to become a little too knowing. Ultimately, it might have been bad for business.

What was far more important was that Chow had served his purpose as the decoy. Chow had enabled Haddadi to get his hands on the greater prize – Joanna Mason. A year ago, his best friend, one of Iran's finest military heroes, General Ruak Shahlai, while serving his country in Yemen, had fallen into the hands of her father, Staff Sergeant Matthew Mason. Shahlai's whereabouts were still unknown, but Haddadi had no doubt that the British and Americans were holding him in one of their so-called 'dark sites', which were just torture chambers by another name.

He looked at the blonde girl sitting next to him and smiled. Matt Mason's daughter was exactly the leverage that he needed to arrange a trade for Shahlai. Once the British knew what he had, they would agree to the handover and his friend, General Ruak Shahlai would return to his home where he would receive the hero's welcome that he deserved.

If not, then Haddadi knew he had only one option. If Matt Mason's country did not agree to Iran's terms, then his daughter would die.

FORTY-SEVEN

Al Dhafra, Dubai

Matt Mason didn't say a lot as Frankie flew them to the Al Dhafra Air Base in Dubai. Redford knew Mason well enough to leave him alone with his thoughts. She couldn't imagine what the guy was feeling right now. His only daughter was the last remaining hostage from the *Falcon* and there weren't a lot of explanations that made sense as to why. Chow had been an obvious target – first James Beeby had seen him as an opportunity to make some money, later the Iranians used him as a way to strengthen their relationship with China by handing him over. But holding onto Joanna didn't make a whole lot of sense unless someone was intending to sell her for money, and Redford didn't want to even think about that outcome right now.

Meanwhile, Chow was in shock. The experience of being kidnapped took a lot of people a lifetime to get over and Redford didn't imagine being hurled off a container ship into the ocean helped speed that up any. But the main thing was that she had him back in her custody. If Chow had been returned to China, then the consequences could have been profound for US intelligence.

Currently, Chow's technology was contributing to over thirty per cent of all the CIA's interceptions of illegal arms shipments, not to mention narcotic and human trafficking. Losing that capacity would have been bad, handing it to the Chinese would have been a disaster. If only Joanna Mason had been there too, Redford would have called it a good day at the office.

An hour later, they touched down at Al Dhafra and an ambulance took Chow directly to the military hospital to get checked over. Mason shook his head when the paramedic asked him to accompany them. He wasn't in any mood for doctors and the paramedic could see from his expression that it wasn't an argument he was going to win. Redford suggested to Mason that he come with her to the debrief room instead. He agreed to that.

'You know we'll find her?' she said as the military jeep drove across the base, through the area controlled by the UAE Air Force, past the mosque and into the US Air Force zone. She wasn't entirely sure that she meant it.

Mason nodded solemnly, as though he wasn't sure he believed it either. They drove in silence past scores of high-altitude surveillance drones and tactical fighter aircraft before they turned past the base branch of Starbucks and stopped outside a single-storey prefab building. Redford took Mason through security and into a fully-equipped command centre that had been assigned for her immediate use. She offered Mason a seat as she patched into a call with Langley.

Redford's boss, Stella Clarke, Deputy Director NCS for Community HUMINT, and Norman Bassett, the head of

Middle East and North Africa Analysis, appeared on the screen. Moments later, Mason saw another face he recognised that made his heart sink. He'd read about Dominic Strous's promotion to Minister of State for Middle East and North Africa in the papers before he'd left the UK. The man who'd signed his dismissal papers from the SAS was the last person he wanted to see.

Redford looked concerned. The presence of two top-ranking CIA officials and a British minister on the call meant that something serious had gone down.

'First up, congratulations on recovering Wei Lun Chow,' Clarke began. 'Outstanding work, Agent Redford.'

'Thank you, ma'am,' Redford replied. 'But Matt Mason deserves a lot of the credit.'

'Not for the first time,' Bassett chipped in. 'I'd like to shake that guy's hand someday.'

'Mason's here with me now, sir,' Redford said, pointing off-camera.

Mason stood and moved in front of the lens. He noted Strous shift awkwardly in his seat as he nodded to the group of faces on the screen. 'Sir. Ma'am,' he said, deferentially to the two Americans before he turned to Strous. 'Minister.'

'Mr Mason,' Strous said pointedly stressing the absence of any rank. Mason glared back.

'Damn good job, Mason,' Bassett interrupted, but there was no joy in his voice. 'I worked with some of you 22 guys back in Iraq and I don't mind saying you were the best goddam fighting outfit I ever saw.'

'Sir,' Mason said. He may have left the Regiment but he still felt an enormous pride for it and he appreciated how big a compliment that was from a spook, let alone a Yank one.

'But I'm real sorry about your daughter,' Bassett added.

'Sir,' Mason said. Again he appreciated the sentiment.

'Actually, I'm glad you're here, Mason,' Strous said, 'because you may as well hear what we're about to say. In the last hour, we've received some pretty disturbing intelligence concerning your daughter.'

'Intel from who, sir?' Redford jumped straight in.

'I'm sorry to be the bearer of bad news, Mason,' Strous continued as though Redford wasn't there, 'but the Iranians have made it known to us, via various backchannels that I can't discuss, that they are indeed holding Joanna.'

Mason's eyes closed and his head fell into his chest. He felt like he'd been punched in the gut.

'Do we know what they want, ma'am?' Redford said. She knew all about Strous, how he had backstabbed Mason and made him the fall guy for the shit that had gone down in Yemen. The guy was a snake and she preferred to deal with her own people.

'They're proposing a trade,' Clarke replied.

'A trade?'

'Joanna Mason in exchange for Ruak Shahlai.'

'No,' Mason grimaced. He couldn't help himself. The name Shahlai cut through him like a knife.

Twelve months ago, Mason and Redford had stopped the Iranian general, Ruak Shahlai, from blowing up a tanker off the Saudi coast that would have created the worst environmental disaster for a generation. After they apprehended Shahlai, he was taken into custody. No record existed of the arrest and never would because he was being held at a dark site run by American agents on the Thai/Burmese border; a place that officially didn't exist.

'How did they know?'

'Our best guess is they got lucky,' Bassett said. 'The Chinese asked them for help bringing in Chow, and when they saw the manifest, they ran the usual background checks and Joanna's name came up. Someone there must have realised they had something valuable.'

'So all this is because of me,' Mason said, stony voiced.

There was a moment of silence in the room as though nobody wanted to be the one to confirm Mason's statement.

'I'm sure she wouldn't blame you, Mason,' Strous said.

Redford glared at Strous, while Clarke resumed. 'You have to let us take care of this now, Mr Mason.'

'No way, she's my daughter,' Mason said, looking towards Redford.

Redford saw a desperation in Mason's eyes. They'd been through a lot of shit together and in all that time, he had never once asked her for anything. Matt Mason was always the one with the plan, the one with the solution, the one taking responsibility. But as she looked at him now, she saw that he was asking her for help.

Redford looked back to the screen. She had an idea, but Clarke was still her boss and if she didn't play it right, her job could be on the line. 'If I could offer a suggestion?' she said.

'Go ahead, Agent Redford,' said Clarke.

'The reports suggest we've picked up nothing new from Shahlai for months. We should take the offer to trade.'

Bassett was already shaking his head vehemently. 'Negative, Agent Redford. If Joanna Mason was a US citizen, maybe, but—'

'With all due respect, Special Agent Bassett,' Strous interrupted, 'Shahlai was our catch.'

'Which is why, with all due respect, Dom,' Bassett retorted conveying nothing of the sort, 'I figured you might wanna take the initiative on this.'

'Afraid not, the PM won't touch another "British hostage in Iran" situation,' Strous said.

'Because he dropped the ball on the last one?' Bassett said pointedly.

'Okay, let's move this on,' Clarke intervened, trying to calm the situation.

Redford agreed. Arguing about the British prime minister's previous diplomatic failures wasn't getting them anywhere. 'Ma'am, we could send Mason in alone with Shahlai to do the trade for Joanna.'

'Go on,' Clarke said.

Redford continued, 'Shahlai has ceased to be of value. Joanna Mason's return is the priority.'

'And if it goes bad? How do we mitigate the fallout?'

'Shahlai doesn't exist. The US and UK governments would deny any knowledge. Matt Mason was acting alone, a British veteran recklessly attempting to save his only daughter. Tragic but ultimately, foolhardy.'

'Foolhardy is right,' Bassett said. 'Only a madman would agree to go into—'

'I'll do it,' Mason stopped the American in his tracks. 'You bring me that bastard and I'll take care of my own business.'

Bassett paused. 'You're a crazy son of a bitch, Mason. If things fuck up, you and your daughter would be pawns in whatever sick game Tehran comes up with next.'

Everyone looked towards Clarke, who was rocking her head to one side with a shrug as though weighing up the pros and cons. Redford's assessment of Shahlai as an asset was accurate. The old man was spent, broken over months of relentless rendition to the point that he was no longer considered a threat to US interests. Additionally, the new administration was less keen than the previous one about operating black sites in foreign territories. Recently, she'd come under pressure to reduce capacity where possible.

'I don't have a problem with moving Shahlai on,' she said finally. 'But beyond that? I agree with Norm, the US cannot be seen to be involved in handing over a prisoner who doesn't exist for the citizen of another nation, albeit an ally. We could deliver Shahlai, but beyond that, we have to step back. That's the deal.'

'Right, in which case, that's settled then,' Strous looked pleased. 'I'll inform the PM you've got it covered. Send me details as soon as you have them.'

Strous hung up, leaving the Americans alone on the screen. Mason sniffed and cleared his throat. 'I appreciate everything you're doing for me and my family, ma'am. Sir. But like I said, I'll take care of my family from here.'

'Okay, Mason,' Bassett said before he logged off. 'May God go with you, son.'

The screen went black and Mason looked at Redford. She wasn't sure what to say to him. She'd just come up with a plan that put him in indescribable danger and she had no guarantee that it would even result in Joanna's release. She'd meant it when she'd described it as foolhardy, but still her gut had told her that it's what Mason wanted. He looked at her for what felt like forever before he finally spoke.

'Thanks,' he said. 'I appreciate that.'

She breathed a sigh of relief because she knew he meant it, but she worried that what he was about to take on was too much. Even for Matt Mason.

PART SIX

PART SIX

FORTY-EIGHT

Basra, Iraq

Mason dragged hard on his hand-rolled cigarette, listening to it crackle as he closed his eyes and savoured the taste. He'd almost forgotten how good smoking felt over here. There was something about this place that made it better than anywhere else he'd ever been. Maybe it was the lack of humidity or the pleasant warmth that hung in the evening air, but either way, the effect was spectacular. He always smoked twice as much when he was in the desert.

He flicked away the butt and watched it spark across the warm asphalt. Other than the faraway glow of the city to the east, there was no light to be seen. This was typical of the Yanks. Total overkill. In preparation for their imminent arrival, they'd commandeered the whole place and cut the power. If you'd been looking down from a satellite in space at that precise moment, all you'd have seen would be a dark, black space where the Basra airbase used to be.

The silence was broken by the sound of a four-engine turboprop in the sky above. Mason looked up and saw a C130 Hercules circle once before coming in to land, its powerful front lights brightening up the runway before it touched down and taxied to a halt three hundred feet from him. The tailgate lowered slowly, creating a space big enough to fit a truck through and he saw Agent Redford appear from inside. Next to her, Mason could just make out another human figure, cuffed at both ankles and wrists, head covered by a black cloth bag. Redford took him by the elbow and guided him down the ramp, flanked on either side by two lines of fully armed Navy Seals.

Mason shook his head. 'You sure you got enough cover?' he said, sarcastically.

'You can never have enough cover,' she replied. 'Ready to say hello?'

Mason looked back to the cuffed figure standing between them. He'd never expected to see the man underneath that bag ever again. Last time they'd met, Mason had come as close to killing someone in cold blood as he ever had; an act of revenge for the death of Andy Foster, a brilliant young soldier, the first and only man ever to die under Mason's command. For a long time, Mason wondered if he should have executed the man responsible for Andy's death when he had the chance – in the wreckage of a blown-out house in Yemen a year ago. Redford had been the one who had stopped him, convinced Mason that pulling that trigger would only give the bastard the martyr's death that he craved. But how grateful Mason was now to Redford for that, because now, he needed him alive.

Redford ripped off the bag and Mason stood face to face with General Ruak Shahlai of the Islamic Revolutionary Guard. The old man, once a formidable bull of a man, now looked drawn and haggard, his clothes hanging off him like rags. Shahlai's eyes focused, zeroing in on Mason's face for a brief moment before he tilted his head back and breathed in the desert air like he was glugging down a glass of champagne. Slowly, he looked back to Mason and offered a courteous bow.

'Of course it would be you, who have brought me home, Staff Sergeant Mason. *Tashakor.*'

'I heard you were homesick,' Mason replied, dryly. 'Heard you couldn't stop talking about Tehran.'

Shahlai didn't respond. Mason knew that Shahlai had divulged secrets during his time in captivity. Mason could see it in his eyes. They'd lost the fire they'd had when the two men last met. This Shahlai looked so much older, smaller, weaker, no longer the formidable adversary. His face was lined and his beard had thinned so it now looked grey and patchy. He looked at Mason again, seeming weary and tired. Mason was pleased to see that he no longer held the powerful charisma of a man who had once commanded an army. A year of rendition would do that to anyone. Torture killed the soul of even the strongest man and Mason knew it because he'd been on both ends of it. Torture was brutal, but worse than that was how torture left you riddled with guilt and shame for your own weakness. It was any man's worst nightmare and, as far as Mason cared, it was exactly what Shahlai deserved.

'I hope they hang you,' Mason said, coldly.

'Okay, Mace,' Redford said, holding up a hand as if to say 'enough.'

'What do you care?' Mason snapped.

'Nobody hates this piece of shit more than me, Mace,' said Redford. 'But right now, you need him, so let's keep it civil.'

Headlights appeared at the end of the runway and an old, white Mitsubishi minivan pulled up alongside them. Redford assessed the driver, a square-headed, mid-twenties Iraqi with a neatly trimmed beard. Mason gave her a reassuring nod. He'd flown into Basra the day before specifically to find Ali and ask for his help. Before Ali copped a leg full of shrapnel from an ISIS IED, he'd been an Iraqi Special Forces soldier. Mason had trained him himself during a stint in Baghdad before he left the Regiment. Now Ali was driving a taxi in Basra for a living, but as far as Mason was concerned, he was the one man in Iraq who he knew he could trust.

Redford handed Mason the keys to Shahlai's cuffs. 'He's officially yours.'

Mason took the keys from Redford and acknowledged the significance of the moment.

'We have you covered every step of the route,' she continued. 'There's a Dragon Lady up there, providing full reconnaissance, and three teams shadowing you through Basra with a Navy Seal QRF in place should you need them.'

'Combat aircraft cover?' Mason asked.

Redford's face grimaced for a moment before she kept her composure. 'Of course. As we discussed.'

Mason forced a smile. He appreciated the effort she was making and he would have loved what she was saying to be true, to have had all the things that she was describing. But they both knew what she'd just said was bullshit, said for the benefit of Shahlai. They didn't want to risk him trying to pull something. Better to make him think he was surrounded. But the truth was this was a deniable op. There was no cover. There was no high-altitude drone, no Quick Reaction Force. If anything went wrong, then Mason was on his own. The official story would be that Mason was a lone wolf who had ventured into Iran on a personal mission to rescue his daughter. A regrettable tragedy.

'Okay, let's do this,' Mason said.

Mason wasn't fazed by working alone. Sometimes, he actually preferred it because it meant there was less to go wrong. But in this case, he'd have much preferred a support team. As long as the Iranians were expecting him to have the full weight of American support, they were unlikely to try to pull anything. But if they caught a sniff of the reality, that Mason was flying solo, there was no guessing what they might do.

He nudged Shahlai towards the passenger seat, putting him up front next to Ali. Mason climbed in the back from where he could keep a close eye on the general. Two minutes later, they were on the highway towards Basra.

Mason looked out as they passed through the city. He'd been in Basra a dozen times over the last eighteen years, so he knew the place like the back of his hand. Three days after he and Kerry got married, he was sent to Iraq for the first time. He'd been eighteen when 3 PARA were tasked with occupying and securing the Rumaylah oilfields to the west of Basra after the fall of Saddam. A week later, they'd entered the city with a unit from the 1st Armoured Division. Back then, the people of Basra had been pleased to see them. For a lad who'd never been further than Aldershot in his life, it was a head-swivelling experience. More so the next day when Kerry called to tell him she was pregnant with Joanna. He'd been on patrol not far from where they were now. He laughed sadly to himself at the irony that Joanna was the reason he was back here again.

'I wonder why you need me, Staff Sergeant,' Shahlai said without taking his eyes off the road ahead.

'Shut the fuck up,' Mason replied.

'Agent Redford said "right now, you need him." Interesting choice of words. Don't you think?'

'I think that if you don't shut up, then I'll make you shut up,' Mason turned around and ground the barrel of his Beretta into Shahlai's temple until he was sure it felt very uncomfortable. Shahlai held up his cuffed hands in surrender.

Mason kept the gun trained on the Iranian as the minivan drove across the new bridge, over Shatt al-Arab, the River of the Arabs. The crumbling remains of Saddam Hussein's palace stood over the piles of rusting shipwrecks that littered the waters below, slowly decaying in the confluence of the Euphrates and the Tigris that poured out towards the Persian Gulf. Long ago, the river was a frontier at the far edges of the Ottoman and Persian Empires but today it's the dividing line between northern Iran and southern Iraq.

As they got closer to the official border crossing, Mason saw the remnants of war all around. Shattered tanks and unexploded ordnance scattered over the cratered ground on either side of the road. When Saddam had marched his armies through here during the Iran–Iraq war, tens of thousands of people died in the fighting. Now, the barren desolate battlefield remained untouched; an eerily preserved monument to a long and bitter conflict.

It was fucked up that he was back here now. Only a couple of weeks ago, he'd been building control towers, fixing fences, training rangers in the name of saving elephants from poachers on an African game reserve. Now he was back in Iraq and he was facing Ruak Shahlai again. His old life had drawn him back in despite all his best intentions. He wondered if he would ever find a way to escape it. Maybe not. Maybe this was the life that was meant for him, maybe he was destined to live it until it was done with him, not him done with it. It was all too much to process right now, but soon he would have to face up to it.

'We are here,' Ali said, as the border-crossing came into view.

Mason peered through the windscreen. The official crossing had been shut for months, so the place had a spooky end-of-the-world feel to it. Breeze-blocks were piled up on the tarmac, dividing the lanes. Fifty metres ahead, two domed, concrete towers, spanned by a beam painted in the red, white, and black of the Iraqi flag, marked the end of the road. Beyond that, lay the Islamic Republic of Iran and, as long as the Iranian's were true to their word, Mason's daughter, Joanna.

'Turn it around and keep it running, cos when I come back through there, we're not stopping. Understood?' Mason said to Ali.

'Of course, Mace,' Ali replied. 'You sure you go alone?'

'I'm sure,' Mason replied. 'Someone's gotta drive.'

Mason went around to the front of the vehicle and dragged Shahlai out. Mason pushed Shahlai ahead, walking close behind him over the last section from the vehicle to the border post. Shahlai shuffled along in his ankle cuffs, while Mason explained how things were going to work.

'When we get to the barrier, you wait until I say "Go". You understand?'

Shahlai's eyes narrowed. Ever since he had seen Matt Mason's face at the airport, he had been trying to work out why he was there. Mason had been the one who apprehended him in Yemen a year ago. But then he had been handed over and processed by the Americans. All his interrogators in that cruel torture chamber had been American too. *Why now would they just hand him back to the British?* Added to that, Shahlai had been watching carefully along their route to the border and he had seen no sign of cover. A man of his experience knew how to spot such things. He was in no doubt that he and Matt Mason were alone.

'When I say go,' Mason continued, 'you walk ten metres. Then you stop. Until I say go again, and you walk another ten metres. Then you stop. If you do not stop, then I will give the order to shoot and I have fifty men in position ready to shoot.'

Shahlai nodded slowly, still wondering why Mason was lying to him. By now they'd reached the concrete towers and Shahlai saw that the border's sentry points were unmanned. Not that remarkable, he thought. It didn't take much persuasion to convince an Iraqi to leave his post.

Sixty metres of no-man's-land stretched out in front of them. A single-lane, brown dirt strip, wide enough for a truck and not much more. It was lit by bright floodlights overhead and at the other end of it, Shahlai could see his beloved Iran. Mason checked his watch, they were three minutes early. He ducked down behind a pile of concrete blocks for cover and dragged Shahlai alongside him. Three minutes was just long enough to smoke another cigarette.

FORTY-NINE

Iraqi–Iranian Border

Seventy metres away, Joanna Mason tried to steady her hand as she adjusted her hijab, so she could see a little better. She didn't like the way the headscarf felt one little bit. Since she'd arrived in Iran, she'd felt uncomfortable even if she had been treated relatively well. There were no more plasticuffs, no more long periods locked up in the dark without food and water, and she'd been free to visit the bathroom at her leisure. The general had acted respectfully and spoken politely to her, offered her whatever she wanted, insisting only that she dress appropriately to the culture of Iran. In the circumstances, Joanna had accepted the hijab as a tolerable compromise, better to wear a veil than a blindfold.

She'd spent the previous night in a large house a few hours north of the port, the first time in weeks that she had felt the softness of a mattress and pillows. Yet, she'd slept only fitfully, haunted by dreams about the man who had tried to rape her on a dusty Ethiopian roadside and about the women who had perished next to her in a container at sea. In the end, she'd decided it was less tiring to just stay awake and prepare for what was to come.

Joanna had already decided that her death was not imminent. There didn't seem to be much point in her captors going to the trouble of transporting her to Iran only to then execute her. They could have easily ordered the kidnappers to do that for them. On balance, it seemed that they must have had a use for her. In the hours before dawn, as she listened to the adhan called out by a muezzin from the nearby mosque, she thought about what that reason might be.

At first, she wondered if she was going to be used as part of an Iranian PR stunt, dragged in front of cameras, accused of spying, hauled up in a kangaroo court and sentenced to prison. She considered whether they might force her to make a hostage video denouncing the West and, in her darkest moments, she even feared that she could be married off to a disgusting old man. But finally, when they came for her and the car took her further north, towards the border, she realised what her true purpose here was. She was nothing more than collateral.

The general's pistol pressed into the small of her back again. She'd have a bruise tomorrow. She almost chuckled at the triviality of that thought. Nervous laughter to cover the fact that she was feeling scared.

'If you do as I have told, Miss Mason,' Haddadi said, his breath was hot and stank of stale coffee and cigarettes, 'then you will live. If you don't . . .'

The gun stabbed at Joanna again. She wanted to lash out and punch the general in the face but she knew she wouldn't last five seconds. There were rifles pointed at her from every angle. Whomever she was being exchanged for must have been important to the general because he had brought a whole platoon of IRG. Thirty highly trained, special forces soldiers were in position, covering every inch from where she stood, to the crossing, ten metres away.

She shuffled forwards, past the deserted Iranian customs post, closer to the barrier that blocked the entrance to a strip of dirt road that spanned a deep manmade channel. This, she realised was the no-man's-land that separated Iran from Iraq. Behind her, she heard Haddadi's digital watch make two beeps. She guessed that meant that it was now midnight since the evening prayer had finished hours before. It made sense that whatever was about to occur had been scheduled on the hour.

'Ten metres, like I said,' Haddadi said. 'Or my men will shoot.'

As she ducked below the barrier, Joanna's breath rattled with nerves. Her hand reached out to steady herself, shaking a little as the hijab again slid down. She cursed the headscarf, pushing it back up onto her head. She could feel her breath getting faster. Shallower. She had to get a grip. She stood still for a moment and closed her eyes. She had to control her breath, remembering the way that her dad had taught her. Blowing out all the air from her lungs, she counted to five before she slowly took it back in again. It worked. She felt a little better. Calmer. She repeated it a couple of times and told herself that she could do this. She could walk across the bridge and she could handle whatever was waiting for her on the other side. She was a Mason and Masons survived.

She began to walk slowly, focusing on where she was putting her feet, counting her strides. Ten metres. Then stop. Wait. Count to ten. Then ten metres more. Haddadi's instructions had been clear. She was not to run, not to turn back, just walk steadily, ten metres at a time, six times until she reached the other side.

After she'd counted out the first ten metres, Joanna stopped and blew out another breath. She allowed herself to look up, already counting out ten seconds in her head. For the first time, she saw what was coming from the other side.

An old man was standing in the middle of the road, forty metres away from her. His beard was long and grey, and he looked tired and thin. His hands were cuffed in front of his body and although Joanna didn't know him, something about him made her feel sad. The man looked up and as he saw her, his brow furrowed as though he was trying to remember who she was. His scrutiny made her feel uncomfortable. Even more so as his eyes widened and a sinister smile crept across his face. He nodded to her as though he had known who she was all along. Joanna shook her head at him. *You don't know me, old man.*

'Go!' She heard someone shout an order from beyond the man, from the Iraqi side of no-man's-land.

Ten seconds were up and the old man began to walk towards her again but Joanna hesitated. She had recognised the voice. She lost her breath again as her whole body began to shake. Her bottom lip trembled and her knees felt unsteady, wobbling underneath her. That voice. That was the voice she had dreamed of hearing ever since this nightmare began. That was the voice of her father.

She forced her feet to move, though they felt heavier than lead. She tried to control her breathing again, but she was too far gone, already descending into full-blown panic. The old man had already reached the end of his second ten metres so that now only twenty metres separated them. But Joanna wasn't interested in him any more. She was trying to see past him, to the other side of the bridge, to catch sight of her dad. Yet, all she could see was darkness. There was nobody to be seen. *Where was he?*

The next ten seconds felt like hours as she waited to move again. Every sinew of her being wanted to run. She wanted to sprint to the other side and jump into the arms of her father, but she knew that to do that would be suicide. Haddadi's men were training their rifles on her, maybe hoping to get a shot at her dad. Of course, that was why she couldn't see him. He was taking cover. That was what he would have told her to do. Complete the task, there'll be plenty of time to celebrate later – as long as you're still alive.

From across the bridge, she heard her father shout again, 'Go!' The old man began to shuffle forwards again. Halfway across the divide, they would stop alongside each other. This time, the sound of her dad's voice filled Joanna with a new confidence. The shaking stopped and she strode forwards as the hijab began to slip again. She tore it off and flung it onto the dirt. She wasn't in Iran any more.

Shahlai walked alongside her and stopped. His eyes burned into her with a threatening rage, but she stared defi-antly back at him. *You don't know me, old man.*

'A woman's head should be covered,' he said.

'I don't know you,' Joanna said, 'but if you're here, then you must have done some really bad things.'

'Go!' she heard her father call out again.

Ten seconds were up. It was time to move. Shahlai's eyes looked up towards heaven. She heard her father calling out for them to move but she didn't. Her eyes remained locked on Shahlai. She felt nothing but hatred for him. He represented everything that she was angry at. He represented the men who had captured and brutalised her. The same evil men who had taken the Filipino girl away on the *Falcon*, the same men who had executed Jim, the same men who had tried to rape her in the dirt, the same men who had smuggled innocent women to become slaves. He was part of the same toxic cancer and so as he lowered his gaze again, she remained still, waiting for him to answer her.

'There is no judge but Allah,' he said.

Joanna sucked her teeth. 'Well then,' she said. 'You should just shut the fuck up, shouldn't you?'

Shahlai's face contorted in unbridled rage. No woman had ever dared to speak to him that way. His cuffed hands shot out and grabbed a hold of Joanna's shirt. Instinctively, Joanna crouched down low to get better purchase, digging in her heels and using her body weight to push him away. But Shahlai had enough strength to overpower her and she toppled over and fell to the floor. He was on top of her in an instant, getting a firmer grip before he started to drag her back the way she had come. Pulling her back to Iran. Taking her back to her captors.

Joanna kicked and screamed, writhing and squirming in the dirt as she tried to get free. Her hands flew out in all directions, desperately looking for anything that she could grab onto, but there was nothing. She scraped along the hard floor as Shahlai took long, purposeful strides back over the bridge.

Shahlai pulled her with everything he had. Joanna saw him glance over his shoulder towards the Iranian side, perhaps expecting someone to come and help him, but as far as his countrymen knew, there were as many British and American soldiers over the other side as there were IRG on theirs. Nobody wanted a firefight.

'She is alone,' Shahlai cried out. 'There is only one man there. Come! Come!'

If General Haddadi or any of his IRG soldiers had considered for a moment that Shahlai was right in his assessment, if they countenanced that Matt Mason stood alone on the other side of the bridge, unsupported and without backup, then they didn't consider it for long. As Shahlai called out again for assistance, his left shoulder exploded in a halo of blood and bone. He released his grip on Joanna and took another round to the gut before he fell to the ground. The Iranian soldiers could see from the bullets' trajectories that they had not come from the same place as the man who was now standing in the middle of the bridge screaming to his daughter to 'Run!' They had been fired from a second position, adjacent to the bridge.

Immediately they opened fire, showering the position of the mystery sniper with hundreds of rounds. Bullets ricocheted off the concrete blocks that flanked the crossing, ripping apart the Iraqi sentry posts and the corrugated iron customs buildings beyond it. They continued to fire for over a minute until they had laid waste to everything in their sights.

But their efforts were ineffective because the sniper was already gone. She was running back towards Matt Mason's position to offer him support. If Mason had looked behind him, he would have seen her familiar face and her long red hair, but he was already on his feet, running into no-man's-land towards his daughter.

'Rapid fire!' he cried out as he ran full steam towards the bullets.

Nobody who was there could have understood what happened during the sixty seconds that followed. As Mason sprinted towards his daughter, he launched two smoke grenades into the air, landing them ten metres beyond her, engulfing the whole bridge in thick white smoke. The IRG soldiers turned their guns around and fired into the fog, unsighted, hoping to make contact with whatever they could, but Mason had already hit the deck and was crawling on his belly, while the bullets whistled over his head. When he reached Joanna, he grabbed the first part of her he could and dragged her back towards Iraq.

Behind him, Redford had taken Mason's order and was laying down rounds, switching her rifle to automatic, firing as much cover over Mason's head as she could. When Mason appeared again from the fog, dragging an unconscious Joanna by her ankles, Redford saw the trail of blood that followed them. She knew then that Joanna had been hit.

'Withdraw!' Mason screamed.

He threw Joanna over his shoulder and sprinted to the minivan. Redford gave another five seconds of cover before she turned and ran after them. The smoke had spread across the bridge, but she could just make out the red taillights of Ali's white Mitsubishi minivan. As she jumped inside, Mason was tearing off Joanna's clothes, looking for the source of the wound. Up front, Ali hit the gas and the van tore off towards Basra.

FIFTY

The Road to Basra

The minivan span around the concrete barriers and bounced up onto the hard tarmac road. Ali's heart was racing as he checked the rear-view mirror to see if anyone was following. Of course, they weren't. A platoon of Iranian IRGC crossing into Iraq would be enough to spark a war, but even so, he put his foot to the floor. Just in case.

In the back of the van, while Mason hugged his daughter tightly in his arms, Redford was already radioing the Basra airbase to put the medical team on standby. Joanna Mason was safe, but she'd suffered a significant wound that was beginning to soak through the back of her shirt.

'Mace,' she said, touching him on the shoulder. 'We should get something on that wound.'

Mason put Joanna down and wiped away a couple of tears from his eye.

'Sorry, love,' he said, turning Joanna around to take a closer look.

He pulled the shirt gently away from her shoulder, teasing the wet material away from the skin, while

Redford retrieved the small green med-kit that was tucked in behind Ali's seat. Mason wiped away enough blood to reveal a neat hole, just above the scapula, where a round had hit Joanna from behind. The exit wound had made a mess of the flesh around her upper chest and he was pretty sure that the collarbone was broken. But if two days ago you'd offered him his daughter back with nothing more than that, he'd have happily taken it. The wound would heal and she would be right as rain again in a few weeks. He moved a strand of hair away from her face and kissed her tenderly on the forehead.

'Thank you, Dad,' she whispered.

'Let's get you fixed up,' he said.

Mason packed the wound, pushing a bundle of gauze into the entry hole before strapping it with a length of bandage. Joanna sat next to him, staring ahead, occasionally wincing in pain. As he finished the dressing, he saw how the rise and fall of her chest had begun to speed up, slowly at first but then all at once, Joanna began hyperventilating.

'Dad?' She gasped. 'Da… Da…'

Joanna's breath was getting shorter and shorter as she gasped for air. Her skin turned pale, her face went a dour shade of grey and a hint of blue crept across her lips. Finally, she began to lose consciousness.

'Jo,' Mason said, prizing open her eyelids, slapping her cheeks. 'Joanna, can you hear me?'

Mason put his hand on his daughter's neck, feeling for her pulse. Her trachea was now displaced to the left-hand side of her throat and she started to gurgle as her airway failed and her eyes rolled back in her head.

'Fuck. I've seen this before in Afghanistan. She's having a tension pneumothorax,' Mason said to Redford. 'Get the seats down. Lay her flat.'

Redford collapsed the seats while Mason lowered Joanna down onto her back.

'Take the bag,' he said, passing the med-kit to Redford. 'I need the chest decompression kit.'

The bullet had perforated Joanna's pleura, the membrane that lines the inner part of the chest wall. The resulting hole was letting air flow into the space in her chest but there was no way for it to leave again. The resulting build-up in pressure was compressing all of her internal organs, squishing her lungs and heart and pushing her trachea to one side of her throat. If the pressure built up much longer, then she was going to go into cardiac arrest right there in the van.

Redford rifled through the kit until she found what she was looking for. She passed Mason a decompression needle while he counted his daughter's ribs, working down from her broken collarbone until he felt the spot between her second and third intercostal space. With one hand, he tore off the sterile sheath, and with the other, he thrust the needle into Joanna's flesh.

'AAAArgh,' Mason screamed. It was one thing to do this to a soldier on a battlefield, quite another to perform it on his daughter. The feeling of the needle penetrating Joanna's tissue felt barbaric, but he knew this was the only way to save her. As soon as he felt the needle pop, the air rushed out like a tyre with a puncture. He stopped before it went too deep. He'd seen a medic nearly kill a guy before by being too eager. Then he returned his attention to her side.

'Oh fuck, I don't wanna do this,' Mason said to Redford.

Redford knew as well as Mason did what he had to do next. 'You want me to do it?'

'No,' Mason said. 'I'd never forgive you.'

Mason unsheathed his knife and counted his daughter's ribs again. When he felt the space between ribs five and six, he eased the tip of the blade inside.

'I'm sorry, baby,' he said.

The blade sliced into Joanna's chest wall as blood oozed out, covering Mason's hand. He gagged as the blade slid inside her until he was sure that he'd penetrated the muscle layer. He withdrew the knife again and thrust his finger into the hole he'd made, pushing it deep inside his daughter's chest, through the pleura, through the muscle until he felt it pop into the cavity behind.

'Bag,' he said, but Redford was already on it, passing him the chest drain, a long tube attached to a clear plastic bag.

The van hit a pothole in the road, sending everyone inside flying. Mason hit his head on the roof. 'Keep it fucking straight,' he roared.

'Sorry, Mace,' Ali said.

Mason withdrew his finger and inserted the long plastic tube into the hole that he'd created, dropping the bag onto the floor by his feet. First, the tube and then the bag began to fill with blood and Joanna's eyes popped open as she took a deep gasp of air, refiling her lungs again for the first time in over a minute.

Mason cradled her head, feeling around her throat, relieved that her trachea was sliding back into place. He kissed her on the forehead as the colour returned to her lips and skin.

'Get us to a fucking hospital!' he screamed to Ali.

Mason knew that Joanna wasn't out of the woods yet. A secondary infection was now the worry.

Redford was already calling back to the base, ordering them to send a chopper. By the time they reached the banks of the river, the heli was already landing in the middle of the bridge. Ali screeched to a halt and, together, they lifted Joanna out of the minivan and into the helicopter. Seconds later, they were flying back over Basra, low over the ground, contouring the road below, as they took the fastest route to emergency medical support back at the airport.

Mason stroked his daughter's hair as she gazed silently back at him. The onboard medic had already given her an oxygen mask. Soon she would receive intravenous antibiotics and begin her recovery, but first, she had to process the adrenaline that was pumping through her.

'You're gonna be fine,' her father kept saying over and over. 'You're gonna be fine.'

She looked up at her dad. He looked pained. On edge. She had never seen him in operational mode before, but now she understood him a little better. Of course, it had been him that had come for her. She'd always known that he would be the one who would save her. She reached out until she felt his rough, calloused hand, and she used what little strength she had left to squeeze it lightly.

'Am I going to die, Dad?' she whispered through the mask.

'No, darling.' Mason was crying, but they were tears of joy because he was telling her the truth. 'No, you're gonna be fine.'

PART SEVEN

PART SEVEN

FIFTY-ONE

Kowloon, Hong Kong

'It is not enough to import only sea cucumbers,' Wang Oo Chin said, with an arrogance that made his sister's teeth itch. 'Hong Kong is changing fast and there are greater opportunities now for real Chinese people. It's time we claimed what is ours.'

There were times when Li Lan found her brother's sense of entitlement and naked ambition an inspiration and a sense of pride. Oo was certainly more on her wavelength than their middle sibling, Bo, who was already pretty drunk on the other side of the table. Li Lan was the real brains behind the family business, but Oo was a good salesman. He was also the one who had sent business-class flights for her and their parents as soon as Li Lan had called to say she wanted to visit.

Li Lan's scheme with Al-Shabaab had begun unravelling soon after she heard the horrific news that Aku had been shot dead on the *Neptune*. Al-Haq had contacted her to confirm the second shipment, the girls to Iran, had landed without issue, but still, the Somalian had sounded angry about losing Chow. He blamed Li

Lan. No matter how much she protested to the contrary, Al-Haq had insisted that someone had betrayed him and until he found out who, he was withholding payment. Li Lan decided to wait for the dust to settle and in the meantime to visit her brothers.

She looked across the table to Oo again, still pontificating about how business should be conducted. She had to admit that there were also times, like now, when she found him exhausting. Her attention drifted around the restaurant, settling for a moment on a redhead sitting alone at the next table. There was a time not long ago when you would never see a Westerner dining in Sham Shui Po. The district around the Kowloon docks had always been an ugly, industrial backwater, but recently it had blossomed into a fashionable postcode, and artists and digital nomads were moving in gradually. As a little girl, she'd hated trips to Asia, but now it was good to be back, surrounded by people who looked like her, spoke like her. It felt safe. She couldn't think of anywhere she'd rather be.

The team of waitresses arrived again at the table with fresh plates of food. Li Lan thought that, judging from their similar dumpling-shaped bodies and cropped hairstyles, they were probably sisters. Oo's frosty reaction to the youngest one made Li Lan wonder if he'd had sex with her before now. As the eldest waitress laid down a plate of lobster tails in the centre of the table, the meat dripping with green onions, ginger, and garlic, Li Lan returned her focus to the conversation.

'Do you agree, Father?' Oo was saying, looking earnestly to their father for affirmation.

Li Lan's father smiled distractedly. He seemed more interested in the lobster than Oo's plans for expansion of the business into West Africa. In light of recent events, Li Lan had convinced her brother that the shipment coming in from Mozambique should be the last from East Africa for a while. The office in Pemba was now defunct. It was no longer safe for Wang Trading Company to operate there and, besides, ivory was finished in the East. The future was on the other side of the continent, in countries like Togo and Benin, where officials could still be paid to look the other way and plentiful supplies of elephants were just waiting to be harvested.

'You know your father is retired,' their mother scolded, already piling more food onto her husband's plate.

Li Lan caught her brother's eye as they exchanged a weary look. Their mother was right. Tradition required Oo to seek his father's approval, but in reality Oo and Li Lan called the shots. The old man hadn't been involved operationally for several years.

'Okay,' Oo said, helping himself to some lobster, 'I'll email you the details, Dad.'

Bo waved to one of the waitresses and ordered another Tsing Tao, much to the chagrin of his mother.

'Go easy,' she said.

'It's been a hard day,' Bo slurred. 'I deserve another drink.'

Li Lan smirked. Bo was a waste of space. A classic Chinese second son, living in the shadow of his older brother. Li Lan was more of a son than Bo would ever be. When she had received the news about Aku's death, she had acted decisively. A call to Oo had convinced him that it was necessary to extract their parents from Zanzibar immediately. Li Lan knew that it wouldn't be long before someone connected Aku's death to the Wang Trading Company container on the *Neptune*. Sooner or later the authorities in Zanzibar would come asking questions. Their parents didn't know the real reason for their trip of course. They were labouring under the false pretence that they were there to celebrate the birth of Oo's latest offspring. But Li Lan knew they weren't going back to Zanzibar anytime soon. They were safer in Hong Kong now.

Oo's phone rang and he looked up to his sister as he answered. They'd been expecting the call and before Oo hung up, they were already on their feet.

'Where are you going now?' Bo said as the waitress filled his glass.

'Just a little business to take care of,' Oo replied.

'Some paperwork, Mama,' Li Lan said to her mother, who was frowning with disapproval. 'Twenty minutes. Order more scallops for when we get back.'

Li Lan and her brother stepped out into the humid evening and Oo unlocked the Mercedes SUV parked on the street outside. They took the back roads, avoiding the traffic on the short journey to the docks. Oo showed his pass to security and they parked up on the quayside. A forklift was offloading a white container emblazoned with the Wang Trading Company logo outside of their warehouse. They got out, and Oo directed the driver where to lower the box while Li Lan signed the docket for the foreman.

The paperwork showed that the container had been loaded and reloaded several times since leaving Mombasa.

It went first to Seoul, South Korea, where an arrangement with a corrupt official ensured that it would pass through customs without investigation; and then to Shanghai, where it was offloaded again before being transferred to Hong Kong. Once the forklift was gone, Li Lan watched her brother break the seal and throw open the container's doors.

Immediately, the sky lit up with flashlight beams. Li Lan heard dogs barking and the sound of people shouting at her to stay where she was. Someone gripped her hands and yanked them behind her back, handcuffing them together. Men and women in dark blue uniforms surrounded her, while a camera flashed in her face. She turned her head to the side, trying to look away from the glare, and saw a familiar face standing in the shadows. It was the red-haired woman from the restaurant. She was walking towards her, holding up an official-looking badge.

'Wang Li Lan?' she said. 'I'm Agent Redford from the CIA. I've been working closely with the AFCD.'

Li Lan looked again at the uniforms. Now she recognised the logo of the Hong Kong Customs and Excise Department. Several of the officers were already inside the container where they had discovered rows and rows of elephant tusks hidden underneath a pile of sea cucumbers.

Back in Mombasa, as Wei Lun Chow began to recover from the shock of his capture, Mason had called in some payback for securing his release. He'd asked Chow to use all the power in the SinoCheck algorithm to look for the Wang Trading Company container that had left Pemba two weeks earlier. Chow had scanned every box routed through Mombasa over five days, searching for anomalies in the paperwork, loading volumes, delivery routes. After grinding through thousands and thousands of data, the algorithm had eventually identified what Chow was ninety-nine per cent sure was the Mozambique ivory. The container left on another ship shortly before the *Neptune*, routed first to South Korea and then on to Shanghai and finally, Hong Kong.

Redford had liaised with China's Ministry of Foreign Affairs, who received the intelligence gladly. Over the past five years, the Chinese government had been targeting ivory smugglers as a way to publicly show that they are no longer participating in the ivory trade. It was one of the few areas in which Beijing was prepared to work internationally. China was committed to showing the world that wildlife conservation and supporting others in that effort – even if that meant imprisoning Chinese citizens – was an example of how seriously they took their responsibility as a global superpower. As a sign of good faith, they'd even invited Redford to come on the raid.

'You're going to spend ten to fifteen years in a Chinese cell, Ms Wang,' Redford said as the AFCD official took Li Lan and Oo away. 'But I want to make something else very clear to you. The international warrant for your arrest will remain live. Forever. There's no statute of limitations on human trafficking and terrorism.'

Li Lan stood stunned, nodding as what was happening to her began to sink in.

'If you or any of your family ever step outside China again,' Redford continued, 'I'll make sure you rot in a cell for the rest of your life. And that includes your father, Mr Wang.'

Li Lan realised that her family were doomed. Back at the restaurant, her father and Bo were being ignominiously dragged from their restaurant table in handcuffs. The whole family, as directors of the Wang company, would be charged with ivory smuggling, something they would all certainly serve jail time for. Not only that but they would be publicly shamed for their involvement in a practice that was once celebrated but was now socially frowned upon. After their release, they would be forced to remain in China and to live with the shame. They had lost their money, lost their business; but, more importantly, they had lost their face, forever.

As the officer took Li Lan away, Redford took out her phone and dialled.

'Hey,' she said. 'It's done.'

She hung up again and watched Wang Li Lan get bundled into the back of a police car. In one fell swoop, a central arm of the ivory trade had been delivered a knock-out blow, a lucrative arm of the Al-Shabaab's financial network had been closed down, and a spanner had been thrown into the gears of Sino-Iranian relations. Plus, she still had Chow. All in all, against the odds, it had been a pretty successful week.

FIFTY-TWO

Poole, England

A young lad dropped onto one knee and slogged a huge six over the mid-wicket boundary. While the bowler stood, hands on hips, grunting his disapproval, Peter Hopkins passed by on the other side of the fence and quietly applauded the audacity of the shot. He'd been quite the cricketer himself as a schoolboy, and sometimes he still missed the cut and thrust of being out there on the square, facing down his adversary with a bat in hand. Willow and leather seemed an entirely more civilised way to settle your differences than the bullets and bombs that filled his working life.

He turned off the main road into an industrial estate and briefly caught a glimpse of the sea, past Sandbanks, way out in the distance beyond the De Grasse building. The security gate was unmanned and the car park was empty. When he unlocked the front door, he found a fortnight's worth of junk mail and final demands piled up behind it. He turned off the alarm and walked along the corridor to his old office, glad that this would be the last time he'd ever come here.

He flicked the light switch and sighed when nothing happened. The electricity had been cut off days before. De Grasse had been declared insolvent and the administrators were already disposing of what few assets remained so that they could settle as many of the company's debts as they could. A month from now, a new business would occupy these offices and De Grasse Maritime Security would be forgotten. Hopkins opened the blinds and as the room filled with daylight, he saw what he'd come back for – a file of contacts that he'd put together, containing useful numbers and email addresses for fixers and mercenaries from around the world.

The sound of the front door slamming made him jump. He hadn't been expecting company. *Maybe one of the administrators was doing a site visit.* He opened his office door to let whomever it was know that he was there, but the person walking down the corridor was no accountant.

'James?' Hopkins said, surprised, and a little disappointed, to see his old boss again. He'd hoped to avoid any unpleasantness.

'It's all fucked, Pete,' James replied. He sounded drunk.

'I'm not staying,' Hopkins said, ducking back into his office again.

Since Joanna Mason had returned safely to the UK, a full investigation into her abduction and subsequent ransom had been launched by MI6 and the Metropolitan Police. James Beeby had been questioned and released on remand, his passport confiscated, and his accounts frozen. For his involvement in the kidnapping, he was looking at ten years in jail but with the way the public felt about terrorism these days, the charges coming down the pipe for his association with Al-Shabaab meant that he was likely to get double that. It was no wonder the guy was drunk.

'I'm going to jail,' James slurred, stumbling a little as he came through the door.

'I think so,' Hopkins agreed, packing up his things. 'No less than you deserve, James.'

James nodded slowly, albeit he still looked a little begrudging of Hopkins's damning judgement. He looked around the room at what had once been the empire he'd built, the creation that defined his professional life. Now it was just a shell, a broken dream, a reminder of his own failings.

'Is Mason's daughter okay?' James asked.

'It's a bit late for that, don't you think?' Hopkins scoffed.

'They're going to kill me, you know?'

'Who's going to kill you, James?'

'Al-Shabaab,' James said, producing a hip flask from his pocket and taking a swig. 'Fancy a nip?'

'Bit early for me,' Hopkins shook his head. 'Why are Al-Shabaab going to kill you, James?'

'Issued a fatwah against me, apparently,' James said casually, as though someone had simply said they didn't like his shirt.

'Al-Haq?'

'Probably. Blames me for everything.'

'Well, it is kind of your fault, James. You were the one who came up with the idea and you were also the one who coordinated its execution. People died because of you. A lot of people died.'

'Bit harsh, mate,' James said. Hopkins couldn't tell if he was joking or not.

Hopkins packed away the folder and gathered his jacket while James watched.

'Stealing the company's secrets?'

'Jack and I are setting up something. BG'ing mostly. Close contact, high-worth individuals. Wei Lun Chow's going to be our first client.'

Hearing Chow's name stung James, but he tried not to show the pain. 'BG'ing? Nice. I could use a bodyguard, myself.'

'You can't afford us.'

Hopkins enjoyed saying that. He enjoyed seeing James's life in ruins. He'd meant it when he said that prison was what he deserved. For James Beeby's whole life, he had done what he wanted without consequence, but now he was going to pay the price for his arrogance.

Hopkins walked to the door, pausing for a moment before he took a final look at James Beeby. The man was going to rot in prison and nobody would miss him. He closed the door and walked back along the corridor, stepping over the junk mail again before he left De Grasse for the last time.

As he passed the cricket pitch, the bowler was exacting his revenge, sending the batsman's middle stump cartwheeling through the air. Hopkins chuckled to himself. All good things come to an end. But something new always comes afterwards. He and Jack were going to put De Grasse behind them and begin something new, something better, something that would stand for more than just money and greed. For the first time in a long time, he was excited and optimistic about what the future would hold.

FIFTY-THREE

Kismayo, Somalia

Matt Mason chewed on the last bite of another dehydrated protein bar before he carefully stashed the empty wrapper in his duffle bag. He was careful not to leave any trace of his presence. Since he'd taken up his position, hiding in a thicket of thornbush along the edge of the forest next to the Jubba River, he'd eaten nothing but protein bars and now, two days later, the taste of peanut butter was starting to repeat on him. He took out his binoculars and scanned the compound across the water, quietly promising himself a plate of lamb chops with a cold beer when this was over.

Operations like this usually required months of planning, but every now and again a situation arose where you had to act fast. The trick was to know when to wait and when to go. Mason's decision was influenced by a number of factors. The first, simple fact was that the CIA had received reliable intel that placed his target here, at home in Jilib, the de facto Al-Shabaab capital in Somalia, one hundred kilometres north of Kismayo. It seemed that there were some high-ranking members of the organisation who thought it was time for the man to disappear. The second was that Mason had been presented with the opportunity to get into the country by Dahir's cousin, a merchant who regularly imported produce from Kenya. He'd smuggled him over the border in one of his trucks. The third and final reason was that Mason simply didn't want to wait any longer. The fury in his belly was still burning red hot and he wanted revenge.

Mason took out his satellite phone and dialled a number from memory. After a few rings, someone answered on the other end and gave him the confirmation that he'd been waiting for. He thanked the person and put the phone back in his pocket, opened his bag, and withdrew a Beretta M9 pistol with a suppressor which he concealed underneath his robes. The magazine contained seventeen rounds but with any luck, two would suffice. When he felt ready, he placed a dark maroon turban over his head, tightened the belt on his macawis, and wrapped a large chequered cloth around his shoulders. Mason would never pass for Somali, but in the fading light of the evening he was dark enough to be easily mistaken for an Arab.

It was a short walk from the river to the edge of town, where Mason blended into a crowd of people moving steadily along the main track to the north of the compound. It was already dark and on one side of the road hundreds of women, their heads covered in brightly coloured shash and dirac, walked together en masse, clapping and singing in a high-pitched trill. Across the street, the men banged make-shift drums fashioned from metal plates and plastic jerrycans. As they approached their destination, Mason saw a bright light cast from lines of electric bulbs strung across trees that surrounded a clearing. Beneath the lights were rows and rows of tables piled high with freshly cooked samosas, koftas, and rice. The smell of barbequed meat hung thick in the air as women appeared as if from nowhere, carrying jugs of fizzy soft drinks, which they administered to men sat cross-legged on carpets scattered over the dusty ground. Scores of children, up way past their bedtimes, ran in and out of the adults, playing games, shrieking and crying out with delight.

Mason moved among them, past another crowd who stood listening while a young man sang into a microphone. Another group of young men danced in circles, peacocking and trying to outdo one another with ever more flamboyant moves. Suddenly, the hum of the crowd was drowned out by a cacophony of car horns beeping in celebration as hundreds more people arrived for tonight's party. The people were predominantly Somali, but Mason saw many Kenyans, Eritreans, and Arabs too. Tonight, anyone who was anyone in the Horn, it seemed, was going to Razir Al-Haq's daughter's wedding.

Mason quietly pulled away from the centre of the festivities and slid unnoticed into the shadows. He vanished into the darkness, away from the lights, rolled a cigarette and waited, listening to the singing and drumming continuing across the way. After a short while, a man dressed in a green turban and a black, woollen macawis appeared. He took out his phone and dialled, and a second later, Mason's phone rang once in his pocket. The man put his phone away again. No more introductions were necessary. Mason saw the man's eyes flick towards the duffle bag. He laid it down on the floor between them.

'Be my guest,' he said.

The man nodded eagerly, but as he reached out for the bag, Mason put his foot on top of it.

'Just one thing,' Mason said.

'What?' the man replied.

'You cross me and you'll regret it. Understand?'

'I know who you are,' the man said coldly. 'I know how you do.'

'Good.'

Mason moved his foot and the man looked inside, barely able to hide the excitement in his face as he saw what a million dollars looked like. When Mason had explained to Wei Lun Chow what he was planning, the Chinese billionaire had been more than happy to donate the money to Mason's cause. It was a fraction of what it would have cost in ransom money and it promised a much more satisfying result.

'Okay. This is as we agreed,' said the turbaned man.

'Yes, it is. Now, can we proceed?'

'Of course. Please follow me.'

The man lead Mason back towards the lights, past another crowd of men dancing to the beat of a group of drummers. The noise from the drums was almost deafening, but nobody seemed to mind. People sat around looking happy, everyone high on free food and sugary drinks. They continued past another group clamouring to catch sight of an acrobat performing somersaults and flips and a fire-breather launching flames high into the night sky. The crowd clapped and cheered, shouting their approval. It felt more like a festival than a wedding. Soon they reached a large canvas tent and the turbaned man waved for Mason to wait while he spoke to a guard who stood blocking the entrance. At first, the guard seemed to struggle to hear over all the drumming and shrieking and cheering, but he must have heard enough because he looked up again towards Mason as he nodded to the turbaned man. In turn, the turbaned man waved Mason forward again as the guard moved aside to allow him to pass.

Inside the tent, Mason saw a man sitting cross-legged on a woven rug in the middle of the space. He breathed a sigh of relief when he saw the deep scar that ran from his forehead to his chin. There was no doubt that it was him. It was Razir Al-Haq, the man who had kidnapped his daughter, who Mason had paid a million dollars to be alone with. The Somalian barely looked up, simply waving for Mason to sit, assuming that he was just another sycophant looking to curry favour on his daughter's wedding day. Withdrawing his pistol, Mason sat down as requested.

When Al-Haq finally looked up at his guest, he seemed confused. Confused by the presence of an Arab in the tent, even more so by the presence of a Beretta M9 pointed at his head. Still, he remained silent, trying to work out why both were there.

'ISIS?' he offered.

Mason shook his head slowly and replied in Arabic, 'Not even close.'

Noticing Mason's distinctly Iraqi pronunciation, Al-Haq tilted his head to one side and considered again who there might want him dead. He could think of nobody.

'This is your daughter's wedding?' Mason asked, now speaking English.

The Somalian saw that his earlier guess had been very wide of the mark. 'Yes, my youngest daughter. She is fifteen.'

Mason smiled. 'When my daughter was fifteen, she was sailing dinghies.'

'Women do not do such things here, Mister . . .'

'Mason.'

Mason saw a flash of recognition cross Al-Haq's good eye, but he decided to spell it out. Just in case.

'Matt Mason? You tried to take my daughter, Joanna from me,' Mason said.

Al-Haq nodded. His eye darted around nervously.

'The way I see it, you owe me,' Mason continued.

Al-Haq could see his pistol on the other side of the tent, way out of his reach. He considered crying out for help, but the sound of the drumming outside was so loud that he knew nobody would hear. There was no way out of the situation he found himself in and he didn't like how Mason's finger was tightening on the trigger.

'Anything,' Al-Haq said, raising his hands. 'But please. It is my daughter's wedding day, show mercy.'

'As it's your daughter's wedding,' Mason said, lifting the Beretta, 'I'm gonna give you a chance.'

Mason took a deep breath and savoured the moment. He was enjoying himself. Al-Haq was sweating in his finery and shifted uneasily on his cushion, adjusting his turban, made from golden silk, perched on his head like a crown. Mason poured himself a cup of mint tea from the silver teapot laid out on a tray between them and took a mouthful. After a moment, he set the cup down again, returning his attention to Al-Haq. Satisfied that he had the Somalian's full attention, he continued.

'You can save yourself today or you can save your daughter,' he said with a terrifying lack of emotion. 'But not both.'

Al-Haq cowered. 'No. Please.'

'Which is it?' Mason's finger wrapped tighter around the trigger.

Al-Haq tried to turn his face away from the gun. 'Please,' he whimpered. 'I have wronged you, Mr Mason. But please—'

'Which?' Mason didn't move.

Al-Haq held his palms innocently in the air. His palms open out, pleading for mercy from his uninvited guest. He clenched his teeth in discomfort, cursing his misfortune. This was a most regrettable situation he found himself in.

'Okay, please,' Al-Haq said finally, bowing his head in deference, his voice pitched slightly higher, the words coming out faster. 'I accept your exchange. For what you have suffered. Take my daughter. But please, I beg you, do not shoot me.'

Mason nodded and forced out a smile, but his eyes betrayed a feeling of genuine disappointment.

'That's what I thought you'd say,' he tutted before he fired two rounds into the centre of Al-Haq's forehead.

Mason stood again and walked coolly out of the tent. The guard on the door was nowhere to be seen. In his place, the turbaned man stood waiting anxiously. Mason didn't have to say anything to confirm that the deed was done, the turbaned man simply nodded his acknowledgement and led Mason back the way they had come. Mason walked unnoticed past the revellers, through the party that raged on all around, and back into the anonymous darkness beyond.

When they reached the area where the cars were parked, the man stopped by a motorbike. He turned to face Mason and handed him a key. 'You must go. In less than ten minutes someone will find him and Al-Haq still has many friends.'

Mason gunned the bike and blasted off in the direction from where he'd come. He didn't stop as he sped along the main road, past the compound, riding south, keeping the river on his right, until the port at Kismayo. He ditched the bike outside the harbour gates and ran along the pier until he saw the familiar face of a large Somalilander waiting for him on the deck of a thirty-foot speedboat.

Dahir fired up the boat's three-hundred-horsepower engines and Mason broke down his Beretta, scattering the parts into the water. Two hours later, they were doing sixty knots, and as the sun rose over the Indian Ocean, they passed into the safety of Kenyan waters. Dahir brought the boat to within a hundred metres of land and slowed it to a stop.

'End of the line, Mr Mason,' Dahir said, his face breaking out into a wide smile.

Mason shook his friend's hand one last time. 'I owe you one.'

'Oh, don't you worry, my friend,' Dahir laughed. 'Your friend at the CIA has been very generous. You don't think I do this shit for free, do you?'

Mason laughed. He'd already agreed with Redford that Dahir would be the one to receive the bounty the Americans had put on Al-Haq's head. Mason smiled at his friend one last time and dived overboard into the crystal clear sea. He swam to shore and walked out onto the white sand. Dahir's boat disappeared from view along the coast and Mason felt the silence return. All he could hear now was the sound of waves lapping on the shore. He sat on the sand and watched the dawn lighting up the sky all around him.

He realised that he had rediscovered something of himself in Africa – that he wasn't quite ready to retire just yet. He still had plenty of fight left in him. But that fight could wait because, first, he had to go home and take care of his own. He was homesick for the first time in a long while and knew that it was time to return to Hereford. He had to be there with Joanna while she recovered and he wanted to see his son, Sam. The most important thing now was for them all to be together.

His phone buzzed in his pocket. He already knew who was calling.

'Hey,' he said.

'How did it go?' Agent Redford asked.

'Exactly as planned, mate,' Mason replied. 'Exactly as planned.'

'Good,' Redford sounded curt, almost business-like. 'Did you consider my offer?'

Mason paused, but he already knew what his answer was. On Redford's suggestion, Norman Bassett had offered him a job. It meant working with the Yanks, but it also meant getting back to doing what he did best. He'd miss the peace that he'd found on the game reserve with the elephants, but deep down he knew that wasn't his destiny. He was hard-wired for this kind of life and nothing was going to change that. It was better to accept who he was and just get on with it. That was true peace.

'Yeah, I'm in,' he said.

'Okay then,' he could tell from the way she said it that she was pleased but not surprised by his decision. 'You better get your ass off that beach and back here, stat. We have a lot to do.'

'Roger that,' Mason replied. 'Let's do this.'

GLOSSARY OF TERMS

AFCD - Agriculture, Fisheries and Conservation Department (HK)

Al-Shabaab - Somalia-based jihadist fundamentalist group operating in East Africa

AK-47 - aka Kalashnikov - Gas-operated assault rifle

C130 Hercules - American four-engine turboprop military transport aircraft

CCP - Chinese Communist Party

CIA - Central Intelligence Agency (US)

CTF115 - Coastal Surveillance Force

HUMINT - Human Intelligence

IRGC(N) - Islamic Revolutionary Guard Corps (Navy) (Iran)

ISIS - The Islamic State, aka Daesh

LPVO - Low-powered variable optic scope

MI6 - UK's Secret Intelligence Service

MQ-9 - Unmanned aerial vehicle, aka drone

MoD - British Ministry of Defence

MTO - Maritime Trade Operations

Narinco - Chinese state-owned arms manufacturer

OC - Officer Commanding

Panamax – New generation of container ships capable of navigating the Panama Canal

QRF – Quick Reaction Force

RAF – Royal Air Force

RKG-3 – Soviet anti-tank hand grenade

SAS – Special Air Service – The elite special forces unit of the British Army

Spetsnaz – Russian Special Forces

SPIE – Special Patrol Insertion and Extraction

TPLF – Tigrayan Peoples Liberation Front

Acknowledgements

Most of this book was written in lockdown and so we'd like to thank our fantastic editor Eve Hall for all the great advice she delivered via Zoom calls from various locations over the past year. We always felt that we were in very safe hands.

Our agent Gordon Wise is, as always, our point man, providing us with lifesaving cover whenever we're on-task. We're also delighted to have Sophie Ransom publicising this book. The squad feels stronger for having her on board.

We owe a debt of gratitude to Jo Dickinson for steering the good ship at Hodder & Stoughton over what have been some stormy seas during the pandemic, and to her amazing team for all the hard work they put in to keep it on course. Many thanks in particular to Alice Morley for her tireless work in marketing Matt Mason and to Priyal Agrawal for getting the final manuscript over the finishing line. Thanks also to Mara Anastas and Jake Allgeier at our US publishers, Open Road. We're looking forward to introducing Mace to America.

Special thanks are reserved for our endlessly generous early readers who offered us so much valuable feedback along the way – Donald MacIntyre, Andy MacIntyre and Katherine Colombino – a million thank yous.

And we couldn't have written this book without the generosity of several people on whose very specific expertise we called for help – SLt Alice Lancaster, WO1 Simon Hanson, Annabel Vose for their naval know-how, Joseph Hanlon for his expert insight into the political situation in Mozambique and John Thompson for allowing us to peek inside the fascinating world of maritime security – we owe you all one.

And lastly, thank you to Jules and Ruth. You give us so much support every day, we thank you from the bottom of our hearts for all that you do.

In the best books, the ending often comes as a shock.
Not just because of that one last twist in the tale,
but because you have been so absorbed in their world,
that coming back to the harsh light of reality is a jolt.

If that describes you now, then perhaps you should track down
some new leads, and find new suspense in other worlds.

Join us at www.hodder.co.uk, or follow us on
Twitter @hodderbooks, and you can tap in to a
community of fellow thrill-seekers.

Whether you want to find out more about this book,
or a particular author, watch trailers and interviews, have
the chance to win early limited editions, or simply browse
our expert readers' selection of the very best books,
we think you'll find what you're looking for.

And if you don't, that's the place to tell us what's missing.

We love what we do, and we'd love you to be part of it.

www.hodder.co.uk

@hodderbooks

HodderBooks

HodderBooks